I0690723

Every Story a GEM!

THE RUBY FILES

Volume Two

AIRSHIP 27 PRODUCTIONS

The Ruby Files Volume 2

Editor: Ron Fortier
Associate Editor: Fred Adams
Marketing and Promotions Manager: Michael Vance
Production and design by Rob Davis

Published by Airship 27 Productions
airship27hangar.com
airship27.com

ISBN-10: 1-946183-18-0
ISBN-13: 978-1-946183-18-7

Printed in the United States of America

10 9 8 7 6 5 4 3 2 1

THE **RUBY FILES**
Volume Two

TABLE OF CONTENTS

MARS McCOY IS DEAD

By Alan J. Porter

"**O**h, Captain wasn't that a battle?" android Lieutenant Betty 12 brushed the back of her hand across her forehead as she looked up at the tall imposing figure standing at the ship's controls.

Ignoring the question, the Black Bird 5 commander spoke into the glowing valve illuminated microphone protruding from the column in front of him, "Captain Mars McCoy calling the Black Hole, Captain Mars McCoy calling Space Ranger HQ; the Gamma Men are defeated, they are in full retreat and are turned back to Sriton Six. Have captured Giant Killer Clonux and have him in the grip of the magnetic ray and are bringing them to the Black Hole. Captain McCoy signing off now." The captain's voice was oddly monotone for such important news, and anyone watching him deliver this message would have been perplexed by his almost vacant stare, almost as if he was focused on something out of sight. His curvaceous female second in command seemed to be equally focused on the same point; almost as if the pair had been reading from a prepared script and were awaiting further instructions.

'You have got to be kidding me? Where do they come up with dialog like that?" Richard Ruby snorted. "Not exactly Shakespeare is it?"

"Well I'm sure the Bard never had to write a department store promotion, Ricky."

"Oh I don't know, I bet at one point he was a working stiff just like the rest of us. Well maybe not you, my ever delightful Carla."

"Oh do behave! Now stop gawking at the pretend space man and come on, I need to find the perfect pair of gloves to wear at Daddy's shindig."

Richard Ruby shook his head in mild disbelief as he watched Carla St. Clair disappear into the depths of the Colmenero's Department Store. Why was he spending his Wednesday afternoon in the millenary section of New York's most fashionable, and expensive, shopping emporium looking for "the perfect pair of gloves" when he should really be hanging out down in Belle's Jazz Club? The answer was at that moment making a sharp right turn between the silk scarves and the mink stoles.

Carla St.Clair, the society dame he didn't deserve, for some unfathomable reason seemed besotted with him. Or was it the life he led? He mentally shrugged, either way he enjoyed being around her, and the glimpses of this rarified world she inhabited occasionally came in useful. Heck, even the toffs had their problems that only a gumshoe like him could solve. After all that's how he'd met Clara in the first place.

A bump in the back bought Ruby out of his moment of introspection. He turned and was about to show his displeasure, when he saw who it was. "Lt.Betty 12" was dressed in a tight fitting short sleeved silver top that showed all the right curves, and a silver skirt short enough to just about protect her modesty while simultaneously displaying her long shapely legs to their fullest advantage. The curve of her legs emphasized by the heels of her ankle length silver boots. Her smiling face was framed by something that looked like an aviator's cap with bits of old radio gear stuck on it. While it covered most of her head, Rick could still see wisps of jet black curls escaping from around the edges. Rick smiled at the vision in front of him; if this is how dames would dress in the future, he was looking forward to getting there.

"Oh I'm sorry," she almost cooed and placed a hand on his arm, "I'm late back on set."

"No problem," Ruby replied, "do you mind me asking something?"

"I guess not." But the way she was fidgeting seemed to suggest that she was, in fact, in a rush.

"Why are you shooting a space movie in a department store?"

"It's not a movie. Well not like one you see in the theater. It's just a way to promote the store. Something to do with toy ray-guns or something. Seems Mr. Colmenero really likes the Sunday funnies and wanted to try something new to get kids into the store."

"So that's why you are wearing that get up?"

"It's a job," and with that she headed back towards the corner of the store that was temporally acting as the cabin of the interplanetary rocket ship; Black Bird 5.

"A working stiff, just like the rest of us." Ruby muttered to himself.

It took him a few minutes to locate Carla, who by that time had a dozen pairs of gloves of various materials, styles and colors, laid out on the counter in front of her. As he approached, she looked up and smiled. "Where did you go off to?"

"The twenty-fifth century."

"From what I saw a few minutes ago, when she passed me near the scarves, it seems to be an attractive place." Carla commented.

"Hey, who needs the future, when I have you in the here and now, baby."

"A good try Ricky, but the only way you can redeem yourself is to help me decide on which pair......"

The sudden sound of a gunshot reverberated across the floor of the department store, halting all transactions and conversations. It was quickly followed by screams and calls for assistance as several of the more delicate clientele fainted. But above it all rose one shrill scream, a scream of panic and terror.

Rick winked at Carla. "Now that's my sort of dialog."

"So my tame detective, are you just going to stand here making quips, or are we going to see what that was all about?"

"Whatever it was, I'm betting it wasn't in the script."

"Richard Ruby, even for a private investigator, you can be incredibly insensitive at times."

"If he's anything like I used to be, the gallows humor helps."

Carla turned round to see a small man, probably not much taller than five feet, although his battered and stained fedora added a couple of inches. The fedora was in marked contrast to the sharp, well-pressed suit he wore, which looked like it had come straight off the racks at Colmenero's. His voice was squeaky, which went with the almost rodent like appearance of his features. Before Carla could ask his name, Ruby supplied the information.

"Jimmy Weasel! As I live and breathe, what the hell are you doing in a place like this? All dressed up like a window dummy too!"

The smaller man grimaced then quickly broke into a smile. He clasped Ruby's arm for a second before giving him a hearty slap on the shoulder. "I work here. I sort of shift between being Mr. Colmenero's body guard, and acting as the store detective in case of any unforeseen incidents."

"And I'm guessing this is one of those 'unforeseen incidents."" Ruby pointed over towards the temporary movie set.

"Yeah, I was here because Mr. Colmenero wanted to watch the filming today, but looks like I'll be doing a little bit of detecting too."

"Need a second pair of eyes?"

"Thought you'd never ask. Come on."

The two walked across to the set, without a word or a backwards glance at Carla St Clair, leaving the socialite staring after them wondering what had happened to her shopping date.

"Murder, that's what happened."

"I won't have talk like that in my store!" the large imposing figure that could only be Alfredo Colmenero said approaching them. Standing closer than was polite; he was trying to use his physical size to intimidate Ruby and the store detective. That may have worked on shop clerks but to this pair it just showed that the department store owner was a pompous ass. But he was the pompous ass who paid Jimmy's wages so the employee bit his tongue and showed due deference. "Sorry, Mr. Colmenero, sir."

The corpulent Colmenero ignored the apology and looked over the battered fedora straight at Ruby with an accusing stare. "So is this the schmuck who shot up my store?"

"Ah, no," answered Weasel. "This is Rick Ruby, an old friend from my days on the force. He's a private gumshoe these days."

Colmenero scrutinized Ruby appraising not only the man, but his disheveled clothes and nonchalant demeanor as well. "What sort of reputation?"

"Whatever reputation gets the job done," Ruby smirked.

Colmenero stared in stony silence, then slowly the beginnings of a smile appeared at the corners of his mouth. The smile evolved into full bore laughter that was accompanied by a hearty slap on the back. Rick winced at the impact; the big man didn't know his own strength. "I like your style Ruby."

Rick didn't dignify the comment with any response beyond a barely visible shrug of the shoulders.

"Do you intend assisting Mr. Veasel with his inquires?"

Ruby's eyebrow's arched at the use of Jimmy's real name, no-one called him that. On the force the only place he'd seen the name was on Jimmy's badge.

"I'm thinking about it."

"If I offered to cover your time and expenses, would it help you come to some sort of decision?"

Ignoring the store owner, Rick Ruby looked across at his friend, "I guess you just got that second pair of eyes."

"Excellent," Colmenero turned and walked away. Just before he turned the corner the store owner looked back at the two detectives and offered a parting instruction, "Just find out who had the gall to make a mess of my store." Then he was gone.

Rick looked directly at Jimmy. "All he seems bothered about is a few bullet holes, but you said there had been a murder?"

"Yep," Jimmy responded, "and it doesn't add up. His attitude, the victim, everything. Something's not right."

"So I guess the first question is who's dead?"

Jimmy Weasel, slowly removed his hat, an action almost as infrequent as the use of his given name, and solemnly announced, without the faintest hint of irony or humor, "Mars McCoy, Rick. Mars McCoy is dead."

It seemed that what any number of twenty-fifth century ray guns had failed to achieve, had in the end been delivered by the business end of a good old fashioned .38. The space ranger lay in a pool of his own blood, his body looking anything but heroic.

"Well, definitely looks like murder from this angle." Ruby said as he approached the body. He squatted down and started to reach forward with the intention of searching the corpse for anything that might constitute a clue.

"Don't touch anything." The voice came from behind Rick and was delivered in a way that meant it was an order, not a suggestion.

"Hello, Bob." Rick responded without turning round.

"Detective Perry to you, gumshoe. Now get up and back away from the crime scene; we don't want you contaminating it more than you already have."

"OK you got me." Rick grinned, and straightened up.

Once he regained his feet, Rick turned and looked straight at police detective Robert Perry. As always the man was impeccably dressed, nothing out of place or displaying even the slightest crease, wear-mark or stain. His tie done up as tight as the man's own morals. Rick Ruby didn't like being around Detective Perry and the feeling was mutual.

"So Ruby, what makes you say this is a murder?" asked the policeman.

"Well it sure looks like one. Guy gets shot in the middle of a department store. Not exactly your typical shopping experience."

"When it was called in by the store it was described as an accident."

"If it's not a murder, why are you here?" Rick asked, "You're a homicide detective aren't you?"

Perry took a not unsubtle deep breath of exasperation. "Homicide or not, it's still an unexpected and suspicious death. But unlike you I'm not jumping to conclusions."

"Who called it in?"

"Sorry?" Perry looked across at Jimmy Weasel as if noticing him for the first time.

"It was a simple enough question, who called it in?"

"No idea, they didn't leave a name."

Now it was Weasel's turn to show his frustration. "Male, female? Young, old?"

"What's it to do with you anyway, Weasel? What's your involvement?"

"Listen curtain rod, you may be the cop on the beat here, but this is my turf. As Colmenero's store detective any contact with the cops should go through me. So I'll ask again, who called it in?"

"A woman, sounded young. That's all we know. So Mr. Store Detective, what do you know?"

"Not much, first we knew anything is when....."

Rick had tuned out the conversation, and wandered off. Weasel and Perry wouldn't have anything to say that could add anything more at this stage. He left them to argue over evidence, and who should clear the mess up.

The person that really interested Rick Ruby at this moment was Alfredo Colmenero and just why he'd been so quick to hire Ruby rather than let his store detective and the cops handle things. There was something more going on here than the shooting, accidental or not, of a character from the funny papers, and Rick was convinced that Colmenero knew just what that was. But to find out more about Colmenero, he first had to relocate Carla St.Clair.

It didn't take long. A quick circuit around the ladies fashion floor and he soon heard her voice floating across from behind a rack of coats made from the skin of various dead furry animals. Ruby never understood the attraction of fur coats, but then again he wasn't a dame; and even if he was, he could never have afforded the creation that Carla was currently trying on. As he approached she looked up and gave him a slightly patronizing smile, as if welcoming the return of a petulant child that had finished play-ing with his toys. "So how was the spaceman?"

"Dead."

"Oh. How did that happen?""

"I think the .38 bullet sized hole in his chest may have had something to do with it."

"Murder, then?"

"Maybe, maybe not. The store owner thinks it was an accident."

"Some accident," Carla shook her head slowly telegraphing her apparent disbelief at this proposal. "Why would Alberto think that?"

"I think he knows more than he's saying, and..." Ruby suddenly stopped. "Alberto? You know the guy that owns this joint?"

"Oh yes, he's an old friend of Daddy's."

Rick Ruby looked at his lady friend for several seconds. "Is he really? Now that gives me an idea."

"Oh oh. Why do I have the feeling that you are about to ask me a favor?"

"Because, that's exactly what I'm about to do."

• • •

"Are you sure this is the right place?" The cab driver looked in his mirror comparing Rick Ruby's crumpled suit with the opulence of the gated residence they had pulled up to.

"Yep, this is the place all right. Come here once, you never forget it."

"I'll bet," the cabby agreed. "So we going in, or what?"

"Just let me out here, I'll walk up."

"What's the matter, don't wanna be seen arriving in a humble old cab?"

"Nope, appearances don't bother me. Don't care what others think."

The cab driver took another glance in the mirror, "I can see that."

Rick Ruby ignored the remark, "I just have a couple of things to think over before I talk to the joint's owner. The stroll will give me time to mull things over."

"Hey buddy, that driveway ain't no stroll, that's almost a forced march."

Laughing, Ruby passed the driver a handful of bills that covered the round trip from the city, opened the door and stepped out.

The front of the house was invisible from the gateway, designed to reveal its splendor as visitors rounded the curve about half way along; a perfect example of the owner's proclivity for emphasizing his wealth and status. Rick Ruby had nothing against money, in fact he rather enjoyed its company; even if most of the time it was just as a passing acquaintance. He had no problems with those who worked hard and earned both success and wealth. He even begrudgingly admired some whose rise to prosperity wasn't entirely legal, for many of them at least worked hard for their rewards. What he hated was society money, people born to it who wouldn't know the definition of hard work if it came up and hit them a across the back of the head with a shovel. The owner of this particular place was just such a social animal. If it wasn't for one thing he would never have stepped through these gates in the first place all those months ago. Well two things actually, the prospect of a large paycheck, and the owner's daughter, a certain Carla St. Clair.

As much as he may have been reluctant to get involved in a cases like this, Ruby never forgot that one such had brought Carla into his life. He knew it would never go any where, but he enjoyed both the attention and the reflected wealth that being around Carla produced. With her he saw another side of life and learned very quickly that rich people are still just people. They do the same stupid and dark things that poor folks do; they just tend to hide it with more style.

And talking of hiding things with style, Ruby mused as he passed an all too familiar Dusenberg sports car parked on the drive way. I wonder what that fop Vandemeer is doing here? Pretending to cadge a few drinks, while snooping around for the latest gossip no doubt. Ruby shook his head, as he passed the long sleek ostentatious white car, noting that it was the only one parked with its hood pointing back down the driveway, as if positioned for a quick getaway. A little further around the drive, as he came to the front of the house, he noticed a second car parked in a same way. This one wasn't anywhere near a match for the playboy's ride; a stock Ford sedan with a couple of goons sitting in the back seat and a driver waiting at the wheel. *Now that's more like it,* thought Ruby as we walked past the vehicle feigning a complete indifference to its presence.

Ricky Ruby reached the entrance to the grand house, and started to grasp the bell pull. As always the same thought flashed through his mind, *Why does anyone need a door that big? Do they get that many visitors who are ten feet tall and three feet wide?* But before his hand reached the brass, the massive doors swung open in anticipation of his arrival. The butler had seen the shadowy outline of a man approaching the door and had elected to provide an extra service by opening the door before the guest rang the bell. A good servant always anticipates the needs of his employer and their guests. However when the butler saw who the visitor was, his obsequious smile disappeared to be replaced with a look of contempt. "Oh it's you. The tradesmen's entrance is at the rear of the house, as you well know."

"Hold that thought, Jeeves. I'm here as a guest this evening. You may check with Miss St. Clair."

The butler, ignored the barb, simply nodded his head towards the interior of the house, indicating that Ruby should enter.

"Thanks," Ruby's smile widened, "I know how much this means to you." With a jaunty wave of the hand he walked past the disgruntled servant, feeling the stare of disapproval stabbing into his back as he joined the party, which by now had been in full swing for a couple of hours.

This was another aspect of so-called society life that Ruby had never understood. This wasn't a party; it was just a bunch of stiffs wearing expensive clothes, sipping cocktails, nibbling on servings of unpronounceable food that wouldn't satisfy a fly. All they did was talk, while some string quartet played in the background hardly making enough noise to penetrate the buzz of conversation. For Ruby, a party meant jazz loud enough you had to shout over it, free flowing booze, dames who could dance and do other things with you. Maybe even the occasional knock down drag out punch up over who should, or shouldn't, be dancing with a particular broad.

Ruby passed on the champagne flute that was offered as he walked from the hallway into the large formal sitting room. He decided he needed a proper drink, and he knew where to find it. He made a bee line across the room for the door that led to old man St. Clair's study. Without a backward glance he pulled the door open and slipped into the darkness of the oak paneled room. He allowed his vision to adjust to the lower light levels, before heading towards the desk.

He scanned the room looking for something in particular. It wasn't there, it had been moved; in its place a collection of framed photographs; a couple of which elicited a low whistle from Ruby.

He eventually found the decanter, now located in the bottom drawer of the desk, along with a couple of glasses. He poured himself a generous portion and placed the decanter on the desk when a voice came from behind him. "Use a coaster, or you'll mark the desk."

Ruby cursed himself for not keeping an ear out for anyone entering the room behind him. A sloppy mistake, but one tempered by the fact that the owner of the voice was perhaps the only person who could sneak up on him in this house.

He turned, smiled, and raised the glass in the direction of the new arrival, "Want one?"

"I thought you'd never ask," Carla St. Clair grinned and perched casually on the edge of her father's expensive mahogany desk. "You always knew where Daddy kept the good stuff, so it seemed like the natural place to look for you."

"Guess I'm way too predictable."

"And in many ways that's what I like about you." She leaned over reaching for the small gold chain hanging from the desk lamp. "Let's take a look at how well my scruffy P.I. cleans up for an appearance in fine society."

Ruby's hand shot forward and gripped her wrist, halting her movement. "Ow, that hurts."

"Sorry, but I want the light off."

"You're not normally shy, Ricky, but if that's the way you want to play tonight, that's fine with me too." Carla rubbed her sore wrist, then draped her arms around Ruby's neck, the breath from her lips hot on his ear.

"Not now, doll. I want to keep an eye on those mooks out there," he nodded towards the window.

"What's so interesting out there? It's just an automobile."

"With people just sitting in it. If they are guests, why are they still sitting in the car? And why is it pointing back down the driveway with the engine running?"

"Okay, that is strange" Carla whispered in his ear. "So what do you expect will happen?"

"No clue, but I think it will happen soon."

The pair sat in a frozen embrace, staring out the window for several minutes. Neither said a word, when suddenly Ruby pointed towards the bushes on the side of the drive way. "Now where is he going?"

Carla followed Rick's gaze in time to see the corpulent figure of Alberto Colmenero step out from between the bushes, do a quick a surveillance of driveway and then cross over to the waiting car.

"Interesting," said Ruby.

Colmenero was carrying something in his hand. As he reached the car he handed over a large stuffed envelope, spoke a few quick words to the driver, did another double take, then stepped back into the bushes.

Ruby slipped from Carla's arms and headed for the study window. "See you later, doll. And thank your Daddy for the drink."

"Where are you going.?"

"To follow that envelope."

"How?"

As he slipped through the French doors that connected the study to a gravel path that lead to the driveway, Richard Ruby had to admit that Carla had asked a damn good question. Running up and jumping on the Ford's running board would only get him shot. He needed transport and he needed it fast. He'd told the cabby to head back to town and the car full of goons was already half way down the driveway and would soon disappear from sight.

Sprinting across the driveway he saw the solution; Vandemeer's Dusenberg. It was pointed in the right direction and the fop wouldn't mind if he borrowed it. He'd be sure to return it in the morning.

Ruby reached the white car and scrambled into the driver's seat. He hit the starter button and the car burst into life with a low growl like a caged beast. With a crashing of gears and a rushed engagement of the clutch, the big car spun its rear tires and then lurched forward.

Ruby didn't own a car, no need when the streets of New York were your world, but he knew how to drive. Admittedly it had been a while but if a buffoon like Raymond VanDemeer drove the fancy auto, how tricky could it be?

Still the Dusenberg wasn't your average Ford runabout, and it seemed

The big car spun its rear tires and the lurched forward.

that the playboy owner had a love for speed and gadgets. When Ruby mashed his foot on the gas pedal the thing seemed to almost literally take off. The startled P.I. was pushed back into the seat with surprising force. After a few minutes of levers being pulled and accompanying grinding and crunching sounds, Ruby seemed to find a gear where the engine was purring at a pace Ruby didn't find too frightening. He left things where they were and focused on just pulling on the wooden steering wheel in an effort to follow the direction taken by the Ford.

He knew these hoods and who they worked for. New York's hired muscle was actually a relatively small pool from which to draw, and over his years on the force, Ruby had got to know most of them, if not personally at least by sight.

Once he thought about that he knew with certainty where this car load of muscle was headed. He backed off further, and let them get out of sight. After all even these guys would soon catch on to a large white sports car following them.

This was one of those occasions when a hunch turned out to be right on the mark. Ruby parked the sports car a block from where he assumed the hoods would be heading.

Sure enough as he turned the corner he spotted the car he had been tailing parked, neatly in front of Mama Rizzoli's, a pasta restaurant with a reputation that had nothing to do the quality of food that it served. Ruby considered walking in casually as if he were just another customer, but then decided that that wasn't such a good idea. Discretion being the better part of valor, he ran across the street keeping to the shadows that lay between the feeble pools of light thrown by the occasional street lights. Civic pride was apparently not on the top of the agenda in this part of the city. Sticking to the gloom, Ruby pressed up against the front wall of the pasta house, and then risked a quick look through the window.

What he saw resulted in a raised eyebrow and a bemused look. From his quick glance he saw a couple of the hoods from the Ford sitting at a table chatting it up with a larger than life mob boss, the envelope in question lying on the table between them. The problem was it was the wrong mob boss.

Just as that registered on Ruby's mind he caught the slight movement in the shadows of his peripheral vision. Spinning around, he came face to face with the driver of the Ford who hit him across the temple with an old-fashioned cosh. Ruby's last thought before slipping into blackness was *this is gonna hurt*. He was right.

• • •

"Well if it isn't Mr. Richard Ruby, private investigator. And what would you be doing snooping around this part of town?"

"Lining myself up for a massive headache it would seem."

"Ah wouldn't be thinking of getting too smart with me answers if I was you, or you might be finding other parts or your anatomy will be hurtin' as well."

Ruby shook his head to clear the fog. He made a move to reach the glass of water on the table in front of him and discovered his arms were lashed to the chair back.

"As I was askin' Ruby, what are you doin' here?"

"I was going to ask you the same question. Since when did the Irish develop a taste for pasta?"

The large man on the opposite side of the table pushed his chair back with a sudden violent motion and came to his feet with a grace and speed that belied his apparent bulk. He leaned over the table placing his hands on the edges and pivoted forward so his face was just inches from Ruby's. "We're not here to discuss my eating habits. I'll ask again. Why are you snooping around here?"

Ruby considered his predicament and decided that the best course of action might be to tell the truth, hoping that it might lead to more information about what was going on, and less chance of bodily injury. "That envelope." He gestured with his head toward the envelope sitting in the middle of the table.

"What about it?"

"I followed it here."

"And?"

"Listen I'm working a case for Colmenero, the guy who owns the department store in mid-town."

"I know who he is." The Irishman's voice dropped even deeper into a scowl, as if just hearing the name left a bitter taste in his mouth.

"Well I saw him pass the envelope to these guys at the St. Clair party," Ruby once again used his head to nod in the direction of the goons he'd tailed. "Seemed like a blackmail drop to me, so I decided to follow and see who was behind it. Must admit I didn't expect it to be you O'Malley, I thought it was a strictly Italian affair."

"You think I'm blackmailing him?" The Irish mob boss stood upright, placed his hands on his hips and erupted into laughter. "Ruby, you're an idiot. And that's going ta save your life."

Rick Ruby was even more puzzled now. *Just what the hell was happening here? The Irish working with the Italians, a blackmail scam that wasn't.*

O'Malley stopped laughing, his voice serious and flat. "Listen Mr. P.I. You're in way over your head. Do us all a favor and back away."

Then the big Irishman gestured to his goons. "Show Mr. Ruby the back door, and make sure he is in a fit enough state to walk out of the alley and find his way home, what happens between here and there, I don't care." With that he turned his back on Ruby and exited the room.

• • •

Before he could mutter any sort of reply, Ruby felt himself hauled bodily upwards still tied to the chair. Ruby struggled with his bonds in an effort to both see the human forklift behind him, and upset his balance in the vain hope that he might drop his burden. He failed in both. He was carried through the restaurant, and the kitchen, past inattentive staff, and saw the back door to the alley swing open in front of him. Then he was airborne. He and the chair sailed out into the alley. Twisting, Ruby managed to rotate so that the chair was beneath him when he landed. Having something between his back and the concrete provided a little bit of a barrier as the energy of the impact broke it apart. *Rather the chair than my back.* The destruction of the chair also freed him from his bonds as the ropes around his arms and legs had nothing left to bind him to. But any thought of escape was short lived. A large hand grabbed his collar and hoisted him aloft, and once more threw him down the alley.

His landing spot was at the feet of the hoods who had been in the restaurant and others he assumed had been loitering outside. Kicks and punches rained down on the private eye. All Ruby could do was pull himself into a tight ball, and pull his arms up to protect his face, hoping to minimize exposure of the most sensitive areas of his body. The blows seemed to continue for a long time, although in reality it was probably only thirty seconds at the most. It was enough, or at least that's what the deep brogue voice told his attackers. Suddenly the beating stopped and he was all alone in the alley.

The mob boss had instructed that Ruby should be able to walk out the alley. Perhaps "walk" was a bit of a stretch at the moment, but he manage to stagger with dignity. Half crouched, half crawling, Ruby found his way back to the spot where he had left the white Dusenberg. The car was no longer there. Pasted to a nearby lamp post was a piece of paper with a simple message, "Next time, just ask! - V."

Ruby muttered an expletive under his breath calling into question the validity of Raymond VanDemeer's parentage, and staggered away in the direction of his office. His years on the streets of Manhattan had imprinted its geography on his mind to the extent that he navigated its sidewalks almost on instinct. No matter his physical condition he could always find the quickest route to his office, like some sort of six foot disheveled homing pigeon.

• • •

It wasn't unusual for the light to be on in Ruby's office in the early hours of the morning; but that was usually when he was actually inside there himself. Spotting the glow illuminating the frosted glass pane in his office door, Ruby groaned at the possibility of his evening getting even worse. The last thing he wanted was another confrontation, especially a physical one. He doubted whoever was in his office was going to invite him to sit down, rest, dress his wounds and pour him a shot of whiskey.

Ruby's reaction was to turn tail and head back down the stairs towards the Jazz Club that occupied the building's first floor. Let whoever it was that was ransacking the office just get on with it, he reasoned.

His resolve lasted for all of five steps before he turned on his heels and headed back up the stairs to the dimly lit hallway outside his door. Crouching low, Ruby kicked the door open, then tucked and rolled through the opening coming to his feet in a crouched position ready for a fight.

"Heck, Ruby! You scared the shit out of me!"

"I scared you! What the hell are you doing here at this time of night Edi? I was sure it was the micks deciding to finish off their night's work."

"What are you talking about the Irish for? They've got nothing to do with the shooting. Do they?"

"You know, at the moment I just don't feel like asking them, again."

"Again?"

Ruby stepped further into the office and his face was illuminated by desk lamp. Edi Rose Adams gasped.

"What happened to you? I thought you were at that society dame's place at some posh party. Did you insult the butler or something?"

"I stopped off at Mama Rizolli's on the way home."

"But you mentioned the Irish. What would they be doing at Mama Rizolli's"

"You know that's a damn good question." Rick Ruby winced as he collapsed into one of the office chairs. They weren't what you would call comfortable or plush, but it would provide him enough support to keep him upright. "But right now I'm more interested in a strong cup of Joe."

Edi headed for the small sink at the far side of the office. "Of course.

One coffee, strong and black, coming up."

Ruby watched his secretary while she fussed about preparing his drink. No matter which way you looked at it, she was a stunning woman, the sort that every man looked at when she entered a room, actually every woman looked too. She had a commanding presence. Her looks were matched by the strength of her personality. In many ways she was Ruby's equal, a fact that she often reminded him of. It was just a shame about the whole religion thing.

Edi passed Rick the coffee and then perched on the edge of the desk; she leant forward to get a closer look at Rick's face. As she unknowingly provocatively encroached into Rick's personal space he smiled when he got an up close view of the pin of a blackbird with jeweled eyes that he'd purchased for her birthday last year, and she persistently wore on her blouse just above her left breast. The smile was not a good idea. Stretching the muscles on his battered face made him wince in pain.

Edi caught the change in expression, "You know you should get someone to take a look at those bruises."

"Yeah, I guess so." Ruby said though he had no intention of seeking medical help and she knew it.

"Well, while you were partying with the hob-nobs, and playing pattycake with the micks I've been doing a little sleuthing of my own."

"Listen, Edi, no matter how often you ask, I'm not taking you out on a case with me, and if you want a reason why," he pointed up at his battered and bruised face and simply shrugged.

Edi also shrugged then slowly leaned back across the desk, the hem of her skirt riding up to expose the stocking tops of her shapely legs. Reaching behind her she picked up a stack of papers.

Straightening up she passed the papers to Rick, who was surprised to see that they were loose newspaper pages. "What am I looking at here?"

"Selected extracts from the various gossip columns over the last year."

"Gossip columns! Why would I be interested in that sort of stuff?"

"You'd be amazed what you can learn from gossip," Edi smiled. "Like who is sleeping with who."

"OK, now you've got my interest."

Edi retrieved the papers and pulled a page from the bottom of the stack before handing it back to Rick. "Look at the photo."

"It's a girl popping out of a cake at some guy's bachelor party. So what?"

"Take a closer look at the girl."

"Only because you insist," Ruby joked pulling the paper closer to his bruised face getting his eyes to focus on the dame in the picture. "Nice chassis."

"Her face," Edi gave an exasperated groan.

Ruby continued to study the photograph. The newsprint wasn't of the greatest quality or clarity, but he could just about make out the features of the cake model. "Damn, is that...?"

"Yes, it's your Lt.Betty-12, and take a look at the appreciative audience too. At the back on the right."

"It's just a blur of faces. Just a bunch of fat rich white guys. How am I meant to make any one out?"

"Try this."

Ruby reached out and took the magnifying glass Edi was holding out. "Jesus! Really? What am I? A cut-rate Sherlock Holmes?"

The smack across the side of the head was as quick as it was unexpected.

"Yeouch! What was that for?"

"Don't blaspheme!"

"What?"

"You took the Lord's name in vain. Don't do that!"

"Jes...., Geez I'm sorry, Edi. Slip of the tongue." Edi just stared at her boss, then after a few seconds pointed her well manicured finger at the newspaper photo.

"Yeah, the stiff in the picture. Got it." Ruby peered intently through the magnifying glass studying the collection of faces in the background. He panned back and forth across the image, his brow furrowed in concentration. Once, twice, three times, then on his fourth pass he paused. Moving the magnifying glass up and down over one spot trying to get it to focus in on one particular face. "Hold on, is that who I think it is?"

Edi nodded, "Colmenero."

Ruby shook his head, "Not sure what that proves other than he was aware of her existence before hiring her to dress in a silver mini-skirt."

"Then take a look at this one from a few months later." Edi handed him another tear sheet.

"Oh now they look cozy," Ruby smiled, "not too bright of him being photographed with the young lady hanging off his arm was it?"

"I guess not," agreed Edi, "but take a look at her face, she doesn't exactly look happy about it."

"You're right. Lover's spat maybe?"

"If it was, it was a long one. This is from just a few weeks ago." Edi offered him a third sheet from the stack.

"She looks down right petrified in this one."

"Look at the crowd watching her and Colmenero leaving the night club."

Ruby picked up the magnifying glass for a second time and scanned the photograph. It didn't take him long to spot a familiar face. He emitted a low whistle. "Well it seems that whatever was going on, she had a hero."

Edi nodded; "Mars MacCoy Space Ranger to the rescue!"

• • •

"Thanks, anyway." Rick replaced the phone receiver with a firmness that was perhaps a little more forceful than needed. "That's it. Two days calling every booking agency on the island and no-one's got a record of those two working together before. So how come they knew each other?"

"Maybe he saw her pop out of a cake too?"

"Who popped out of what cake?" the voice came from behind Edi. Rick Ruby leaned over to peer around his secretary. "You know Ruby you should keep your door locked, you never know what sort of low life could just walk in."

"You got that right," Ruby muttered, hoping it was pitched low enough so only Edi picked it up. Raising his voice back to a normal pitch, Ruby asked in an overly jolly tone, "And what can we do for you this fine morning officer Perry?"

"You can start by not getting cute with me, Ruby."

"Yes, sir!" Ruby's sarcastic response seemed to go past Perry.

Ruby looked Detective Robert Perry up and down. He didn't like the guy, and he was far from alone in that sentiment, most of the other cops in town didn't much like him either. Maybe it was the way he was always so immaculately dressed, or his insistence on doing things by the book. But the word was that this stuck up prig got results. And for that reason alone, Ruby was prepared to listen.

"I'll ask again, who popped out of a cake?"

"The girl."

"What did I say about being smart with me?"

"No, the space girl from the shooting, it appears she knew Colmenero."

"Of course she did, you idiot, he hired her."

"I think he hired her for more than just that in-store movie thing."

"Are you trying to insinuate something?"

"I'm not insinuating anything," Ruby smiled, "I'm saying he knew her all right, in the biblical sense!"

"Do you have any proof of that?"

"Not yet."

"Well don't bother doing whatever grubby things you do to find out stuff like that." the cop's tone became serious. "It's irrelevant. Their private life is just that, private."

"Yeah," Ruby smirked, "but I'm a private investigator."

"Leave it, Ruby."

"But what about the shooting? A guy is dead."

"The official police position is that it was an unfortunate on-set accident caused by a malfunctioning prop. Unfortunate, but that's all it was, an accident."

"I don't get roughed up over accidents!"

"What do you mean, Ruby?"

"Nothing, he doesn't mean anything," Edi interjected. "Just one of his stupid phrases." She glared at Ruby, and slightly moved her head from side to side.

He got the message. "We'll take your request on advisement Detective. Now if you'll excuse us we have other cases to work on."

"Fine. Just stay away from this one. It's over and done." With that Perry turned on his heel and departed.

Ruby watched the door as if waiting for the immaculate detective to re-appear. When he was convinced that the it would remain closed, he turned to Edi. "What was all that head shaking for?"

"He didn't need to know about your run in with the micks."

"Why not, that proves there's something else going on here. You don't buy that accident BS do you?"

Edi smiled. Ruby knew that smile, a seductive knowing smile she used when she had the better of him. The smile she used when she'd thought of an angle he hadn't covered. Her *I'm a better detective than you smile.*

"Go on." Ruby capitulated knowing it was easier to just ask than try to tease it out of her, which is what she wanted. Sometimes he'd play the game, but not today, he wasn't in the mood. "What did I miss?"

"Maybe it was an accident," Edi explained, "just not the accident the cops think it was."

"I'm not following?"

"They think the accident was the gun going off. Well what if the gun was meant to go off and the accident was who caught the bullet?"

"So instead of asking who shot Mars McCoy we need to be asking why they wanted to shoot anybody in the first place?"

"You got it, buster."

• • •

Richard Ruby enjoyed walking the streets of Manhattan. He felt connected to the rhythm of the city. Today he wondered if he had lost his mind. Every step just seemed to confirm that he had no idea what he was getting himself into.

In Ruby's experience there were a few places that were more intimidating in the daylight than at night and Mama Rizolli's was one of them. Maybe it was the shuttered windows; maybe it was the two goons lounging by the door. As he stepped up, Ruby glanced at the large gentleman standing to his left. A slight shiver ran up his back, while the face was vaguely familiar he knew that he'd already made a personal connection with those large clenched fists and their distinctive oversized knuckles.

"Afternoon." Ruby's greeting went unnoticed. When the goon made no attempt to stop him, Ruby continued into the restaurant. They obviously considered him no threat. Ruby guessed that none of the people with heads bent over steaming bowls of pasta were actual paying customers in the traditional sense. A large section of tables remained unoccupied, providing a no-man's land between the door and the object of his visit. If anyone wanted to reach Giancarlo Vinolli they would have to get through that open space.

Rick Ruby kept walking. No one stopped him, but the occupants of the large round table at the rear of the establishment stopped eating, set down their silverware and eyed him. Ruby felt like a rabbit being examined by a flock of hawks.

Ruby started to speak then realized the restaurant was quiet. No murmur of voices; no slurping of drinks or chewing of food. Not a single clink of glasses or silverware on china. He froze.

"I'll give you one thing; you've got some nerve walking in here." The only thing pointing at Ruby was the bread stick in Vinolli's chubby hand. "So why did you risk another beating?"

"I'm looking for Jack O'Malley."

Vinolli laughed. " Does this look like an Irish bar to you? Why would you think that mick scum bag would be hanging around here?"

"He was here the other night, when your boys gave me a few take home presents. In fact he's the one who ordered the beating."

Vinolli suddenly stood up, pushing his chair backwards with such a force that it tipped over and then put his hands flat on the table and leaned forward.

"Nobody tells my boys what to do, except me! And anyone who says different is up for another beating. Do you get that?"

"Sure," Ruby said. "Sorry if I made a mistake. Look I just need to ask O'Malley a question."

"So go ask him."

"Do you know where I can find him?"

"How the hell should I know?" Vinolli moved to sit and one of his goons quickly set the chair upright and slid it in behind him. Once seated, Vinolli reached for another breadstick. Waving it casually towards his mouth, he took a bite, then looked at Ruby. "What are you still doing here? Get out!"

Rick turned and walked away. As he passed through the door, he glanced at Fat Knuckles. The big man suddenly leaned towards Ruby and whispered "Murphy's," then returned to the upright position acting as if not a word had passed his lips.

Murphy's, Rick sighed, there must be hundreds of places with that name in the city. How in the hell would he find the right one, assuming it was a business, and not a person the doorman was hinting at?

Ruby found his answer about ten minutes after entering the Irish part of town.

• • •

The explosion blew him off his feet.

Rick Ruby picked himself up, and started brushing masonry dust and glass shards off his suit. As he patted himself down he glanced across the street at the source of the explosion. Above the gaping hole that had once been a bar front, a scared sign hung perilously from a single remaining nail. Swinging to and fro it declared that this had once been Murphy's Bar. This was probably the place he'd been looking for.

Ruby sprinted across the road, weaving his way between cars and trucks that had come to a sudden halt when the bar exploded. Scrambling over the rubble he joined the growing crew of people searching through the debris for survivors. Without thought for personal safety, the eclectic group of New Yorkers pitched in, shifting rubble, lifting broken timbers, pulling and sorting debris. They worked for hours next to each other, all focused on the grim task. Amazingly everyone pulled out of the wreckage was alive. Most had scratches, and a few had broken bones, but no lives had been lost.

After what seemed like an eternity, the police and fire crews arrived and began to organize the rescue efforts. The volunteers kept working. Daylight turned to evening as the search continued. It must have been an hour after the last person had been recovered when the fire chief got on the bullhorn and declared the search over. Only then did Ruby look over at the person who had been working next to him the past few hours. As their gazes locked the man's eyes opened in recognition.

"Jesus, Ruby, what the hell are you doing here?"

"Looking for you."

Jack O'Malley looked at Rick Ruby as if he'd gone mad. "And why would you be wanting to find me after our last little encounter?"

"Well..... I... "

"Never mind what it was, I'm glad you chose today to pay us a visit. We all appreciate your help."

Rick gestured at the debris. "So who woulda done this. The Italians?"

"You mean Vinolli?"

"Yeah."

O'Malley shook his head. "No way, not at the moment. More like it was the Jerries."

Ruby was confused. "I know we have a few black shirts goose stepping around the island, but they would never mess with you."

"Not those delusional wannabes, I mean the real Jerries. Nazis."

"Nazis, here? In New York?"

"Sure, you think that the war is only happening in Europe? Think again buddy, the Germans and the Brits are having their private little war right here in the good old US of A."

"So what's that got to do with you?"

"The jackboots wanted my help in pulling a little trick on Brit interests here in town, but as the old country is neutral in this particular disagreement, I refused. I'm guessing this was a little demonstration as to what happens if you say no."

O'Malley took Ruby by the arm and steered him back on to the sidewalk. "I don't know about you Ruby, but I could do with something to get rid of all that dust in me throat?"

"But your bar was just destroyed," Ruby stated the obvious.

"An Irishman never has far to walk to find a drink."

• • •

O'Malley wasn't joking. The next bar was literally just around the corner. It was packed shoulder-to-shoulder with locals, rescuers, cops, and newspaper reporters trying to get a human interest angle on the afternoon's events. Yet they seemed to just walk up to an empty booth at the back of the bar. A quiet, private oasis in the midst of all the chaos. Once settled in, a barmaid appeared and placed two shots of whiskey in front of them. The big Irishman looked up at the girl, smiled and gave the merest indication of a nod as she melted back into the crowd.

Ruby looked around the bar, recognizing a lot of faces, most from his days on the force; an equal mix of New York's finest, and not so finest. This was where the thin blue line faded to more of a grey tint. The distinction between honest cops and those on the take became impossible; but a who's who of bent policemen wasn't Ruby's concern today; he just wanted to talk to O'Malley. As he started to ask his first question, the Irishman raised his hand in a simple gesture of silence.

O'Malley looked at Ruby with a serious expression. "Listen flatfoot, don't ask me why, but I like you. Always thought you were one of the better guys when you wore the blue. This thing you are starting to poke your nose in, it has the potential to get ugly. We are sorting it out, so I'd suggest you just head back to your office."

"We? Whose 'we'?"

"Look, Ruby, drop it. If you want to keep breathing."

"You and the Italians! Geez whatever this is must be important to get you working together. But what sort of pay off is big enough to satisfy both gangs?"

"Not everything is about money!" O'Malley's responded.

So it was something personal. Ruby realized he'd have to tread carefully. "Look, I'm sorry about jumping to conclusions. The thing is I was hired to do a job, and that's what I intend to do - my job. If I can do that and stay out of your way I will. If you know of another direction I should be looking, just tell me and I'm out if your hair."

O' Malley stared at Ruby for several minutes. When he spoke, the pain had been replaced by a slight hint of humor. "Okay, Ruby, you've got moxie. Not many have the gall to ask me direct questions, so I'll give you one hint; but after that I don't want to see you around these parts again. Do I make myself clear?"

"Crystal."

"When you get back to your office, get that cute secretary of yours to check your social calendar and give your friend St. Clair a call."

"Carla St. Clair?"

"No, you idiot. Her father."

• • •

"My father!"

Well that didn't go as well as Ruby had hoped. He pleaded with the now irate Carla St. Clair. "Look doll all I asked was if you could set up another meeting with your father."

He pleaded with the now irate Carla St.Clair.

"Based on the advice of an Irish gangster."

"True, but..."

Carla's stare become venomous; her voice icy cold. "Richard Ruby, how dare you even suggest that there is any connection between that criminal and my father? He probably got my father's name from the newspapers and used it to send you off on a wild goose chase."

"I'm sorry, Carla, but I don't think that he lied. O'Malley was pretty clear about your father having some connection to this murder case."

"Well you can forget using me to get to my father. In fact you can forget any future invitations to the house." Carla spun on her heels, and exited the offices of Richard Ruby Private Investigator, punctuating her departure with a slammed door that rattled the frosted glass.

"Well that was awkward."

Ruby turned towards his secretary, weakly smiled and shrugged his shoulders. "Well I guess its Plan B then."

Edi chuckled. "You don't have a Plan B, do you?"

• • •

Ruby looked up at the wrought iron double gates and the imposing stone lions that stared down at him in apparent disapproval. *Well I guess it turned out be Plan C.*

The sound of an approaching car was the signal for Ruby to slip behind one of the bushes adjacent to the gates. The large metal gates of the Lionsgate Country Club swung open in response to an unseen hand flicking a switch somewhere inside the compound. The large black car slowed almost to a halt to make the sharp turn off the road onto the long graveled driveway. Ruby slipped out from behind the bush and crouched low alongside the car, hoping it would act as a shield from prying eyes.

The driveway was lined with an avenue of trees that provided the skulking detective with sufficient cover to reach the impressive club house without being seen. But now what next? Edi would not be impressed by his lack of planning; but he often got the best results when he just went with the flow, and let opportunity present itself. The large black car had finished unloading passengers and bags of golf clubs and other sporting equipment. As one of the club valets shut the trunk, the car moved off. That meant it had either a chauffeur, or was being valet parked. Either way it pointed to a back entrance for staff. Staying hidden behind a convenient row of bushes, Ruby followed the car around to a side parking lot, then watched as the driver disappeared down a small set of steps.

Ruby followed. The steps led down to a door marked Staff Only. He pushed the door open and walked in. The corridor was empty; he could hear voices and the clattering of various pots and pans from behind doors. Without hesitating he strode purposefully along the corridor banking on the axiom that if you act like you belong somewhere people rarely question you. Turning a corner he passed two maids deep in a whispered conversation who barley gave him a second glance. Turning another corner he spied a rack holding what appeared to be short white jackets worn by waiters. He swapped his sport coat for one, and headed for what he believed to be the general direction of the club's main facilities.

"You! Where do you think you are going?"

Ruby froze. The shout had come from a large stocky man in a chef's uniform whose bulk seemed to fill most of the corridor.

"I was just..." Ruby was frantically trying to improvise an answer, when the chef interrupted.

"I don't know you."

Ruby took a breath, ready to make a run for it.

"Are you new here?"

"Er, yeah, just started a couple of days ago. Still trying to find my way around."

The chef smiled. "It is a bit of a labyrinth down here. Took me almost a year to figure my way around. Where you heading?"

"The dining room I think, I was actually going to look for Mr. St. Clair, someone gave me a message for him."

The Chef's focus shifted slightly as if he was consulting some sort of internal time table. "He will have finished his luncheon by now. You're most likely find him in the Show Room."

"Show Room?" Ruby was confused.

"Of course, you probably don't know where that is, do you?" Ruby was puzzled by the Chef nodding his head as he asked the question. *Why would he be nodding, it didn't make sense, unless it was to someone behind.* Rick Ruby spun on his heels just in time to see the cosh descending and then everything went black.

• • •

Ruby shook his head. He wasn't ready to open his eyes just yet. His head felt as if he'd gone ten rounds with Joe Louis, and he wasn't ready to welcome any light into his spinning world just yet. But wherever he was he knew one thing, it was cold!

When head stopped spinning, Ruby opened his eyes. His view consisted of a row of half butchered pigs dangling from a series of vicious looking meat hooks. Beyond them wooden shelves piled with hams and bacon joints.

Ruby shivered. Cold storage. He raised his hand towards the lump on his head where the cosh had landed. He winced in pain at the touch. Still, whoever had thrown him in here had helped speed up his recovery, the cold having reduced the swelling and eased the pain. Instead of an ice pack, he had a whole room of frigid air. But he didn't plan on staying much longer. They hadn't tied him up or restrained him obviously assuming he'd be out longer. But his skull was a lot thicker than most bad guys estimated it to be.

Pulling himself to his feet, Rick Ruby started to reconnoiter the room. It was only ten feet square and didn't contain more than the pig carcasses and shelving he'd already spotted. It was, of course, completely sealed with no windows or vents. The only means of entering or leaving was via the bolted door.

Ruby contemplated hammering on the door, on the hope that he might attract the attention of someone working in the kitchen. But given the chef's involvement he discounted getting aid from that quarter; it would be safer to assume that every member of staff was involved in whatever it was that was going on here.

So what else to do? Wait it out? The cold would get to him eventually.

Ruby stiffened, hearing a noise outside. He held his breath as if to dampen the noise his own existence so he could hear more clearly. There it was again, the dragging of a foot across a tiled floor. The scrapping got closer. If they thought he was still out, they might not be taking too many precautions when they opened the door. They wouldn't be expecting a fully conscious man armed with..? Ruby looked frantically about and then he smiled and reached out.

The door creaked open and a figure stepped into the freezer, at which point the newcomer's face made heavy contact with a vigorously swung side of bacon.

Hoping his unconscious visitor was a lone kitchen worker, Ruby gambled that there wouldn't be a reception committee waiting for him as he stepped out of the meat locker.

The locker was located at the back of a larger general storage room stacked with cans and various other supplies needed by the kitchen of a large entertainment establishment. Ruby figured that he was still in the Country Club and that he had about ten minutes before the kitchen worker would be missed. *Now to find this mysterious Show Room.*

He spent the next twenty minutes frantically going up and down various stair cases and corridors that ran behind the scenes. Amazingly Ruby's luck held and he didn't encounter any other members of staff as he traversed the premises.

All the access doors that connected the passages to the club's main rooms were labeled on the staff side except one. By a process of elimination, Ruby figured that the plain door he now stood before was the entrance to the Show Room. He pushed the door open and his eyes widened. He hadn't known what to expect but it wasn't this.

Now he knew why they called it the Show Room.

It was laid out like most of the burlesque clubs and jazz joints with which Ruby was all too familiar. At the far side of the room was a small stage on which several girls were dancing, accompanied by a trio of musicians situated off to one side.

The main floor area was a little more upscale than the dives he frequented. Instead of stained tables and broken chairs, it was covered with leather sofas, and booths upholstered in deep velvet cushioning. Hostesses moved among the guests offering various drinks, cigarettes, and what, from a distance, looked like pills.

But what really caught Ruby's attention was that everyone in the room was naked!

The hostesses, the dancers, the musicians, and the patrons. The women on stage weren't actually dancing either. They were rubbing their hands up and down each other's bodies as they gyrated.

The people occupying the booths and sofas were doing the same thing; some in pairs and others in groups. Rick Ruby had stumbled into a full blown orgy.

More importantly Ruby recognized a few faces among the sea of writhing, heaving, flesh. Faces that he'd seen in the society pages of the metro newspapers; even a few faces from the St. Clair party a few nights before.

St. Clair! The Chef had said he would be in here. *Was he part of that mass of bodies?* He got his answer almost before the thought had finished percolating.

A gun barrel pressed against his spine. He'd been so absorbed by the sight in front of him that he'd let his guard down again. "Enjoying the view, Mr. Ruby?" It was St. Clair. Ruby assumed the question was rhetorical and made no attempt to answer.

The lack of response provoked further pressure from the gun barrel against his back, and another voice he recognized emphasized the point with the command, "Turn round."

Ruby slowly rotated until he stood face to face with the Chef. "You are becoming a nuisance. What are we going to do with you?"

"Oh I bet you have some ideas, something involving a kitchen implement no doubt."

"Don't tempt me."

St. Clair reached past Ruby and silently closed the door on the hedonistic scene behind them. "So, what do you think we should do with you?"

"Your call, but I'm sure Carla wouldn't approve."

St. Clair's fist flew at Ruby's jaw with sudden violence. "You never mention my daughter's name again. If you go near her, I will leave you to the tender mercies of my culinary friend here."

Ruby rubbed his jaw. "You pack a good punch for a trust fund dandy."

"Even private schools have boxing teams."

"Fair point. So what are you going to do to me?"

"Nothing. I'm going to let you go. In fact I'll have my chauffeur drive you back to your office."

"What!?" The cry of disbelief came from Ruby and the Chef simultaneously.

St. Clair gave them both a patronizing smile. "You two dolts live in a world where the only language you understand is violence. There are better ways to curtail someone's activities than locking them up. Frustration can be just as an effective restraint as ropes."

"I don't get it." complained the Chef.

"Oh, I do," Ruby looked at St. Clair with unadulterated hatred. "Who am I going to tell about what I just saw? Anybody I can talk to works for someone who was in that room, or knows someone who was in there. This may be a big city, but runs with a very small clique. Yes, I saw what I saw. I know your dirty secret, and there's not a damn thing I can do about it!"

"Precisely," confirmed St. Clair, "Now can I offer you that ride home?"

• • •

"That was some fancy car you rode home in last night?"

Rick looked up from his desk as Edi opened the office door. He hadn't slept. He had spent the last few hours trying to both erase certain images from his mind, and to figure a way out of the impasse he caught in. He grunted.

"So, was that your fancy society girl-friend?"

"It was her father's car."

"Really? I thought he hated your guts?"

"Let's just say we came to an agreement last night."

"Must have been an interesting discussion."

"You have no idea."

"Want to talk about it?"

"I don't think you'd approve." Rick watched Edi walk across the office and start to brew what would become an endless stream of black coffee. "Oh no, you definitely wouldn't approve. On any level."

Edi returned and placed the steaming coffee cup in front of him. "So that moment of inspiration yesterday turned out to be a dead end then?"

"You could put it that way. Let's just say that avenue of enquiry is no longer available to me."

"So what now?"

"The two of you do nothing." Detective Perry stood in the doorway.

"Why if it isn't my good friend Officer Perry fresh from getting his shoes shined and his suit pressed."

Edi sensed Perry's discomfort and invited him to take a chair. The homicide bull used a handkerchief and wiped imaginary dust off the visitor's chair. Once settled, he came straight to the point. "I don't know what you've been up to Ruby, but it seems you've rattled some gilded cages."

"Listen, Perry I did what you told me. Sort of."

"I'm not interested in how you earn your grubby living. But when a message comes down from on high that I needed to remind you to drop this case, it upsets me greatly. Especially a message that comes from so high that it almost needs a parachute to land on my desk."

"Go on." Ruby waved his hand.

"Officially I'm here to tell you to walk away from this case. A case I thought you'd already dropped."

"Interesting."

Perry leaned back in the chair, and impulsively ran his hands along the seams of his jacket to straighten it. "Isn't it?"

The two men sat looking at each other coolly. Edi was intrigued. These two men never saw eye to eye on anything. Yet they did agree on one thing, justice for the wronged. The longer Edi watched, what she had first thought of as a Mexican standoff, she now perceived as silent communication.

Eventually Perry stood and leaned forward until his face was uncomfortably close to Ruby's. "I'm officially telling you to stay away from the department store owner and his girl. Did you get that?"

Ruby smiled. "Oh yeah, message received and understood, Officer Perry."

Perry straightened up, spun around, and as was his style, left the office without another word. Ruby reached across his desk and picked up the folded slip of paper that was lying where Perry's hands had been resting.

"What's that?" asked the puzzled Edi.

Unfolding the paper, Ruby replied, "If I'm not mistaken it's the opening move in the game of What Rick Ruby Does Next."

• • •

"I can't believe you persuaded me to do this!"

"You've been asking to join me on a case forever, Edi. Well this is it."

"But, it's cold, wet, miserable, boring, and above all more than a little creepy."

"Welcome to the wonderful world of stakeouts."

Edi indicated the area around the park bench they were sitting on. "So why are we here anyway?"

"I just explained that. We are on a stakeout."

Edi punched Ruby's arm. "I meant this particular spot, and you knew it."

"Just trying to relieve the boredom with a little light banter." Ruby nodded in the direction of a brownstone across the street from the park, where they were partially hidden from sight by a line of trees. "I'm interested in who comes out of that door."

"Why that door?"

Ruby handed Edi the folded paper that Perry had left behind. "Because that's the address written on this."

"So who lives there?"

"I don't know for sure. But I can make a pretty good guess as to who might be coming through that door."

"Are you determined to be obtuse all evening?"

"Yep."

Rick Ruby and Edi lapsed into silence, as they continued their vigil. After an hour Ruby felt Edi's weight on his arm as she started to doze off. He was starting to feel a little heavy eyed himself. Then he saw movement across the street: a figure appeared at the foot of the brownstone's steps. He nudged Edi awake.

"We've got movement."

"Who is it?" she asked as she rubbed the last remnants of her brief sleep from her eyes.

"Take a hard look."

Edi focused on the woman that was cautiously making her way towards the building's door, while balancing several overstuffed grocery bags, and was now illuminated by a nearby streetlamp. "It's your space girl. She obviously lives there. How does a two-bit model afford such an uptown rent like that?"

"Because," Ruby offered, "this house is owned by Colmenero Department Stores Incorporated."

Edi looked at Ruby. "You knew, didn't you?"

"I had a hunch."

"Since when?"

"Since Detective Perry used the phrase 'his girl' shortly after slipping us this address."

"I don't understand. He told us to stay away."

"As usual, he did things by the book. He did what he had been ordered to do and passed on the official message."

Edi gasped, "But unofficially..."

"He didn't say anything, but how we interpret what he didn't say... Well that's just between us. Isn't it?"

A sudden gust of wind caused Edi to pull the collar of her coat up in an effort to stay a little warmer. She shivered. Ruby moved slightly to put his arm around her, and as he shifted position, his foot hit a discarded soda bottle that the wind had blown close to the bench. He froze and stared at the bottle for several seconds.

"Edi, do you know where the closest grocery store is?"

"You hungry, or something?"

"Just a sudden thought, do you know where it is?"

"Maybe four or five blocks from here. Why?"

"That's a long way for anyone to juggle an armful of bags."

"So you're thinking she had help?"

"Yep."

Edi shook her head. "But a grocery store delivery boy would have carried the bags up the steps, in fact he'd have taken them inside for her."

Ruby's attention had shifted from the brownstone's steps sweeping his gaze along the street in both directions. "Maybe she had help from someone who didn't want to chance being seen close to the brownstone." He suddenly pointed off to his right. "Somebody like that guy!"

Rick Ruby stood up, playfully patted Edi on the top of her head, forcing her to readjust her hat, "Stay here and keep an eye on that door. I'll be back in a few minutes."

"Where are you off to?"

"Just to say hello to our mysterious grocery boy." Instead of stepping out towards the sidewalk, Ruby slipped behind the bench and disappeared into the trees behind them.

The move left his prey out of view for a minute, but Ruby gambled that as the man hadn't moved since the girl got home, he wasn't likely to move any time soon.

Sure enough he was exactly where Ruby had first spotted him; on another park bench about five hundred yards south of where Ruby and Edi had been staking out the brownstone. This bench also gave a good line of sight to the brownstone.

Ruby quietly walked up behind the seated figure and clamped his hand on the man's shoulder. There wasn't much muscle or mass underneath the bulky overcoat. Ruby squeezed harder, pinching the nerve where the neck meets the shoulder. The man gave an involuntary cry of pain, ineffectively squirmed in a vain effort to break the grip, before turning to look behind him.

"You're getting sloppy, Jimmy."

"Jesus, Ruby, you scared the shit out of me."

"So what are you doing here Weasel?"

"Can't a guy just sit in the park and enjoy the view?"

"Not when that view is the front door belonging to his boss's girlfriend."

Weasel didn't say a word.

"So that's it, you've got the hots for Colmenero's bit of skirt."

Jimmy Weasel's voice took on a menacing tone. "Don't you ever talk about her like that!"

Ruby was taken aback. "Geez, I'm sorry, Jimmy. You've got it bad haven't you?"

"It ain't like that, Rick, she's my sister."

• • •

"Wow, I didn't see that one coming."

"Well you deserved it."

Ruby continued rubbing his jaw, reflecting on both the throbbing pain and the strength of his friend's right hook. "How do you figure that, Jimmy?"

Jimmy Weasel remained stoically quiet. The silence hung between the two them like a bad smell neither would acknowledge.

The door of the office swung open, as Edi appeared with two steaming mugs of coffee in hand. She stopped, looked at the two men, then sniffed dramatically. "Geez you can almost smell the muscles in here."

Rick just reached out his hand for the hot cup of Joe. "You got the special ingredients from downstairs?"

Edi sighed, "Yeah, just like you asked. But I don't have to approve."

"Don't think he was asking for it." Jimmy Weasel interjected.

"Men!" Edi said in exasperation. "So what do you geniuses here have in mind to wrap this thing up?"

Jimmy just shrugged his shoulders, "Hell if I know."

Ruby kept rubbing his chin. Edi looked straight at him. He never was this quiet unless he was thinking. Rick stopped massaging his bruised chin as a smile spread across his face. *Uh Oh*, Edi thought. She knew what that smile meant.

"So, Jimmy," Ruby started, "I know you have a pretty good forearm smash, but how's the backhand these days?"

• • •

Ruby stared up at the stone lions, hardly believing that he was back here again, nor that he'd convinced Weasel to go along with his crazy idea. In a show of childish bravado, at he stuck his tongue out the stone guardians, then yanked on the bell pull by the side of the Country Club's iron gates.

'Well let's hope this works out." he muttered under his breath.

The guard who appeared was not pleased at being pulled away listening to the ball game on the radio. "What do you want? This is a private club."

"Oh I know exactly what this place is. And you couldn't pay me to be a member. But despite my personal misgivings I've got a message for Mr. St. Clair."

The guard's demeanor changed. "Pass it here and I'll see that he gets it."

"Sorry, Mr. Colmenero said I had to deliver it in person."

The guard's eyes widened at the mention of Colmenero's name.

"Mr.Colmenero, huh?"

"Yeah. So can I go in or not?"

The guard must have signaled someone, for the large gates silently swung open.

By the time Ruby had completed the long trudge up the driveway, a member of the club staff was waiting at the main entrance. Walking past the waiting man, Ruby did a quick double take. He was pretty certain the last time he'd seen that face it had been connecting with a side of frozen bacon.

St. Clair was waiting for him in one of the opulent side rooms. "Home way from home?" the private eye commented.

"I'm not interested in your smart remarks, Ruby. You've a hell of a nerve showing your face around here again. What's the message from Colmenero?"

"Ah," Ruby rubbed his chin in feigned embarrassment, "that's where

"Geez, you can almost smell the muscles in here."

things fall apart. You see there isn't one."

"Ruby, you are an idiot. Congratulations for exceeding my already low opinion of you. What my daughter sees in you is beyond me." St. Clair gestured at Bacon Face. "Put this imbecile back on ice."

Ruby felt the all too familiar pressure of .38 Smith & Wesson in the small of his back. "Okay, but before I go, one quick question."

"Just one?" St. Clair shrugged, "Well what is it?"

"How long had Mars McCoy and you been an item?"

"Mars who?"

"The studley looking space man who was popped at Colemero's department store."

"Oh him." St. Clair stalled for a second before continuing. "He was just one of the men who worked here at the club. Sort of a bodyguard for some of the girls."

"Yeah, the sort you could trust around them too, knowing he'd never make a play for one." Ruby waited for a reaction. When he didn't get one, he pushed a little further. "Do you often keep photos of the hired help in your study? For instance I didn't see one of Bacon Face here, but you had plenty of the space man."

St. Clair turned his back to Ruby he quietly and muttered two words. "Kill him."

Ruby tensed as he felt the pressure on his back disappear.

"Not in here," St.Clair added. "Take him to the locker with the rest of the dead meat."

The tap of the Smith & Wesson was back. Ruby obeyed and headed off in what appeared to be in the general direction of the kitchen. As he walked he used a slightly longer stride than his normal gait; widening the gap between himself and Bacon Face. By the time they had reached the labyrinth of service corridors, Ruby was contemplating making a break for it. His thoughts were interrupted by a sudden loud expulsion of breath from behind him, followed by the unmistakable thump of an unconscious body hitting the floor.

Ruby turned and sure enough Bacon Face was making a close and personal inspection of the floor tiles. Stooding over the supine gunman was the imposing Fat Knuckles, with cosh in hand, and an evil gleam in his eye.

"Jesus Christ!" Ruby cursed freely. "You took your time."

Fat Knuckles shrugged. "Sorry."

"Hey give the wee lad a chance." Jack O'Malley's grinning face appeared from behind Fat Knuckles. "This place is a maze. Took a while to figure out which route yer man here," he prodded the inert Bacon Face with his boot in an not too gently manner, "was takin' ya."

"What about the plans that Colmenero supplied?" asked Ruby.

"They aren't as kosher as he thought. There's a few of the twists and turns a missin' especially the back stairs stuff."

"We can ask him about that in a while. But first we got to catch up with The Weasel. Come on."

• • •

Jimmy Vessel was exactly where Ruby expected to find him. The only trouble was that he was dead; a bullet hole in his chest.

"I'm thinking that wasn't part of your plan there boyo."

Ruby snarled at O'Malley. "Shut up. I need to think." Squatting down by the body he took a close look at the wound. "We've got a new player. Don't know who it is yet, but they knew Jimmy, or rather he knew them."

"What makes ye say that?"

"Shot in the chest from almost point blank range. They would have to get pretty close and be looking into his face when they pulled the trigger."

"What are you guys still doing down here?" The voice was soft, feminine, yet full of authority.

Ruby looked past his criminal companions into the face of an angel. Or so she seemed as the corridor light behind her formed a halo affect around her features. He recognized Lt. Betty-12.

"Follow me," she advised.

Ruby, O'Malley, and Fat Knuckles admired the view of the shapely model as she sashayed in front of them, while simultaneously wondering just where the hell she was leading them. The corridors seemed endless and if the girl was trying to confuse them she was doing a good job of it. Turning a corner, she suddenly stopped and pointed to a white paneled door with a small plaque indicating that it led to a dining room.

"This is the back of a servant door that is disguised as part of the paneling in the room on the other side." She put her ear to the door listening for sounds of movement on the other side. "If we time it just right, we should be able to sneak in and surprise a few people."

Ruby nodded. "Your call Betty-12."

"My name's not Betty-12, it's..."

"Oh for gawds sake," O'Malley cut in, "Does it really matter what your name is, do we go in or don't we?"

"Sure we do," and with that she pushed the door open and stepped through. Ruby, O'Malley, and Fat Knuckles followed.

• • •

"Well now, that certainly was a surprise."

Ruby looked over at O'Malley. "She sure got that part right."

Fat Knuckles muttered something obscene under his breath.

Ranged before them in a semi-circle facing the secret door were about a dozen well muscled members of the country club staff all armed with knives of the type found in any gourmet kitchen. Standing behind them were Alberto Colmenero and St.Clair; the latter holding a pistol.

"You have a bad habit of not being dead, Ruby," St. Clair sneered.

"It's a talent," Ruby replied nonchalantly.

"One I intend to curtail. And just to make sure it's done this time, I'll be happy to deliver the coupe de grace myself." St. Clair raised his gun.

"Before you pull the trigger, just answer me one question. How long have you two been working together?"

Alberto Colmenero took several steps back and looked at St. Clair. "What does he mean us two working together? I never ...."

"I never said you did." Ruby raised his voice. "In fact I think you have a different, and more noble, agenda." His gaze then shifted to one of his own party. "Don't you, Betty?"

The girl stared at Ruby, "Where the hell did you get the idea I know what these idiots are up to?"

"Well I would suggest we go talk to your brother, but that wouldn't do us much good would it?"

"What does he mean?" Colmenero blurted out. "Where's Jimmy?"

"Taking a permanent nap in the servants' corridors." Ruby answered, looking directly at Colmenero. "And I'm guessing that piece of information isn't exactly news to your friend St. Clair." Ruby's gaze shifted to match Colmenero's as they both looked at St. Clair. It was at that moment Ruby knew he'd made a mistake. The report of the gun, despite its small calibre, was loud in the enclosed room. He felt the hard shove in his back at almost the same instant that the slug came whizzing past his ear.

As he fell, Rick Ruby witnessed the tableau unfolding before him.

The girl, a small smoking Derringer pistol still in hand, was backing out the door, with St. Clair at her side. The various knife wielding members of the country club staff were still waiting for instructions. Alberto Colmenero stood slack jawed in the middle of the room trying to figure out what was going on. Lying prone on the floor was Fat Knuckles with blood on his shoulder; kneeling over him O'Malley was trying to stanch the flow, while appearing to be shouting at someone behind him.

Ruby shook his head to clear the ringing in his ears caused by the close passage of the bullet that was now lodged in Fat Knuckles' shoulder. The noise cleared just in time to catch O'Malley say something about "boys."

The hidden servants' door burst open and several large figures that Ruby recognized as belonging to Irish gangs charged through. Simultaneously the one he'd seen St. Clair disappear through opened allowing a mob of Italian gangsters into the room.

The room was suddenly very crowded.

Ruby was never sure who moved first, but suddenly the space was full of flying fists, boots, and every conceivable part of the human body that could be used as a weapon. Joining the mix was the occasional knife and kitchen implement, as the two groups of mobsters turned on the country club heavies. As the melee spun around them in a vortex of broken bones and blood, Ruby and O'Malley dragged the unconscious Fat Knuckles with them to the door used by St. Clair and the girl, only stopping to take along the still dumbstruck Colmenero.

Reaching the safety of the corridor seemed to snap the store owner out of his fugue state. "What the hell is going on in there?" he demanded.

"A little Manhattan justice." O'Malley explained. "No-one takes kindly to Long Island toffs and their hired help trying to run rackets on our doorsteps. Even less when they are messing around with our girls."

"But this isn't what I wanted."

"What exactly did you want?" Ruby asked.

"I just wanted to get Dorothy away from the clutches of St. Clair."

"Dorothy?"

"Jimmy Weasel's sister."

"Oh," Ruby nodded, "You mean the space girl."

"Yes, I used her to play that part."

"She was a better actress than you gave her credit for. She played you; and it would seem her brother too."

"Okay, so now we've got the who's who sorted out," O'Malley butted in, "let's go find the little bitch, and St. Clair."

"His office."

• • •

"What is it about this office St.Clair?"

"Well, let's just say it has a certain charm." St. Clair was stood calmly behind his desk, his hand resting on the back of his leather office chair, as if the sudden arrival of Ruby, Colmenero and O'Malley was just another scheduled business appointment.

Ruby did a quick scan around the office, noticing nothing different from his previous visit . "So where's your playmate run off to?"

"I have no idea. She ran out of the front door, and I must admit I have no inclination to determine her whereabouts. She has served her purpose."

"And what purpose was that?" snarled Alberto Colmenero.

St. Clair smirked, "Ah, the poor deluded love sick Romeo. You had no idea, did you? You know, people like you make me sick. Real wealth comes from property, and inheritance, it's a mark of breeding."

"Don't make me laugh." Colmenero's retort was bitter, "You're no better than any one else, in fact you're worse."

"If that's so," St. Clair pointed his finger, "Why were you so keen to join this club, keen to use your wealth to try and buy status and a social position that only true gentlemen are born to."

"Gentlemen!" Ruby snorted, "I've seen what goes on here."

"Well it didn't seem to bother your mercantile friend here; he was an enthusiastic participant as anyone to start with, happy to use his money to indulge in all sorts of pleasures. That is until he took a shine to Dorothy. Started to talk about trying to get her away from the club. It was too good an opportunity to miss. She played you like one of those grand pianos that sit in the windows of your ghastly department store."

"That's not true. You had her trapped, just like all the other girls you recruited off the streets of Manhattan."

"Trapped?" St. Clair's laughter was cruel. "This was her operation, her show. She was the one who procured and trained the girls. I just provided the location and the client list."

"Go on..." Ruby could see that St. Clair was enjoying himself. Over the years the P.I. had discovered one thing about people who thought they were morally or socially superior; they liked to brag about it. St. Clair was on a roll.

"Oh, sweet little Dorothy had all the right contacts: modeling agencies, dance halls, jazz clubs. Anywhere where the pretty young hopefuls would congregate, she was there; whispering how she'd heard of a cushy gig that would get them noticed by rich and powerful. They ate it up."

"So why did she play along with Alberto here?" Ruby nodded to the store owner. "No offense."

Colmenero looked back crestfallen. "None taken. As much as it hurts me, I'd like to know the answer to that one too."

"At first I think she genuinely saw you as a way out. A real sugar-daddy, a way to a rich pampered existence where she could just hang off your arm and live the life she wanted. But then you started to get all noble. You started to talk not just about rescuing her, but rescuing the other girls as well.

She couldn't let you do that. It would ruin everything we had built up here."

"You bastard. I ought to kill ya right now." O'Malley's brogue cut across the monologue.

St. Clair looked across the room at the Irishman. "Ah, the Irish hoodlum. I'd almost forgotten you were there." Glancing at Colmenero now, he continued. "I'll admit figuring out that most of the girls came from the Irish and Italian parts of town was very clever, Alberto. And I must admit to being impressed by your negotiating skills in getting the less desirable elements from the two communities working together. But unfortunately that was the tipping point for dear Dorothy. She had no choice but to get rid of you. A sentiment I fully supported by the way."

Ruby's eyes lit up as suddenly it all clicked in to place. "Damn! The ray gun!"

• • •

"Correct, Richard."

Ruby winced, he hated the patronizing tone St. Clair layered on the rare occasions he used his first name. It made it sound like his name was an insult. For the moment he let it slide by. "But she missed, didn't she?"

"Yes she did," said Detective Perry. He was in the doorway straightening his silk tie. His free hand clutched a pair of handcuffs, into which was manacled the disheveled figure of Dorothy Veasel. She looked like she had been dragged through a hedge backwards.

"Dorothy!" Alberto Colmenero exclaimed. "How could you?"

The girl sneered. "How could I miss? Damned if I know. Shame that the Nancy-boy got it instead. Stupid idiot walked into the line of shot just as I pulled the trigger."

Ruby had shot a look at St. Clair when she had used the phrase 'nancy boy.' The man had flushed in barely suppressed anger. "He wasn't even meant to be there!"

A gunshot rang out and Dorothy collapsed to the floor. St. Clair was waving a pistol around, and screaming to no-one in particular. "It was just another acting job, he was covering for some other joker who called in sick."

Ruby cursed himself for not having searched the desk drawers. There was one in St.Clair's home office desk, so why not here. *Idiot.* Then Ruby noticed the swivel chair was positioned with its back to the desk. He heard Perry go for his own gun. "No!" Ruby called out. "He's got a hostage!"

"Smart boy." St.Clair transferred the smoking gun to his left hand, still keeping it pointed at the police detective, while using his right hand to spin the chair around for all to see who was tied in it.

"Who's that?" asked Colmenero and O'Malley in unison.

Ruby groaned. "Oh Edi!"

• • •

"Edi? I was wondering what the pretty thing's name was." St. Clair placed his hand on the top of the bound girl's head and applied just enough pressure to turn it so Ruby could see the livid bruising blemishing her cheek. "She was less than forthcoming about that."

"You bastard, St. Clair!" Rick Ruby lurched forward, ready to leap at Charles St. Clair and get his scrawny neck in his calloused hands. The sight of St. Clair transferring the aim of the gun towards Edi's head held him back.

"Good boy, Richard."

Ruby swore to himself that if St. Clair called him Richard one more time, he'd pounce, and damn the consequences.

"So this is how it will play out from here," St. Clair continued. "The young lady and I are going for a walk. If anyone has any ideas of jumping me before I reach my car, I will simply blow her brains out. Is that clear?"

"Perfectly!" The voice was female, but it didn't come from either the bound Edi or the wounded Dorothy. Ruby recognized it immediately.

There was another gunshot and the back of Charles St. Clair's head disappeared in a shower of blood and brain matter that made a mess of office wood paneling and expensive carpet. As he died the millionaire's finger tightened on the trigger and his own gun fired.

Edi slumped face down across St. Clair's blood spattered desk. Ruby raced to her and gently lifted her head off the unforgiving surface, cradling her in his arms. "Damn you, you silly girl. You were only meant to hide in the bushes and keep a look out. Jesus. I never intended to get you killed."

"What have I told you about blaspheming?"

Ruby looked down in disbelief.

"Edi! You're alive!"

His secretary smiled weakly pushing blood soaked hair from her eyes. "Sorry to scare you, boss. I ducked when I heard the shot. It just went through my hair and scratched the top of my skull. How about untying these ropes?" She held up her bound wrists. "Then I can check it out."

"You know Ricky, I thought you only had eyes for me." Carla St. Clair walked calmly from behind the thick folds of curtain hanging in front of the office's French windows. The smoking gun that had killed her father hung limply in her hand.

O'Malley stepped forward and removed it without protest. After emptying the chamber, he applied the safety and handed it on to Detective Perry.

"Carla." Ruby shook his head sadly. "Why?"

"To make up for a life time of lies." She nodded in Edi's direction. "And to save the life of the one person who matters to you most."

• • •

Rick Ruby, P.I. spread The New York Times across his desk, smoothing out the pages. This was one of his little rituals, a quiet morning with no clients, a hot cup of Joe and his favorite section of the Sunday paper.

"You're coffee's cold. Let me get you another one."

Ruby looked up and a wide grin split his face. "Shouldn't you be home resting?"

Edi Rose Adams winced, her hand going up to the bandage wrapped around the crown of her skull. "It's just a dull headache now."

"So what brings you to this rat-hole on your day-off?"

"There's no such thing as a day-off with you. But I was thinking a picnic lunch in the park might be a pleasant change."

Ruby never liked picnics. They only meant damp grass and ants. But he decided that today probably wasn't the best time to share that opinion.

"Okay, but let me finish the funnies first."

Rick Ruby's eyes glanced down towards the paper in front of him.....

CAPTION: WE HURLED OUR FLEET ACROSS THE SKY IN A STRAIGHT LINE TO INTERCEPT THE ENEMY'S CURVING COURSE.

CAPTION: BUT IN SPITE OF OUR SPEED -

Officer: It's a losing race Captain McCoy! We can't wring another ounce from these generators!

Mars McCoy: Keep after them! We might get a break! Betty-12 is a prisoner aboard that ship!

Rick Ruby smiled to himself, and folded the newspaper comics section shut. The twenty-fifth century could wait a little longer.

THE END

Rick Ruby Essay

love the streets of New York. The Big Apple is one of my favorite cities. Whenever I'm there I like to stay in mid-town and then walk to wherever I need to be. Uptown to Central Park, including my regular pilgrimage to Strawberry Fields, or to the museums and galleries. Downtown to publishers offices, or all the way to Wall Street for business meetings. I always walk. In all my trips to Manhattan I've never used the subway. This is a city that needs to be experienced at street level.

Walking the streets of New York you see the world in microcosm. All examples of humanity are on display. There is no such thing as a typical New Yorker. But there is one example of a literary character that does exemplify the streets of that great city: the iconic private eye of pulp-noir adventures. A private eye like Rick Ruby.

When I got the chance to pitch a few ideas for a Rick Ruby story, I'd not long completed another story set on these same streets. A story featuring my pulp style masked adventurer, The Raven (now published in The Protectors anthology from Caught Dreams Press ISBN - 978-0985870225). I had really enjoyed doing the period research for that story, and Rick Ruby was the perfect opportunity to carry on in that world. In fact anyone who has read The Raven story will spot a little bit of a cross-over cameo here establishing that both heroes co-exist, in my fictional universe anyway.

Around the same time I'd also been doing some initial research for a projected book on the history of Buck Rogers, a project that is now unfortunately in limbo. I'd not long discovered a small piece of video of a special short, *Buck Rogers and the Tiger Men of Mars*, filmed in 1936 as a promotional piece to be used in department stores selling Buck Rogers merchandise. I just knew I had to add that to the mix.

Airship 27's Ron Fortier suggested switching out Buck for the line's own space adventurer, Mars McCoy to keep that shared universe feel going. A great suggestion, and one that added a whole other layer to the story.

So what better way to start a mystery set on the mean streets of 1930s New York than with the murder of a spaceman?

• • •

ALAN J. PORTER - Alan J. Porter has been writing about the worlds of various pop-culture icons for well over a decade, with non-fiction books on Batman, The Beatles, Star Trek and James Bond. He has also contributed essays to several other books, as well as written numerous magazine articles.

In the world of comics he is perhaps best known as the writer of the Disney*Pixar CARS comic book series from BOOM! Studios. He has also had work published by Tokyopop and Marvel and is currently writing a new series called *Forgotten City*.

As well as writing various short-stories for Airship27.

THE LONG KILL

By Ron Fortier

Greer was wearing that see-through black lace negligee Rick Ruby drooled over. She came into the darkened room and the slivers of moonlight playing through the curtains seem to paint her body in zebra like pattern, alternating between white and black stripes.

"Hi, baby," she breathed and walked to where he sat in the overstuffed chair. "Been a long time, hasn't it?"

The way her hair cascaded down over her shoulders, the curve of her long legs, the tilt of her full breasts beneath the sheer fabric. He could feel himself aroused and reached out for her hips.

She giggled as he took hold of her and pulled her into his lap. The smell of her was all rosewater and lilacs.

"Ouch, is that a rock I'm sitting on?" Her frosty green eyes bore into his knowingly and then her lush, cherry red lips sought his.

The kiss was hot and heavy. He wanted her so badly.

There was a booming gunshot and Rick Ruby jumped awake.

His arms were empty. The room was empty. Sitting alone in the dark, thunder and lightning battled each other outside and his stomach felt nauseous.

Another freaking dream, he realized. Another long ache for a woman who was long dead. Greer Lawson, perhaps the one real love of his love; murdered over seven years ago. Life should have ended right there and then, but as he'd come to understand, it never did. People came and went, lived and died, and the world just kept on spinning.

He was holding an empty glass in his hands and decided to fill it. But the bottle on the lampstand beside his chair was on its side, its alcoholic contents long drained to fuel his fevered dreams of lost loves.

Damn. He put the glass beside the empty bottle and climbed to his feet. His wristwatch let him know it was long after midnight. Didn't really matter. This was New York and there were always open liquor stores if you knew were to find them.

Rick Ruby was a regular customer. He knew where to find them.

• • •

Even at this late hour, the humid heat was oppressive as Ruby made his way along 125th Street pass the Apollo Theater. It was closed up; its entertainers and patrons long since having vacated the former Burlesque venue to find a bar or club where they could alleviate the foul weather with a cool drink. Which was Ruby's mission as he spotted the little hanging sign over Pop Tandy's Wine & Liquor shop on the corner. His idea was to pick up another fifth of Scotch and a bag of ice. Medicine to help cure what ailed him.

"Hey, red," a tall, leggy hooker called out, leaving the shadows of an alley to waylay him in hopes of scoring a few bucks. She was tall, with nice figure wrapped in a gaudy red dress, the top buttons flagrantly undone to display her large, round breasts. "You looking for a little brown sugar to party with."

Ruby stopped and looked her over. Brown indeed in a smooth, soft mocha way with long black hair that curled down to her shoulders. She wore open-toed high heels and clutched a Wolworth's Five & Dime purse under her arm. He studied her face and guessed her age to be in the late twenties range. With hookers it was always hard to judge. Normally he'd have smiled, declined the offer and gone on his way. But she was definitely a looker and a moment of unencumbered passion, along with the booze, might be just what the doctor ordered.

His smile grew.

Then they heard the gunshot. It had come from the liquor store. The prostitute took a step back, recognizing the pop immediately as did the private eye.

Two young men came back peddling out of the shop, each waving a revolver in his hands. Ruby, a former police officer, registered their statistics automatically. One white, tall and hefty, pockmarked face, wearing slacks and a cotton jacket with a baseball cap pulled down over his eyes. His companion was black, short, with kinky hair and a mustache, wearing jeans and a pullover sweater. He was also carrying a paper bag from which dollar bills were falling out.

"Josh," the white thug spoke seeing Ruby and the hooker for the first time. "Look!"

The woman's fear broke and she started back for the safety of the alley from which she'd first emerged.

It was the wrong thing to do as it startled the already frightened gunmen. The one called Josh seeing them for the first time, whipped his gun around and fired. The bullet hit the girl in the leg and she screamed.

As she fell to the hard sidewalk, Rick Ruby moved away from her and dropped behind a parked sedan. In a crouch, he reached back under his light jacket and found the grip of his .38 caliber handgun. He pulled it free and then silently counted to ten.

He could hear the two hoods racing towards them. He glanced at girl, on her side crying in pain, a dark smear over her left leg.

Ruby took a breath, then rose up behind the car, raised his pistol and shot both men dead center before they could stop their forward motion. His bullets punched them off their feet, a look of sheer unbelief in their eyes as they were thrown backwards. They hit the ground simultaneously and they died together.

• • •

"Jesus, Rick, can't you stay out of trouble for one week," Detective Jack "Mac" McGinnis groused, pointing a finger at his former partner.

"Come on, Mac, I told you what happened," Ruby retorted angrily waving his hand at the two chalk outlines on the sidewalk. "It's not my fault these two buttheads decided to stick up Pop's place."

"No, it ain't," the medium built Irishman conceded. "Just their bad luck to do it on the night you were stopping by to buy a fresh pint."

"Pretty much sums it up. Say, how is the old man?" Ruby hadn't even stepped into the shop after shooting the heist duo. Tandy's wife, asleep in the couple's apartment over the store, had awakened upon hearing the gunshots and called the police. By the time the patrol car arrived, Jack was still tending to the wounded hooker whose name was Lola Conklin. Then the ambulances came wailing onto the scene along with more cops, the medical examiner and God knew who else.

Lola had been bundled up and hauled off by medics to the nearest hospital at the same time police photographers were popping flashes at the two dead men on the sidewalk.

Somewhere in that three ring circus of activity, Mac had appeared, his trusty little notebook and pencil in hand. Spotting Ruby, he'd corned his old pal and allowed the redheaded six footer to relate what had gone down. Mac appreciated having an ex-cop as an eye witness.

"Pops is okay," Mac informed Ruby. "The punk who fired at him wasn't a good shot. Hit a few vodka bottles and made a mess, but the old guy is fine. Shook up, but still breathing. Which is more than we can say for those two you plugged."

"It was either them or me, Mac."

"I believe you. But I still want you at the station first thing in the morning to give a complete statement. You know the captain will want a full investigation."

"Especially when he hears I'm the shooter."

"He does things by the book, you know that."

"Fine. Can I go now, it's been a long night as is."

"Yeah, scram. Go on home."

"Home, hell, I'm gonna go get a drink. I need one more than ever now."

Rick Ruby turned and started down the street leaving McGinnis to wish for the hundredth time things would have turned out different for his old friend. Sometimes life just wasn't fair.

• • •

It was almost eleven p.m. two nights later when Rick Ruby entered the Jazz Club; his usual haunt when not camped out in his office/living quarters in the two rooms upstairs. He'd been avoiding the place since the shooting afraid of the notoriety the incident would bring him and his friends who ran the establishment.

The actual name on the neon sign over the entrance was Belle's Jazz Club but the tubes making up Belle's name had long since burned out and times being what they were, May Belle Williams had merely shrugged and let the glaring light announce the remaining two words. An older, attractive black woman, Belle had continued to manage the club after her husband, Parker Williams, had tragically died in an automobile accident several years earlier. Fortunately she was able to rely on her manager, and chief bar tender, Bruce "Broom Stick" Strickland to help run the day to day affairs. In fact he did such a fine job of being the club's front man, most of the patrons assumed he was the owner. Belle was content to leave that misconception in place.

Walking into the smoke filled lounge, the scent of sweat and alcohol mingling like a familiar cocktail, Ruby noted the joint was half full which was typical for midweek. The five man jazz band was on the stage to his right breezing through a lively little number while several young couples were gyrating happily on the dance floor.

A primarily black club, Belle ran a friendly, inviting place and as always, there were a few white couples mixed in among the dozen round tables. Although segregation was still the order of the day when the sun rose up, at night people tended to put aside their politics and come together to enjoy some good booze and music.

As he approached the bar, Ruby saw Belle behind the counter with Broom Stick, a ledger book open in her hands. He assumed they were talking business.

"Can a fellah get a drink around here?" He propped himself up on the padded bar stool and slapped his hands on the smooth mahogany top.

"Well if it isn't the prodigal son," Bell smiled; closing her accounting book and handing it back to Broom Stick. "Where you been, Rick?"

"Around," he replied, pulling a pack of Luckies out of his coat pocket, "Things were getting a bit too noisy for my taste."

"Now is that any way for a bona fide hero to talk?" the tall, shapely Belle grinned mischievously.

"What?" Ruby used his lighter to start his smoke and put it away.

As if on cue, Broom Stick, who had since put the ledger away, reached under the bar and pulled out a copy of the Tribune dated the previous day. He opened it to display the bold headlines and held it up for Ruby's inspection.

P.I. FOILS STICK-UP – TWO DEAD!

"Oh, great," he mumbled, blowing out a puff of smoke.

"Thought you might like it for your scrapbook," Strickland laughed, taking back the paper.

"What I'd like is a shot of bourbon, neat. And make it a double."

"Make that two," Belle added and walked around the bar to join Ruby, though in her tight purple dress she opted to remain standing rather than attempt to pull herself onto a stool.

As a grinning Broom Stick poured the amber liquid into the twin shot glasses, the music on the stage ended and a lovely brown goddess entered from behind a side curtain. Tall and willowy, she moved to the microphone clad in a slinky red satin gown with a low cut front that amply displayed her natural charms. She was the color of warm cocoa and her bare arms and shoulders glistened under the ceiling lights. Around her long graceful neck was a slim pearl necklace and two white bracelets encircled both her wrists. Her hair was cut short, framing a classic beauty highlighted by lush full lips, a small petite nose and two deep brown mysterious eyes accented by thin, curving eyebrows.

"Ladies and gents," the sax player introduced her. "The Jazz Club's own songbird, Miss Evelyn Johnson."

There was a smattering of polite applause then the band began to play and the alluring Miss Johnson did her magic. Her voice was sensual and sad as it musically created a tale of hypnotic love and longing.

Ruby, tasting the burning alcohol, recognized the lyrics. Evelyn was singing "In a Sentimental Mood," a Duke Ellington number he'd released a year ago. It was still very popular amongst jazz bands both black and white.

"That girl's got the voice of an angel," Belle whispered over his shoulder. Ruby nodded and continued sipping at his bourbon. The owner was well aware of the on and off affair the P.I. and her chanteuse enjoyed.

"...the stars come thru my room..." the girl's voice was syrup sweet. "While your loving attitude is like a flame that lights the gloom..."

The front door opened and out of the corner of his eye, Ruby noticed three black men entering.

"On the wings of ev'ry kiss..."

Ruby let the words seduce him. Evelyn was no angel, he mused. More like a siren.

There was a loud commotion from the vestibule and now he swiveled around on the stool to see the biggest of the three new patrons marching towards him, his arms out, index finger pointing. "That's him! That's the bastard killed my brother!"

• • •

The band stopped playing, Evelyn's last note hanging in the air. The big bruiser kept shouting as he came on, balling his meaty hands into mallet size fists.

Ruby finished his drink, put down his glass and slid off the stool ready for whatever happened next. Internally he was upset that he just couldn't get a break no matter what he did. For the shooting and now he was about to be assaulted by some relative of the black kid he'd gunned down.

But Belle wasn't about to let that happen in her place.

She stepped in between Ruby and the massive black dude, putting her hand up like a traffic cop. "Now you hold it right there, mistah!" she commanded. The tone of her voice was threatening implying she was not about to back down.

"Out of my way, Miz Belle," the big man warned though he had come to a stop before her. "Ize Leroy Sanders and that man there shot my baby brother Joshua."

"You're brother was a crook, Mistah Sanders," Belle snapped back. "Not only did he shoot a harmless old man, he went and shot a poor girl right on the sidewalk like some mad dog." Sanders face contorted at her words, the rage painting his bulldog black features into something truly ugly. "Rick here merely put him down in self defense. That's the truth of it."

Ruby was genuinely touched by Belle's defense of him.

"That don't manner none," Sanders refused to listen to reason. "When Ma died, I told her I'd watch over Joshua and now this cracker done shot him dead. I aim to give him a whippin' he won't ever forget."

"Not in my club you won't," Belle said folding her arms over her bosom. "Ain't that right, Mr. Strickland?"

Ruby turned to look over his right shoulder to see Broom Stick leaning over the bar pointing a twin-barrel shotgun in his hands. "Yes it is, Ma'am."

"Well, you don't scare me none," Leroy Sanders snarled and then directed his words to Ruby. "You cain't hide behind other folks ala da time, cracker. I'm gonna get you sooner or later."

Rick Ruby stepped up behind Belle looking up at the enraged Sanders. "I'm sure you will. So let's settle this right here and now...."

"Rick?" Belle was momentarily confused.

"....but we take it out back in the alley," Ruby went on. "Just you and me, no guns or knives. We take care of this like men."

The offer surprised the black man. He looked back at his two companions who were just as puzzled. A frown creased Sander's brow and then he finally nodded. "Alrightee. That's fine with me. I'm still gonna whip your white ass three-ways to Sunday."

"You don't have to do this," Belle remarked as Ruby turned and started back to the bar.

"If I don't he'll just keep coming, Belle. Best to deal with it now." He reached behind his back, under his coat, and withdrew the first of his special Colt .38 handguns. The second was hidden in a thigh holster accessible through the open lining in his right pants pocket. He pulled this out and laid it on the bar next to its twin.

"Watch these for me," he told Broom Stick.

"I'll let Lester handle that," the barkeep said, waving to the big bouncer by the front door; his name was Lester Maddox. "Keep an eye on the place, while I tend to this little boxing match out back."

"Will do, boss," affirmed the thick neck former longshoreman, with a smile on his face before looking down at Ruby and whispering, "Good luck, Mistah Ruby."

• • •

Belle led the two men out the side door into the long alley alongside the building. It was used by her vendors to deliver supplies and the sanitation trucks to pick up the weekly refuse. A single dim light hung over the loading bay to the far end of the alley. The only other illumination was from the street lamp to the opposite end; all of which left the wide lane poorly lit. Still, it would be enough for a close-in fight between two men.

Half the patrons of the club exited behind Ruby and Leroy Sanders, along with Broom Stick still clutching his shotgun. People instinctively formed a wide circle in which Leroy and Ruby stepped, each man removing his jacket and then shirt.

The effect was dramatic, as it revealed the mass of hard muscles that made up Sanders' torso. After handing his coat and shirt to one of his companions, he began flexing his arms and throwing punches to loosen up. Meanwhile Ruby, also now draped in white tee-shirt, had his back to his opponent having handed his clothes to Belle, while Broom Stick stood beside her.

"Good luck," Belle wished him.

Broom Stick took a step closer and leaning forward, whispered. "You got to fight dirty like, Rick."

"I know."

With that Broom Stick moved back and raised his voice. "All right, let this here fight start." He held up his shotgun for all to see. "Anyone else gets any ideas of getting involved is gonna get filled with buckshot."

Ruby mentally chuckled; well aware his friend meant what he said. At least his fight, regardless of the outcome, would be with Sanders alone. For that he was grateful.

Like all policemen, Ruby had learned some martial art skills and had been a decent boxer in his time. But he'd never gone up against a monster like this Joshua Sanders' brother before. Broom Stick's words echoed in his thoughts as the brute attacked him, his right arm swinging wild.

Ruby put up both arms to block off the powerful blows. Sanders' first punch hit his left arm and the blow nearly knocked him off his feet. He stumbled back a few feet, pain shooting up the nerves of his arm. *Damn, this guy can hit!*

Sanders started bringing his left around and Ruby decided he didn't like playing a punching bag so he stepped in close and drove his own right cross into the big man's jaw. Instant pain fired through his hand and his knuckles felt busted as if he'd just punched a brick wall. So hurtful was the blow, he failed to react to Sander's second right and it caught him in the chest.

Just like that, Ruby was sent flying off his feet into the crowd behind him. Men and woman tried to scattered as he fell into them, then onto the hard pavement. Stars swam in his vision and he quickly scrambled to get to his feet. He knew Sanders wasn't about to let up now that he'd knocked him down. Bruisers like Leroy were the type to go nuts when fighting and wouldn't stop until somebody was dead.

In this case, that meant Ruby.

He was barely on his feet when Sanders launched another assault. Somehow Ruby managed to fold over, ducking the powerful round house. At the same time, his gaze looked down squarely at the man's crotch and he remembered Broom Stick's words. Bringing his hands up to protect his face, Ruby took a step back, straightened up to full height and kicked Leroy Sanders in the balls with all the force he could muster.

Sander's expression turned cartoonish as his mask of rage was suddenly replaced with a goofy look of utter disbelief. His eyes popped wide and his mouth made an oval shape as an unexpected shriek escaped it.

The crowd jeered as the formidable fighter suddenly folded over, his hands clutching his family jewels. At which point, Rick Ruby whipped his right hand over him and then brought his elbow down onto the back of Sander's skull with a loud crack. Sanders dropped face first onto the hard ground smacking his forehead in the process. He gave out a moan and then passed out.

The gathered crowd cheered and began to press in on Ruby, men slapping him on the arms and back, while their girlfriends looked on admiringly. But the victor was still dizzy from the blows he'd taken and found his vision starting to blur and his feet getting weak.

Belle and Broom Stick pushed everyone away and Belle caught the wobbly shamus under one arm. "You okay, sweet-pie?"

"Just a little woozy," Ruby grinned hoping he didn't pass out right there on the spot.

"All right, people," Broom Stick said. "Fight's over, let's get back in the club and have some fun."

Following his suggestion, the crowd started back into the club. At the same time Leroy Sanders' two companions came over and began the arduous task of getting him up off the pavement.

Broom Stick, using his free arm to bolster Ruby along with Belle, looked back at them and warned, "When he comes to, you tell him this is done. Rick whipped him fair and square and he'd best remember that."

Neither man commented and continued their struggle to get the hulking sleeper to his feet. Broom Stick didn't envy them the job.

Once back inside the Jazz Club, Ruby had regained some semblance of equilibrium, though his arm, shoulder and back ached severely.

"I'm okay, really," he affirmed detaching himself from Belle and Broom Stick. "But I could sure use another drink."

"Coming right up," the bartender nodded.

Belle was handing Ruby his shirt when the alluring Evelyn Johnson appeared holding a warm, wet towel in her hands. Without a word, she applied the moist cloth to Ruby's face and slowly washed the dirt and grime from his cheeks.

"Oh, baby, did he hurt you bad?"

"He'll live," Belle laughed, aware of her singer's affection for Ruby. "Look, Eve, it's getting late. Why don't you call it a night and help get tough guy here up to his room upstairs."

"I got a better idea," the sultry Miss Johnson replied. "Rick's gonna come home with me where I can look after him good and proper."

Ruby, fumbling to button his shirt, looked up the beautiful brown face and smiled. Now there was the kind of nursing any man would happily take advantage of. Maybe his luck was about to change for the better.

• • •

A twenty-minute cab ride later and Ruby and Miss Johnson were entering her small but elegantly appointed Harlem apartment. The fresh air had done wonders to restore Ruby's well being though he still moved cautiously as his ribs on his right ached fiercely. If that was the case come morning, he'd have to go see a doctor for sure.

"Why don't you go make us a drink," Eve suggested peeling off his fedora and tossing it in the closet by the front door. "I'll go find some rubbing alcohol in the bathroom."

Ruby complied and directed his footsteps to the small bar along the wall facing the square living room with its sofa, coffee table and cushioned chairs. As he was filling two glasses with ice, he admired the framed pictures tacked to wall to either side of the liquor bottles. They were photos of Eve with some of the great jazz musicians of the time and Ruby identified several of them immediately.

He had just squirted seltzer over the glass' bourbon content when he heard his hostess approaching. He looked up and beheld a vision of true, graceful beauty.

Evelyn Johnson was standing by the sofa dressed only in a red chiffon negligee and matching slippers. The thin nightgown did nothing to hide the full, lush body beneath it and Ruby caught his breath involuntarily. A thin sash pulled the material taut against her full bosom and two dark spots the size of quarters were clearly outlined through the material. In her hands she held a brown bottle and white cotton washcloth.

"Well, are you going to get over here and let me look at you?"

He gulped slightly, blinked and then grinned. He went over and held out one of the glasses. She put her first aid stuff on the coffee table and her leaning over afforded him a generous peek into the valley between her breasts.

She took the offered drink and took a sip, her brown eyes sparkling. "Hmm, that's good. Now why don't you take off your jacket and shirt and

"...get over here and let me look at you."

let me look at how bad you're banged up."

Ruby did as ordered, throwing tie, shirt and torn jacket over the closest chair. Over these he carefully laid his shoulder holster rig and back-up pistol. Eve frowned, she hated guns. In the light of the overhead ceiling lamp, Eve leaned down to examine an ugly purplish bruise on his right side. She touched it gingerly with her long fingers. "Does that hurt?"

"Well, it don't tickle," he gasped slightly, becoming very aware of his being half naked and her alluring attire. Eve wore a subtle lilac fragrance perfume and the scent was extremely pleasant and as she raised her head he started to bring his down.

"Whoa, tiger, one thing at a time," she chided slipping herself away from him and uncorking the bottle of rubbing alcohol. She dabbed some of clear liquid onto the folded washcloth and then setting the bottle down set to washing the bruised area.

"Yeow," Ruby cried feeling the instant sting of the antiseptic alcohol on his flesh.

"Don't be a big baby," Eve admonished continuing to rub the hurt flesh in firm but gentle caress. After a few minutes, she straightened, dropped the towel onto an empty glass ashtray on the coffee table and slapped her hands together indicating her job was done.

"How does that feel, Rick?"

"Better, really." He took a step and slid his arms around her waist. "You're a regular Florence Nightingale," he joked.

Pulling her against him, he felt her breast flatten against his broad chest. She gave him a sly smile and brought her arms up around his neck, her voice becoming thick. "Is there anything else I can do for you, sir?"

He brought his mouth to her painted lips and they kissed. At first it was tender and mischievous but the feel of her against him began to make his blood hot. His hands moved down to grab her round buttocks through the thin chiffon.

Both of them were quickly giving into desire as Eve's tongue went into his mouth and her fingers worked up the back of his neck to dig into his red hair. Their lips parted but he continued to rain kisses on her; along her cheeks then down her long, smooth neck where he could feel the pulse of her throbbing. Meanwhile his hands had climbed back along her naked back, hooked the straps of her negligee and as he lifted his face from her neck, they easily peeled off the garment exposing her ample charms.

Rick Ruby had no idea how they managed to get from the living room to Eve's bedroom and he really didn't care. One minute they had been going at each other like starving dogs and the next she was laying naked beneath him in her bed, her head and shoulders propped up against several pillows. The only light came from the streetlamps outside filtering through half-open curtains allowing him to drink her dusky brown beauty.

Eve was all woman and he devoted himself to exploring every wonderful inch of her until in the end, both of them bathed in a light sheen of sweat came together and rode a tide of ecstasy that carried them to heights of unbridled pleasure.

When their lovemaking was finished, Ruby collapsed on his back, the ache in his ribs still there but now ignored, his heartbeat slowly dropping to normal. He felt Eve's hand on his chest, turned to look at her in the dark and together they drifted off to sleep.

It was the most satisfying, contented sleep Rick Ruby had had in months.

Too bad it had to come to end with a bang.

• • •

There was a loud noise that woke him up. There was shuffling of feet and in the dark he heard Eve scream. Instantly Ruby shoved his hand under his pillow only to realize he wasn't home and there was no gun hidden there. The last vestiges of sleep evaporated quickly as the lights went on in the bedroom and he looked up to see the barrel end of a gun pointed down at his face.

"Get up, Ruby!" A gravely voice ordered. "And do it nice and slow." His vision cleared as he started to sit up, pulling off the bedspread. Ruby saw that Eve's bedroom had been invaded by three heavy-set goons, two of which were holding her between them on the other side of the bed like Neanderthal bookends wearing cheap suits. Poor Eve was doing her best to cover her nudity despite both thugs holding her arms in vice-like grips.

"Hurt her and I'll break your necks," Ruby warned.

"Shut up and get dressed," the fellow pointing the gun at him barked. "We're the ones giving the orders here."

The private-eye reached over to the wooden chair by the bed to grab his boxer shorts and gray socks, complying with the big man's directive. He had recognized the hood after a few minutes; the square rock-like face with the broken nose and beady black eyes belonged to one Hank Curvallis known on the streets as Dutch.

"You too, sister," the ugly crook waved his gun at Eve Johnson. "Put some clothes on and hurry it up." Her two captors released her and even though frightened, the beautiful black woman remained stoic as she went to her closet and began to dress.

Standing to pull up his pants, the Ruby's mind was doing its best to reason out exactly what was going on. Dutch Curvallis was known to work for a two-bit boss named Walter Granger who operated out of South Brooklyn. To the best of Ruby's recollection, he had never met Granger personally nor had he ever crossed his path before. His knowledge of the gangster came only from what he had read in the papers and information gleaned from his old pals on the police force.

The fact that he and Eve hadn't been shot gave the private dick some small comfort. For whatever reason, they were being snatched. He didn't know why but assumed it wouldn't take long to find out. Nor would the answers to all this be pleasant.

Ten minutes later both of them were being escorted down the front steps of Eve's apartment building where two black sedans were parked at the curb. One of the armed kidnappers grabbed Eve's arm and began tugging her towards the second automobile. She yanked her arm away from him and clutched at Ruby for solace.

"Tell her go peacefully," Dutch Curvallis said, holding his automatic at hip level where both of them could see it. "Or else she dies here and now."

It was twilight and a dark purple sky was slowly lightening over the rooftops to the east and bringing a new day to the dirty, narrow streets.

There were tears swelling in Eve's eyes. Ruby held her tightly and stared into them. "Do as they say, Baby. For me. It'll be all right."

"You promise, Rick?"

"I promise."

Reluctantly he let her go and without another word she turned and went with the two men detailed to watch her. They loaded her into the back seat of the second black car and then drove off.

Dutch pointed to the remaining car where another gunsel stood like a doorman holding the back door open for Ruby.

"After you, Ruby."

Rick Ruby entered the car, sat back in the seat, making room for Curvallis. Once the doors were closed, the driver goosed the gas pedal and they rolled onto the empty pre-dawn streets. Another gunmen riding in the front seat turned and tossed Ruby a small burlap bag.

"Put it over your head," Curvallis said.

Ruby looked at the bag in his hands and the gun still pointed at him. What choice did he have? He removed his fedora, set it on the seat between them and pulled the stiff, rough bag over his head. He felt like a prize turkey on Thanksgiving Day.

"Just sit back and enjoy the ride," Curvallis advised.

Rick Ruby let out a breath and did just that.

• • •

Sitting blind, Ruby forced himself to relax. By the time the car came to a stop, he guessed a half hour had elapsed and he could be anywhere in the city. Being that it was sunrise; the ride had felt speedy as if there was very little traffic to slow them up. He felt the door to his right side open and a hand grabbed his shoulder.

"Okay, Ruby, step out of the car but keep the hood on."

The redheaded private eye complied. Again, both figuratively and literally in the dark, he had no other option. To try something now would be foolish and most likely get him and Eve dead. He had to maintain his own logical course; play along with their abductors until he could learn what the hell was going on.

His escort guided him around the car then said, "We're coming to a door. Take a step over the landing." Ruby did as he was told at the same time he realized the person leading him along wasn't Dutch Curvallis. Maybe the thug who'd been driving the sedan?

Next he was told they would be climbing stairs. Ruby could sense there were men both in front and behind him. He took his first tentative step up and felt a wooden railing to his right side. He took a hold of it to help keep his balance. Walking without sight wasn't easy. He found himself with a new and profound respect for the blind.

Finally he and his guards arrived at a landing and after another few yards, he was pulled forward and told to stand still.

A few seconds transpired than another new voice spoke softly. "All right, Ruby, you can take the hood off."

Rick Ruby blinked when the lights in the small square office assaulted him. Holding the burlap hood in his hand, Ruby put his hat back on and took in his surroundings as he learned do to on the police force. A typical business office with no windows, rectangular desk at one end, lots of filing cabinets everywhere, two straight back chairs before the desk and the walls covered with old calendars and several cheap paintings of sailing ships. It was the kind of efficiency set up one would find in a hundred factories and warehouses throughout New York.

Those items taken in, Ruby then gave his hosts his scrutiny. Dutch Curvallis was standing just behind him to the left with another tough guy. Both of them had their hands folded neatly in front of their bodies. Seated behind the desk was Walter Granger, the gang boss. Ruby had never met him personally, but had seen his mug in enough police files and newspaper accounts. Granger was a fit looking fellow in his mid-fifties with silver-gray hair and a matching mustache trimmed neatly. Some women might have found him ruggedly attractive in a brutish way. He wore an expensive blue pin-striped suit, a white shirt and black tie with a diamond stick-pin at its center.

Granger was lighting a cigarette with a wooden match and looking at Ruby with large, brown eyes like a teacher inspecting his newest student. "Go on and grab a chair," he said shaking the match dead and tossing it in a tin ashtray. "Would you like a smoke or maybe a drink?" He indicated the half empty bottle of bourbon to the left of the ashtray. Directly in front of him was a folded newspaper.

Rick Ruby tossed the hood he was holding back at Curvallis and took a seat in one of the chairs. "No, thanks, I'm fine."

"Suit yourself," Granger blew out a puff of smoke.

"Where's my friend?"

"You mean the cute little darkie we snatched you with?"

"Where is she, Granger?"

The mobster smiled inhaling another drag. "How is that dark meat, Ruby? Any sweeter than white tail."

Ruby started out of his chair, his hands balled into fists.

"DON'T!" snarled Dutch Curvallis.

Ruby looked over his shoulder to see the goon was pointing a gun at him, the look on his stone face showing every intention of pulling the trigger if he didn't back off.

"Sit down," Granger ordered a second time. "You listen up, shamus. You and your…ah…lady friend are gonna stay healthy as along as you do what I tell you. Are we clear on that?"

Reluctantly Ruby sat back and let his temper ease up. "Yeah, I hear you."

"Good, then we can get down to business."

"Business?"

"This new partnership you and I are about to go into, Ruby." Granger crushed out the remains of his butt in the ashtray and then picked up the newspaper before him. He held it up for Ruby see. It was the same edition of the Tribune Broom Stick had shown him the night before. The one with the story of his gun battle with the two stick-up men.

"You're quite the Wyatt Earp, aren't you Ruby?"

"What do you mean?"

"Don't be modest, taking down two hop-heads and dropping them cold like that. That wasn't luck that was nerves and shows you know how to use a heater when you have to."

Ruby was getting more perplexed by the minute. "So, I'm a good shot. What of it?"

"Well, there you have it," Granger dropped the paper back onto his desk. "As it turns out I have need of someone with your particular skills, Ruby."

"How so?"

"I need somebody whacked and you're going to do it for me."

"You're nuts, Granger," Ruby blurted out. "I'm not a hired gun." He nodded his back towards Curvallis and the other guard. "Besides, you've got plenty of shooters on your own payroll for those kinds of things."

Granger chuckled. He opened one of the desk drawers and took out two small glasses and began pouring bourbon into them. "Trouble is, most of them are known around town. I need someone no one will ever associate with me if they get caught." He slid one of the glasses toward Ruby. "Someone like you. Smart enough to get the job done and not get caught in the process."

"And what if I say no?"

Granger picked up his drink and leaned back in his chair. "Then I'll have Dutch take you and the songbird out for a long drive in the country and find somebody else."

Rick Ruby needed time to think but he wasn't going to have that luxury. He leaned forward, picked up the other glass and took as sip of the alcohol letting it burn down his throat smoothly. It was the good stuff.

"So who do you want me to shoot?" He knew when asking the question he wasn't going to like the answer.

Granger downed his drink, smacked his lips and wiped them with the back of his hand. "Big Sal Bonadonna and his brother, Little Joe."

If a trap door had opened under Ruby that exact moment, it would have easily duplicated the sinking feeling in his gut. Granger had just fingered the most powerful gangland figure on the South Side. Big Sal Bonadonna had come over from the "old country" as a young man in the early twenties and had immediately been recruited by Anthony Giacana and his crew of bootleggers. Salvatore proved to be a quick learner and was soon moving up the ranks of Giacana's organization until by his fortieth birthday he was the boss' number one man. When Giacana dropped dead of a heart-attack, no one questioned Bonadonna's moving up to take over the family. Under his guidance, it grew larger and more influential in the city's underworld affairs until Big Sal took his rightful place in the Council of Bosses.

The nickname Big Sal was added after his ascendency to top of the mob and it aptly fit his corpulent body brought about by his well known love of Italian food. Some guessed the big man tipped the scales at three hundred pounds. Of course this led many on the streets to wonder if some day he wouldn't keel over like his mentor, Giacana had done. He was certainly eating his way to that fate.

Apparently Walt Granger didn't want to wait that long, Ruby thought.

"You're crazy, Granger. I couldn't get anywhere near those two and you know it."

"What I know, smart guy, is that every Friday night Big Sal and that creepy brother of his always eat at Mama Rosa's on Lincoln and Third. They always get that private table in the back by the kitchen entrance."

"So?" Ruby knew of the restaurant famous for it authentic cuisine. Though he'd never eaten there, he'd passed it often enough in his travels.

"So," Granger continued, "this coming Friday night, soon after Big Sal and his crew are all seated comfortably at their tables enjoying their spaghetti or whatever it is those wops order, someone is going to unlock the kitchen back door for you."

"Who?"

"You don't need to know that. You just need to be in the back alley at eight sharp with your gun loaded and ready to go. Once that door is unlocked, you proceed through the kitchen area, walk into the restaurant and drill those clowns; one, two, three."

"What about his men?" Ruby lifted his hand with his thumb pointing back at Granger's own bodyguards. "It ain't just going to be Sal and his brother there."

"Then you'd better be as good as the papers say you are, Ruby." Granger leaned over the desk and folded his hands together as if in prayer. "You'll have the element of surprise on your side, see. You come out of that kitchen door blasting away and Bonadonna's men won't know what hit them. Shoot Sal and Little Joe and before they can even think to pull their own pieces, you are out the door and high-tailing back the way you came."

"Gee, you got it all worked out, don't you?" The sarcasm dripped like acid in Ruby's voice. "If it's that's goddamn simple, why don't you do it yourself."

"What are you, Ruby, stupid?" Anger flared up in Granger's black eyes. "I already told you, no one can know it was me who set up the hit."

"Or else half the other gangs will be coming after your head, is that it?"

"Ah, now you see the light." Granger smiled cruelly and leaned back again. "Beside, you're the one with the incentive here."

Rick Ruby kept his mouth shut. There was nothing he could say but wait for Granger to spell it out for him. Which he was only too happy to do.

"Cause if you don't do it come Friday night, then Dutch here is gonna take your lady pal and slit her throat from ear to ear.

"Are we perfectly clear on that?"

Ruby nodded, his throat dry.

"Good, you pull the job and I'll call you the next day with instructions on where to pick up the dame." Granger looked past the private eye to his men. "Okay, Mr. Ruby is all done here. Give him a ride home."

Ruby got up and turned his back on Granger. As he did so, Dutch Curvallis tossed him the black hood, a big ugly grin on his face.

• • •

It was almost nine a.m. by the time Curvallis deposited Rick Ruby on the sidewalk in front of Belle's Jazz Club. Then Dutch drove off with his fellow thugs. Holding his fedora, the redheaded investigator rubbed his eyes with the knuckles of his free hand, trying to get them accustomed to the glare of the morning sun. Wearing the damn hood had been a claustrophobic experience he hoped he'd never have to experience again. Holding up his arm to see the time on his wristwatch, he mentally strategized what he had to do next.

His guns were still back at Evy's place and he felt naked without them, but first things first. If he was going save her he would need help and that meant someone he could trust completely. He started down the walkway heading for a small diner located two blocks down the street called the Pot Luck Express.

The eatery was an old train dining car that had once been part of the Long Island railway system. It was one of the more popular spots in the black neighborhood and Ruby hoped to find his old pal Broom Stick Strickland there.

The bell over the front entrance jingled loudly as he made his way into the crowded, narrow interior and was immediately assailed by delicious aromas coming from the stove grills where the owner/cook Pops Wiley worked his culinary magic. His wife, Mary was at the front cash register handing out change to a customer when she spotted Ruby.

"Hey handsome, you look like somethin' the cat done dragged in," she smiled good naturedly, her oval brown face reminding him of a happy pancake. "Rough night, Rick?"

"You could say that, Mary. Is Broom Stick here?"

Mary Wiley pointed over patrons' heads to the end of the long counter to her left. Ruby thanked her and pushed past two exiting customers to reach the tall, lanky bartender. Bruce Strickland was finishing the last of his scrambled eggs and hash browns and nibbling on a last piece of burned bacon when he spotted Ruby.

"Hey, Rick, grab a seat," he said indicating the empty stool beside him.

The last place Rick Ruby wanted to talk was at the bar where passing waitresses and other customers could overhear what he had to say. Luckily he saw an empty booth at the back of the place being cleared by the pretty apron-wearing Maxine, Mary's oldest of three daughters.

He pointed to the booth and moved to it before the girl could signal a new customer. Broom Stick shook his head, grabbed his coffee and followed his friend to the leather covered booth.

"Hi yah, Mr.Ruby," Maxine greeted, putting her washcloth back into its apron pocket. "Can I get yah all somethin' to eat?"

"Sure, tell your Pops to give me four eggs over hard and some sausage. But first I need some coffee in the worst way, sweetie."

"Coming right up." The girl walked off as Broom Stick drained the rest of his own java and looked at Ruby carefully.

"Geezus, Rick, you look awful."

"Thanks for the compliment." Ruby tossed his fedora on the seat and ran his fingers through his unruly red locks. "Keep your voice down, pal. I'm in a big jam. Maybe the biggest in my life."

Seeing he was serious, Broom Stick leaned over the table and lowered his voice. "Okay, then, what gives?"

"Evy's been kidnapped," Ruby said. "And if I don't find some way to save her, she's going to die."

Strickland's eyes widened in his ink-black face and he was about to fire off a follow up question when Maxine suddenly materialized with a full pot of coffee in her hands and a porcelain mug for Ruby. After she filled Ruby's cup, Strickland slid his over and she gave him a second. Ruby thanked her and she walked off, a saucy bounce to her young hips. Once she was gone, Broom Stick leaned over again demanding to be told Ruby's story.

The tired, weary private eye took a long sip of the strong, hot coffee then proceeded to relate the events of the previous night from the time he and Evylyn Johnson had left the club. To his credit, Strickland didn't interrupt once and fifteen minutes later Ruby was finished, as was his coffee.

"Holy freakin' shit," Broom Stick gasped. "What the hell are you going to do?"

Ruby looked him straight in the eyes and replied, "What can I do? I'm going to have to shoot Big Sal Bonadonna.

"And you're going to help me."

• • •

"Okay, then, what gives?"

At first Ruby felt a twinge of guilt digging into his delicious breakfast. Most likely poor Evelyn wasn't eating that well. Still logic dictated Granger and his goons would keep her fed and well at least until after he'd finished his job for them; a job that would prove difficult enough without his having to do it on an empty stomach. No, Ruby required all the energy he could find to get through his predicament and somehow not only survive but save the singer at the same time.

After Maxine had removed his empty plate and left him and Broom Stick with fresh cups of coffee, the two friends once again began verbally hashing out the dilemma Ruby was mired in.

"Well, you certainly can't go to the coppers," the tall, gaunt bartender said stating the obvious.

"Tell me something I don't know." Ruby felt like a trapped rat. Everywhere he turned, he seemed to be hitting another blank wall.

"Man, I got to tell you, Rick, you got more enemies in this town than Carter has liver pills. Seems like every other day somebody is taking a pot shot at you."

The private eye nodded at the truth of his friend's comment. He had never been short of enemies. It was as if he was fated to go through life with only a handful of true friends and most of them invariably ended up suffering or dying on his account.

Friends and enemies is what made the world go round.

And just like that Rick Ruby had an idea; a very slim, wisp of an idea.

He sat up straight and snapped his fingers. "Damn it, Stick, that's it!"

"What is?"

"Friends and enemies. What you said about my having so many people who want me dead."

"I'm not following you, pal? What do yah mean?"

"What I need to find is someone who hates Granger as much as he hates Big Sal."

Broom Stick sat back against the booth and looked at the private eye as if Ruby had just spoken the most profound words of wisdom he had ever heard. "You know, that's so twisted, it do make sense." The black man tugged at his chin. "But who you got in mind, Rick?"

"I'll tell you on the way," Ruby answered, digging a few dollars out of his pants pocket and tossing them on the table for Maxine. "I've got to get to the office and you've got to tell May Belle about what happened last night. About Evelyn and all."

Sliding out of the booth behind the six foot redhead, Bruce Strickland frowned. "Right, you're gonna let me tell Mrs. May Belle Williams about how you got Miss Evelyn kidnapped by low-life gangsters. Thanks for nothing, pal."

"You're welcome," Ruby said racing for the exit while slapping his hat on. "Now get the lead out, will yah!"

• • •

Rick Ruby's office was located right above Belle's. In exchange for helping Belle out as a part time bouncer when the need arose, or doing her bidding whenever she had a problem just this side of the law. For these services he was provided with a dirt cheap rent on a single bedroom apartment and a two room office.

The frosted glass on the front door was stenciled, Ruby Investigations. Entering it, he found his brunette secretary, Edie Rose Adams, bent at the waist at the corner filing cabinet. With her statuesque figure contained in a tight black skirt and starched gray blouse, the scenery before him, accentuating her long shapely legs and tight derriere was tempting to say the least.

"See something you like?" Edie inquired in her smoky voice.

"That and then some," Ruby quipped as she stood withdrawing a yellow folder, closed the draw and turned to face him while straightening out. Edie's long, shiny brown hair tumbled down to her shoulders and he couldn't help but drink in her high cheek bones, heart-shaped lips and dazzling brown eyes.

Edie ignored his sexual taunt, as she always did, and walked back to her desk which guarded the door to his own office. "I was wondering if you were going to come to work today," she said coldly easing back into her chair. "Unless your weekends are going to begin on Thursdays now?"

"Listen, kid, I've had a rough night so how about cutting me some slack here."

At that the haughty brunette gave his clothes a second look and slowly her features were filled with concern. "Rick, what happened to you?"

He leaned over her desk hoping the urgency in his voice would satisfy her for now. "Look, Edie, I really haven't time to explain everything. Just believe this is something serious and I need you to do what I say, no questions asked."

"All right, I guess. What is it?"

"I'm in a jam."

"What's new about that?"

"Edie, please!"

"I'm sorry. Proceed."

He pushed his hat back on his head and sighed. "I don't want you hanging around here. Get me Jack Minch on the line, then cancel whatever other appointments I have for the rest of the day and tomorrow."

"But…"

"No buts. Just reschedule them for next week. I don't care. Then you grab your things and go home. Stay away from here until Monday morning. You got all that?"

Edie stood and came around the desk, she was frightened and Ruby mentally cursed himself for putting her through this. But he had to know she was safe once he instigated his mad scheme.

"What is it Rick, please? You're scaring me."

"I know, doll. It's probably nothing at all, but I just can't take any chances." He took hold of her shoulders gently, getting a whiff of her rose perfume. "Just do what I say and go home. Okay?"

She started to pout and he kissed her on the cheek before she could say another word. "I knew I could count on you, Edie. You're a trooper."

With that he let her go and dashed into his own office. Closing the door behind him quickly, he repeated. "Jack Minch. Get him on the line."

Dames. Did they have to complicate every part of his life?

The venetian blinds behind his work desk were still down, casting his small square office in a gloomy gray state. Moving around his desk, he grabbed the cord and drew them up allowing bright sunlight to flood the office. Outside the street was busy with traffic and the sidewalks crowded with citizens as the Big Apple went about its daily routine. Everything was normal except Evylyn Johnson was out there somewhere, her life in his hands.

Turning his back on the bright light, he saw the red signal buzzer on the base of his telephone flashing. He scooped up the receiver and put it to his ear while falling back into his wooden swivel chair. "Yeah."

"I've got Mr. Minch on the line," Edie announced.

"Thanks. Put him on, kid."

He heard the click and then a man's gravely voice spoke up. "Ruby, you old hound dog, what are you up to?"

"Hi, Jack, I need your help old pal."

"Why do I suddenly feel like someone is about to pick my pocket?"

"No, nothing like that, Jack. Look, you're the best reporter on the city's crime beat. Right?"

"I wouldn't argue that. Why?"

"What can you tell me about the Bonadonna brothers?"

"Whoa, there red, you're talking about some serious wiseguys here."

"I know that already. What I need is details, like their personalities, habits, quirks. You know, the kind of stuff that never makes the papers."

"What the hell have you gotten yourself into this time, Ruby?"

"Look, Jack, I really can't go into details here. The thing is someone is going to get hurt unless I can get a handle on those guys and I'm hoping you're the one person in this entire city that can help me out with that."

There was silence on the other end of the line. Minch was a careful guy who hadn't lived as long as he had by being reckless; especially when his job was exposing some of the gangland figures in the city. It was well known some of his stories had put away several mob bosses and there had been a few botched attempts on his life in the past. So the savvy newshawk had learned to be wary before jumping into any situation connected to the underworld.

At the same time, he had a loyal streak a mile long. "Okay, Ruby, but anybody asks you where you got this stuff...."

"I know, I'll tell 'em I found it out at the library."

There was chuckle on the other end of the line. "Right. You got paper and pencil ready?"

"Just a second." The private eye pulled opened his desk drawer and from it withdrew a yellow notepad and sharpened pencil. He transferred the receiver to his left hand and ear and held the pencil over the pad. "All set, Jack."

"Okay, then, Sal or Salavtore, as he was christened back in the old country, got his start...."

• • •

By the time Rick Ruby had jotted down the pertinent facts from his reporter friend, his secretary had also completed her own assignment. Together they shut off the lights and locked up the outer door. Edie gave him a final hug, cautioned him to be careful and then departed for the elevator. Watching her walk off, Ruby wondered for the millionth time why she just didn't quit and go find a decent job elsewhere. It seemed all he did was bring heartache and grief to those around him.

With a shrug, he turned and headed down the long hallway in the opposite direction. His living quarters were at that end of the floor. Once inside his small rent, he tossed the notes he'd written on the sofa in the combined kitchen-living area. Then in the bathroom, he turned on the hot water tap in the bathtub and watched it start to flow, steam rising up from the spigot. In his bedroom he stripped out of his clothes, tossing his rumpled suit and underwear into a laundry hamper inside the bathroom closet. Exhausted, he climbed into the rising water slowly, the heat burning his flesh until he had to turn on the cold tap to make it bearable. Once half submerged, he leaned his head back and sighed deeply. The soothing hot water drew the aches and pain out of him slowly. Finally he grabbed a block of hard soap off the counter behind him and proceeded to scrub his body clean again.

Once done, he threw on his white terry-cloth bathrobe, took two steps towards his bed and collapsed across it. He managed to pull one of his pillows under his head before falling into a deep, bottomless chasm of sleep.

• • •

BRING!! BRING!!!

The jarring noise wouldn't leave him alone. Rick Ruby opened his eyes. Afternoon shadows were splattered across this bedroom wall and he wondered how long he'd been asleep.

BRING! It was the phone in the living room.

Cursing, he got out of bed and running his hands through his thick hair started through the door. "Hold on, dammit, I'm coming!"

It started to jangle again as he hooked the receiver; the unit was mounted on the wall next to his icebox. "Yeah, I'm here," he mouthed sourly.

"About time," Broom Stick Strickland said. "I thought maybe you'd gone off to find Miss Evy on your own."

"Kind of hard to do when I haven't a clue where they've got her."

"Yeah right."

"I fell asleep," Ruby explained. "Hey, how'd Belle take the news?"

"She weren't none too happy. Nearly chewed my head off and said she was gonna box your ears if you don't get that girl back safe and sound."

"Right. Look, what time is, Broom?"

"Going on four, Rick."

"Okay, I need a favor."

"What?"

"I need to borrow your car." Strickland owned a 1934 Studebaker he kept parked in back of the building.

"As long as you leave her with a full tank, sure. Where you going?"

"Hoboken. Gonna pay a man a visit. I'll be down to get your keys in about an hour."

"I'll be in the club setting up. And, Rick, watch out for Belle."

"Gotcha. Thanks for the warning."

After hanging up, Ruby went back into the bathroom to brush his teeth, then he went into his bedroom closet to pick out his gray charcoal suit, a new white shirt and a navy blue tie. Leaving the jacket on the hanger, he started to dress himself. Once he'd knotted his tie, he went to mirror atop his bureau and gave himself a once over. He actually looked half human again.

From the bottom drawer he removed a leather shoulder harness and slipped it on so that the holster cavity rested comfortable over his left breast. Then he went back to the bed, knelt down and fished around beneath it grabbing hold of a luggage case. Sliding it out into the open, he lifted the latch to reveal a wooden gun box inside of which was a clean, well oiled Colt Automatic 1911 model. His .38s were still in Evy's apartment. He had resolved not to go back there until he brought her home.

Also in the box were three clips filled with .45 caliber rounds. He shoved one of these into the bottom of the automatic's grip and pulled the slide back to chamber a round. Making sure the safety was on, he then pushed the gun into his shoulder holster, closed up the case and returned the luggage back to its hideaway under the bed.

Now properly heeled, he put on his suit coat; made sure the gun was concealed and then went to find his fedora. Killing the lights, he exited his flat and took off to make his rendezvous with Broom Stick. The ride to Hoboken, New Jersey would be a long one and he wanted to get a head start before daylight ended.

• • •

Rick Ruby finished his fifth cigarette and tossed the butt out the open window. His body was getting stiff and if his prey didn't arrive soon, he was going to get out of Broom Stick's car and take a walk up and down the tree lined street called Summer Lane. It was a decent avenue with well kept houses on either side; many of them quaint old Victorians that had been well maintained. He had been to Hoboken many times and with Jack Minch's directions, he'd found the place he was looking for easily enough. Madame Joy Hansen's bordello was the big three story house at the end of the block.

Having been taught the proper way to stake out a location, he'd parked on the opposite end of the street facing in the opposite direction from the house. He'd adjusted the door mirror to giving him a clear view of the cathouse's front stoop and door. Then it was time to sit back and watch who showed up. Of course most of the activity didn't start until way after sunset and he was glad for two things; one that there was a light fixture over the front entrance which clearly illuminated the male customers who went in and second that he'd stopped at a small hamburger joint upon arriving in

Hoboken to grab a bite to eat. He'd left the restaurant with a few candy bars stuck in his suit coat pocket in case his vigil turned out to be a long one.

Still he trusted in Minch's information. If he said Joe Bonadonna frequented Madame Joy's establishment every other night, then Ruby's odds were fifty-fifty the hood would make an appearance. With tomorrow being Friday, the private-eye didn't want to think about how bad his situation would be if the little weasel didn't show up.

He held up his left hand to the windshield letting the light from the nearest streetlamp show him it was going on ten o'clock. Then a big, expensive black Cadillac rolled past him and he caught a quick glimpse of a small man seated erect in the back seat. He eyed the car's progress and held his breath as it stopped in front of the bordello. A big block of granite in human shape exited from behind the wheel, jogged around the back of the car and went to open the back door facing the building. From it emerged Joey Bonadonna, all five feet, four inches of him wearing a fancy fur-collared overcoat and the latest chic Homburg on his head. Even though he was a long distance away, Ruby had actually crossed paths with the mobster on several occasions back in New York; enough times to recognize him even at this distance.

And here we go! Ruby climbed out of the Studebaker and quietly closed the door. Then he started down the sidewalk, keeping to his side of the street. He walked slowly watching Bonadonna talking to a young woman attired in a flimsy negligee for a few seconds before she stepped back and welcomed him and his beefy chauffeur inside. As the door closed again, Ruby pulled out his pack of *Luckies*, shook another loose, nipped it with is mouth and got it going with a wooden match he torched using his thumb's fingernails.

He took a long drag hoping the nicotine would help calm his nerves which were now on edge. Being no stranger to whorehouses, he decided to continue his stroll and give Bonadonna time to get settled in with whichever girl he favored. Having the cold blooded killer naked when he braced him would be to his advantage. Naked men, no matter their psyche, were always vulnerable and easier to manage. Of course there was still the bodyguard to contend with, but he would deal with that obstacle when it was time.

The night was cool and he appreciated the chill in the air. It invigorated him as he walked along. He passed a few people and politely nodded, touching the brim of his hat as he did so. He wondered if they were aware there was a cathouse operating in their fair community?

Once his cigarette was finished, he turned around and crossed the empty street. He started along the sidewalk eyeing the tall house and hoping he could get to Bonadonna without having to hurt anyone. As he neared the cement steps, a taxi cab pulled up in front of the Cadillac and from it two distinguished fellows stepped out. They looked like bankers to Ruby. They were in a jovial mood as they started up the stoop and Ruby hurried to catch up with them so that when the front door opened after one of them rang the ball, he appeared to be one of their party.

"Hello, Mabel," one of the gray-haired greeted, removing his hat and handing it to her.

"Good evening, Judge Thompson," Mabel smiled moving back to let them enter. Ruby grinned inwardly. It seemed Madame Joy's clientele were very prominent members of the city. *If that one is a judge, who's his pal, the Police Commissioner?*

As the older men walked into a lavish, ornate front pallor aglow by a hanging chandelier. There was a black piano player in the far right corner tickling the ivories with a lively tune while the rest of the room was filled with sofas and padded chairs, most of which were occupied with half naked girls and their so-called dates. Ruby's trained eye denoted most of the customers were dressed to the nines.

"Excuse me, sir?" He turned to look at Mabel. She was a pretty blonde with too much rouge and cheery painted lips. "Is this your first time here?"

"Yes, it is," he gave her his best, harmless smile. "I hope that's not a problem. This place was recommended to me by several of my friends."

"Oh, no problem. It's simply that Mrs. Hansen likes to meet any new customer. Just to be safe, if you catch my meaning."

"Clearly." Again with the smiles.

"Fine, then would you follow me please." She indicated an open door to her right and Ruby followed her into a small waiting room with several chairs and a few potted plants.

"Please, wait here and I'll go find her."

• • •

With the hostess gone, Ruby opened his coat, pulled out the .45 and then took off his fedora and hid the pistol behind it. There were footsteps and Madame Joy Hansen appeared at the door and stood there for a moment eying him.

Ruby did the same and was silently appreciative of what he saw. The Madame looked like a slightly older version of Mae West with a ripe womanly body that was barely contained by a silver sheath dress cut drastically at the top to reveal lots of bare bosom. She had a round face with curly hair that had been colored a platinum blond hue and lake blue eyes under two long lashes.

"Good evening, I'm the owner of this establishment," she purred taking a step into the room. "And you would be?"

Ruby took a step forward and tilted his eyes down to his hat, which he then moved aside to reveal his automatic pointed at her. "I'm the fellow you are going to lead to Mr. Bonadonna's room."

The woman gasped and brought a hand up to her throat. "You're crazy! I can't do that." Her eyes were wide with fear.

"Look, sister, either you take me to him or I'll plug you. It's your choice." For Ruby it was the biggest bluff of his life. But he had to convince the Madame he was a stone cold killer or everything was lost. When she didn't react to his threat, he pushed the barrel of his gun into her belly. "What's it gonna be? I ain't got all night."

"No, don't shoot. I'll take you to him."

Deep in his soul, Rick Ruby sighed. He pulled back his pistol and hid again behind his hat. "Then move and remember, I'll be right behind you all the way."

Madame Joy led him back into the main room, past the revelers to the curved staircase that wound its way up to the second floor. As they moved up the highly polished steps, she kept her hand on the railing and mumbled a few words to the gentlemen guests who bid her a good night as they passed on their way out. It didn't take Ruby long to deduce the house did a booming business and he could easily imagine the take each night with so many well-to-do regulars.

At the top of the landing, the busty matron indicated the hall to the right and moved off in that direction, Ruby sticking with her hoping to look like an eager new john. They came to the end of the corridor where it intersected with another and Joy Hansen pointed to the left.

Over her shoulder she whispered, "He's in the big room to right at the end. His boy, Bruno, is right there playing watch dog."

Ruby moved around her slightly and saw the heavy set thug seated on a wooden chair leaning back against the wall by the bedroom door, his face lost behind the pages of a boxing magazine he held in his hands.

"All right," Ruby brought his mouth near the woman's right ear speaking softly. "Just walk up to him naturally like you need to ask him something. Keep smiling. I'll take care of the rest."

"Pal, you're gonna get us both wasted."

The private eye touched her ribs with his .45. "Move."

Doing her best to contain her fright, the woman started down the carpeted corridor with Ruby still behind her to her right side. Her high heels made a rhythmic tapping noise and the man called Bruno looked up over the pages of his magazine. Seeing Madame Joy, he nodded slightly and lowered the periodical.

"Hey, whatcha want, Mrs. Joy?"

"Oh, nothing important, Bruno. I just wanted to make sure everything was okay with Mr. Bonadonna and Polly."

Bruno's mean little eyes scrunched as he began to reply. Ruby moved past the Madame while raising his arm in a long arc before the gangster could fully grasp what was happening. He brought the steel barrel down across the man's forehead with a powerful blow. There was a loud thud, Bruno's eyes rolled white and he fell sideways off his chair unconscious.

Ruby stepped over him, grabbed the doorknob and shoved the door open. The big bedroom was awash in the glow of painted light-bulbs. In a huge bed, filled with pillows and comforters, a naked Joe Bonadonna was trying to raise himself up from under a little brunette with a tight ass and pert, apple sized breasts. She had been straddling him and now looked at the door, her mouth making a perfect O of surprise.

Bonadonna's sharp, pointed face made rat-like by his think mustache and thinning hair on his head was too slow on the up take.

"FREEZE!" Ruby said, pointing his .45 at the couple.

"EEEEK!" the prostitute named Polly cried out before Bonadonna managed to push her off the bed and sit up, pulling a pillow in front of his middle.

"What the hell is this?" he barked in a high pitched voice. "A hit?"

"That's up to you," Ruby retorted. "Do what I say and you keep breathing. It's that easy."

He looked back quickly at Madame Hansen standing frozen by the crumbled figure of Bruno. "Drag him in here. Hurry!" Then he looked to the naked broad on the floor and said, "You, come help her!"

Polly jumped up to obey his order and together, with her boss, they pulled the sleeping man into the room. Hansen brought in the chair as well and then Ruby took one fast glance down the hall and shut the door.

As he turned back to the red colored painted bedroom, he caught Bonadonna starting to reach for the nightstand to his left.

"Don't even think about it, Joe." He held up his gun menacingly. "I'll take off the top of your head before you could grab whatever piece you've got in there."

He brought the steel barrel down...

Bonadonna sat back against the pillows, anger filling his features. Meanwhile Ruby had moved past the bed to the private bathroom in the far corner. Obviously not all the rooms in the old structure were equipped with such amenities and it was the gangster's prestige that afforded him this added comfort.

He pointed to the room and ordered the two women to get inside. They fearfully complied and as Madame Joy was moving past him, Ruby held his index finger over his lips and suggested, "Stay quiet in there and this will soon be over." Whether she believed him or not, the sexy Madame shrugged, entered the room after the naked girl and Ruby closed the door behind them.

He turned and walked over to the bed keeping his automatic trained on Joe Bonadonna.

"So you gonna plug me now?" the crook asked coolly. Ruby begrudgingly admired his backbone.

"No, I'm here to tell you a story, Joe."

"A story? What, some kind of bedtime fairly tale or something?"

Rick Ruby sat on the edge of his bed and tilted his fedora back on his head. "You might say that, only this is one of those where you never wake up again."

"Look, dipshit, cut to the chase. You got something to say to me, spit it out or are you gonna talk me to death?"

"Okay, here it is. Walt Granger wants me to shoot you and your big brother Sal tomorrow night at Mama Rosa's."

That got Bonadonna's attention.

• • •

Rick Ruby spent most of Friday afternoon in Belle's backroom with Broom Stick plotting exactly how he was going to go into Mama Rosa's, shoot Big Sal Bonadonna and get out alive. The only advantage he had was knowing where and when. But that left all kinds of logistic problems to be resolved the least of which being how to disguise himself so that no one recognized him. His shock of red hair was going to be very hard to conceal, unless he wore a bag over his head and he'd had enough of that already.

So he and Broom Stick sat drinking coffee and talking about the Italian restaurant, its personnel and layout. They would be going in the back way through the kitchen area. First problem; what to do with the kitchen help? Then Ruby would walk through the swinging door into the public area. The Bonadonnas always sat at the last table near the kitchen entrance so they would be to his immediate right upon entering the main room. Seated at the next table in line would be the brothers' bodyguards. Ruby had no idea of how many there would be. There were also the innocent patrons to consider.

The more they kept hashing it over, the more it seemed impossible; Walt Granger had sent him on a suicide hit. There just seemed to be no way to make it work.

And then Broom Stick suddenly snapped his fingers and pointed at Ruby with a wild look in his eyes as he said one word; "Candles!"

• • •

It was shortly after 8 p.m. when Ruby and Strickland, seated in the Studebaker at the end of the alley, saw the back door to Mama Rosa's open. A figure looked out over the rows of trash cans, spotted their car in the darkness and then disappeared back inside.

"That's the signal," Ruby said and he climbed out of the passenger side. Broom Stick exited the driver's side, opened the back door and reached in to grab a Springfield 312 sawed off double-barrel shotgun.

"You be careful with my Sweet Angel there," the private eye cautioned. He kept the nasty weapon hidden under his desk during office hours. "Wouldn't want you shooting your foot off."

As they started walking across the road, Broom Stick, clutching the weapon to his chest, chuckled. "My pa taught me to hunt coon when I was ten, I'll have you know. Me and your Sweet Angel we'll be just fine."

Both of them wore knitted black sailor's caps and bandanas tied around their necks. As they approached the restaurant's back door, each of them tugged their caps down over their ears and then lifted the front of their kerchiefs to conceal their faces. Rick Ruby pulled out his .45 from under the old mackinaw jacket he wore.

"You ready?"

"Let's do it before I come to my senses," Broom Stick answered, his voice nervous. He tightened his grip on the shotgun.

Ruby pulled the door wide and his friend dashed in first. The glaring lights of the big kitchen made them both blink as they moved into the working area filled with stoves, sinks and island tables. "Everybody get your hands up!" Broom Stick snapped, doing his best to be heard while at the same time keeping his voice down.

Ruby went around the nearest prep table waving his handgun for all to see. He quickly counted five men, two of them in white aprons, three dressed as waiters. One of the chefs, a huge, pot-bellied fellow with a thick walrus mustache picked up a butcher cleaver and rushed Strickland.

"Who are you to come into my place…"

Broom Stick swung the shotgun around fast, knocked the big blade out of the man's hand and then kneed him in the belly. The man's face went red as he doubled over clutching his stomach. Broom Stick pointed the short barrels at the chef's head. "One more move like that and…boom! You is history. Clear?"

The fat chef gulped and nodded. "Si."

"Good, now where's the fuse box for this place?"

"It is in the cellar at the base of the stairs," one of the waiters offered, pointing to the door in the corner next to the giant ice box.

"All right then, everyone, let's go!" Broom Stick held up Sweet Angel and used it to herd them. "Everyone into the cellar. Now!"

While his black companion was handling the kitchen staff, Ruby had moved along the wall to the swinging door and pushed it open a crack. Looking out, he immediately spotted the Bonadonna brothers seated at the closest table. They were both digging into plates filled with spaghetti and meatballs, a bottle of Chianti on the table between them along with a basket filled with loaves of hard Italian bread.

At the center of the round table was a thick red candle, its flame flickering gently.

Ruby sighed.

Suddenly he sensed a body on the other side of the door and jumped backward. The door swung in pushed by another waiter carrying a tray of dirty dishes.

"Hey, Guido, table four wants another…"

Ruby stepped up next to the man and shoved his gun into his side. "Shut up!"

The waiter froze; saw his colleagues disappearing down the stairwell to the cellar and the masked black man with the shotgun. "SHIT!"

"Quiet!" Ruby ordered giving the fellow a push forward. "Put that goddamn tray down and go with the others."

"Yes, sir," the scared waiter mouthed as he hurriedly put the heavy tray down on the work table and moved to do as he was told. "Just don't kill me….please."

"No one is gonna get hurt," Broom Stick stated as the man, his hands held up, walked past him and down the first step. "As long as you do what we say."

As soon as this last waiter was gone from view, Broom Stick turned to Ruby and gave him a thumbs-up sign. "Give me five minutes to find the box and pull the switch."

"Right, and soon as you hear shots, you get your ass out of there," Ruby reminded his companion. "All hell's going to bust loose."

"Gotcha." Broom Stick disappeared into the cellar.

Rick Ruby again edged himself close to the door and peeked out. He tried to slow his breathing. The palm of his gun hand started to sweat. He kept his gaze totally focused on the Bonadonna boys. He heard a tiny click from the open door of the cellar and immediately shut his eyes. Strickland had cut the power and the lights went out in Mama Rosa's.

Dozens of voices erupted in surprised curses. Ruby opened his eyes. Everything was black…except for the soft yellow glow at each table provided by the candles. He shoved the door open, rushed in and raising his gun fired two quick shots.

The first caught Big Sal in the neck, his mouth sprung open as noodles and tomato sauced gushed out of it. His eyes bulged in shock and then Ruby shot him in the temple. As the big mobster toppled out of his chair, his younger brother started to push away from the table reaching into his coat for his own pistol.

Ruby swung his gun around, looked at Joey Bonadonna and shot him in the left arm. The bullet spun the little crook and knocked him of his feet.

Then Ruby was back pedaling to the kitchen. A huge shadow rose up before him. It was one Big Sal's soldiers and he fired two shots into the man's chest blowing him away. Through the door, he heard running footsteps and as he dashed around the table, a tall skinny figure flew out of the open cellar door to join him.

"Move it!" he cried, letting Broom Stick charge out the back door ahead of him Ruby was two steps behind his pal when the lights suddenly came on again. He never bothered to look back. He just kept running.

They made it to the parked car in seconds. Broom Stick tossed the shotgun onto the back seat through the open window and climbed into the driver's seat, turning on the engine the second he had the door closed. Rick Ruby slid into the passenger seat just as several gunshots rang out.

The cold motor roared to life and Broom Stick stomped on the gas peddle. Ruby saw several men stumbling out of the backdoor, guns in hand. Then they were rocketing down the alley in the pitch black. More bullets flew after them but none of them hit the speeding auto.

The second they flew out onto the main boulevard, Broom Stick flicked on the headlights and the Studebaker sped away into the night.

• • •

By the time Rick Ruby awoke the next morning, the shooting of Big Sal Bonadonna had made all the papers. He could hear newsboys hawking the headlines through the open window in his office. "Gangland Boss Gunned Down!" He did his best not to dwell on his actions while getting dressed. Salvatore Bonadonna had been a cold blooded monster and killing him to save Evelyn Johnson was something he was willing to live with.

He met Broom Stick at the Pot Luck Express and the black bartender seemed fine, though still anxious to know what would happen next.

"I wait for Granger to call me," Ruby explained. "Then they are supposed to let Evy go."

"You think they really will, Rick?"

"No. That's why I got that insurance."

"Well, I hope he calls soon. This waiting is murder." Strickland looked up the second the word fell from his lips. "Sorry."

"S'alright. I want this over with too."

• • •

Rick Ruby guessed Walt Granger would wait until nightfall and he was right. It was shortly after seven p.m. when the phone on his office desk rang.

"Ruby here," he identified himself putting the receiver to his ear and stubbing out the cigarette he'd been smoking.

"You botched the job, Rick," Granger's voice sounded in his ear. "You were told to kill them both. You only wounded Joey."

"Give me a break, will yah. I got Big Sal for you. I thought he was your primary target."

"True, but…"

"But what? You afraid of Joey?" Ruby was playing to the mobster's ego. It was his final trump card.

"I ain't afraid of no one, shamus. Joey is a piss-ant thug without Big Sal."

"Right. So…are you going to cut the girl loose?"

The small light on Ruby's desk cast his shadow on the closed blinds behind him as he held the phone and silently prayed.

"Well, of course," Granger finally spoke up. "But I ain't just gonna dump her on some street corner. What kind of a louse you take me for, Ruby."

"What do you mean?"

"Be outside your building in fifteen minutes. Dutch is going to pick you up so that you can come and get her. You know, play the hero to the rescue routine. How's that?"

"Okay."

"And leave the artillery at home."

There was a click and the line went dead.

Ruby pulled a folded piece of paper from his coat pocket, clicked the line several times until the operator came on.

"Operator. What number do you want?"

He gave her the city number and then sat back in his chair. His nerves were wound tight, his breathing heavy.

There was a ring, then a deep bass voice asked, "Yeah, who is it?"

"This Rick Ruby. Let me talk to the boss."

• • •

Dutch Curvallis was prompt if nothing else. The redheaded shamus had been standing on the sidewalk in front of Belle's only five minutes when the familiar black sedan left the center strip and stopped in front of him. Curvallis came out of the back seat and motioned for Ruby to turn around. "You know the routine."

Dozens of Negroes walking past eyed the two of them curiously as the hood frisked Ruby starting from his ankles up to his armpits, assuring himself the P.I. wasn't carrying.

"Satisfied?"

Curvallis sneered, pointed to the open back door and said, "Get in."

It was Saturday night and traffic was congested. After a few moments of looking out the window to the rear, the driver turned the wheel and pulled out, smoothly entering the flow of cars going south.

When Curvallis merely sat back without offering Ruby the black hood to put over his head, Ruby knew the implication of what that meant. Curvallis didn't care if he learned where they were going because he wouldn't be around later to tell anyone. This was strictly a one-way trip. Ruby had expected as much and knew control of the situation was now out of his hands. His fate, and Evy's, now rested on his scheme and his ability to manipulate the scum he dealt with every day. It was the biggest gamble he'd ever bet on.

They continued moving through lower Manhattan until they reached Battery Park which looked out over the harbor and the Statue of Liberty. The driver circled the entire area until they came to a Flying A gas station that was closed for the night. The sedan turned into the front lot, moved past the two gas pumps and went around to the back where various automobiles all needing some kind of repair were parked. Here they came to a stop.

Climbing out of the car, Ruby could see light shining through the square windows atop the two bay doors. Curvallis marched him to the door situated between the two larger portals with their driver taking the lead. Ruby was aware many of the bosses in the city owned various business and that Granger would have a garage made sense in a lot of ways. What better place to patch up bullet holes or change the color of a hot car the police were looking for.

As they entered, Ruby could smell the pungent odors of gas and oil and other caustic lubricants. Inside the massive working bays were two vehicles set over two eight foot deep cement pits. One was a convertible roadster while the other was a Ford pick-up truck with its hood up, left that way by the mechanic who had obviously been working on the engine at quitting time.

A single light bulb hanging from the ceiling was one of two lights illuminating the interior. The other was a table lamp located on a steel work bench covered with various auto parts and tools. Walt Granger, resplendent in a dark brown suit, was seated on one of the two steel stools with his back to the table. He was smoking a cigar and looking very smug.

"Ah, Ruby, at last. Glad to see you could make it."

The driver from the sedan went to stand against the back wall behind Granger, while Dutch Curvallis remained a few feet behind Ruby.

"Cut the bull, Granger," Ruby was in no mood for frivolity. "I'm here. Now where's the girl?"

Granger turned his head to the right and yelled out, "Bring her out, Otto!"

Hidden in the gloom at the opposite end of the building a rest room door opened and Rick Ruby watched as two people emerged. As they came into the lighted space, he saw Evy being followed by another one of Granger's men whom he recognized from the night they had been snatched. Though she looked worn and tired, the brown beauty did not seem to be injured and upon seeing Ruby, she brightened and ran to him.

"Oh, Rick." He folded his arms around her and she rested her head on his chest.

"Are you all right?"

She moved her head and looked up him with a weary smile. "I am now."

"Rest easy," he comforted her. "This is almost over."

"Indeed it is," Granger chuckled. "Although I must admit, I really thought you were lots smarter than this, shamus."

"Meaning you're going to have us both shot," Ruby retorted. "Sorry, Granger, but you're the dummy here."

An ugly expression appeared on the crime boss' face. He sat up on his stool perch clearly surprised by the private eye's accusation.

"Bold talk for someone about to die."

"Ever play chess, Granger?" Ruby was stalling for time. He had to keep Granger and his men occupied for just a little while longer. Or so he hoped.

"Huh, chess? What da hell are you talking about?"

"Okay, how about checkers. That's probably more your speed."

"You know, you got one hell of a smart mouth, Ruby."

"I'm glad you think so, Granger, because you're going to love what I have to say next."

"Yeah, and what's that?"

"Well, like I was saying. Sometimes in checkers you have to sacrifice one of your pieces in order to sucker the other guy into jumping you. That way he ends up in the place where you can jump him even worse."

Suddenly the back door opened and gunshots rang out. The man behind Granger clutched his chest and fell over. Four men raced into the garage, all of them armed and shooting. Granger leaped off the stool and started to dig into his coat for his own gun.

Meanwhile Rick Ruby had pulled Evelyn down to the floor, draping his body over hers.

Dutch Curvallis had his gun out but never got off a single shot as the strangers cut him down. Then big Otto caught a slug in the neck and dropped leaving only Walter Granger left standing, his .38 revolver barking in his hands.

"I give up!" he suddenly cried dropping his pistol to the ground. "You got me, coppers."

Ruby looked up, saw the shoot out was over and got to his feet, helping Evy do the same.

"Sorry, Granger, but they ain't cops," he informed the mobster as he dusted himself off. Evy still clutched his arm, trying to hold back the tears that threatened to flow. "Like I said, figuring out how to beat you wasn't all that hard."

"Huh?"

"You wanted me to take out Big Sal because you were greedy and wanted to take over his territory. All I had to do is figure who wanted it even more than you."

"You're not making any sense," Granger had his hands up and was looking back and forth between the gunmen and Ruby.

"Oh, I think Ruby made a lot of sense," Joey Bonadonna said as he walked into the garage, his left arm encased in a medical sling. His rich overcoat was draped over his shoulders and he wore his regular homburg.

"JOE?" Granger could barely get the words out. Then he looked over at Ruby with venom in his eyes. "YOU! You set me up!"

"Of course I did," Ruby said. "I went to Joe two nights ago and told him the whole set up. I kind of figured if Big Sal was out of the way, everything would be all his."

Granger looked at Joe Bonadonna in disbelief. "You let him shoot your own brother?"

The little gangster shrugged and held up his palms innocently. "It was strictly business, Wally. You know how that goes. I was getting tired of getting Sal's leftovers and living in his shadows.

"When Ruby came to me and told me what you were planning, it was the perfect solution to my problem. Now Big Sal's out of the way and everyone is gonna think you were the one who done it. None of the other families will blame me for taking my revenge here."

"You lousy little rat…"

Bonadonna gave his men a hand gesture and they opened up on Granger. Six bullets tore into him and he staggered back yelling. Then he fell over onto his back and was still, the cigar falling out to the cement beside him.

Joe Bonadonna walked over, looked down at his dead rival and then ground out the cigar with the tip of his shoe.

"You two are free to go," he said to Ruby and the girl. "Go on, get out of here."

Rick Ruby put his arms around a shaking Evelyn and they started walking past the killers to the exit. As they did so, Ruby looked at one of the men holding a smoking pistol and suddenly wheeled around and punched him in the side of the head. The man fell over unconscious.

The other soldiers all spun around and trained their guns on Ruby. Bonadonna looked at him puzzled.

Ruby straightened his tie and pointed to the man on the floor. "This is the one who opened the back door to Mama Rosa's for us. I just recognized him."

Joe Bonadonna came over and looked down at the fallen gunmen. "Okay, Ruby, it seems I owe you one after all."

The two men looked at each other and then Rick Ruby turned took the singer's arm and they walked out into the night.

As they made their way through the dark parking lot, they heard a single gunshot from behind them.

Rick Ruby held the girl tight in his arms and hoped it wouldn't take them forever to find a cab. He was bone tired and just wanted to go home and get some sleep. It had been one hell of a week.

"Rick, I thought sure I was gonna die. But you came back for me."

"Did you ever doubt I wouldn't?"

"Not for a second, baby." She reached up and kissed him, holding his neck down and pressing her warm lips against his. There was promise in that kiss.

Twenty minutes later he spied a Yellow Cab and flagged it down. Opening the back door for Evy, he thought maybe his luck was changing at long last.

THE END

The Gumshoes

I learned to read with comic books in the late 50s. But as much as I came to love those four color magazines printed on cheap paper, it soon became apparent to me as I neared my teen years that comics were geared to children, again, remember the times, and ultimately I began to look for other, more adult fare. I found it in the lurid paperbacks that enticed us all from the drugstore spinner racks. Companies like Fawcett, Dell and Ace offered up lots of pulpish titles and eventually I would go on to find, in paperback reprints, such iconic heroes as Tarzan, Conan, Doc Savage and many more. But these tales of fantastic adventure were not the first to snare my attention; that was done by the crime noir titles.

I was twelve years old, raging through puberty and there were these covers usually featuring some hot babe in a revealing outfit or pose; a garter belt stocking top exposed on some long, sensual leg hinting at the forbidden fruit that was sex. And these femme fatales were never alone on those covers; either they were partnered with some ruggedly handsome tough guy or standing over a dead body with a smoking gun in their hands. All of it was heady stuff and sold for only twenty-five cents.

The very first private eye I encountered in this pulp-paperback world was the white haired California hipster; Shell Scott. He was created by writer Richard Prather and his cases, told in first person, were so laden with all manner of sexual innuendo, it didn't take me long to fantasize that some day I'd be that tough guy hero with all these gorgeous women falling all over me because I was so damn irresistible. As Bogart said so succinctly, "The stuff that dreams are made of."

As the years went by I'd discovered many more classic private eyes from Brett Haliday's Mike Shayne to the toughest one of them all, Mickey Spillane's Mike Hammer. At the same time I was reading all this crime fiction, it was popping up all over television as well and many of these paperback heroes did get their own series on that little black and white tube. One such was Richard Diamond, Private Eye as played by actor David Janssen. If you haven't guessed yet, he would be inspiration that sparked the birth of Rick Ruby by writing buddies, Bobby Nash and Sean Taylor.

Eventually they would come to me with the character suggesting we do a series of anthologies starring this 1930s tough-guy investigator. They wrote up a bible for others of their colleagues who might want to join the fun and then they got busy writing their very first Rick Ruby stories. Those stories appeared in "The Ruby Files, Volume One" that was released in 2012 and would go on to win the Pulp Ark Award for Best New Pulp Character. Shortly after the book came out, I was exchanging a few e-mail messages with Sean and mentioned how much fun I'd had editing those first four stories; the other two had been written by Andrew Salmon and William Patrick Maynard. Somewhere in that back and forth, Sean suggested I write a Rick Ruby story for the second volume and I said yes; but only if there was an open slot in the book when it came time to produce it.

Being the Managing Editor of Airship 27 Productions, I try to avoid this kind of thing in that being the so-called "Boss" I would never want any of our writers to think I was taking advantage of my position. Anyway, Alan J. Porter submitted a story and Bobby and Sean, per our contractual agreement, both would write stories and that left that fourth slot…empty. But not for long.

I had a blast writing Rick Ruby and entering his world. Thanks to Bobby and Sean for inviting me aboard and I pray you, the reader, have truly enjoyed this second collection. Thanks for your support.

• • •

RON FORTIER – is a veteran comic book creator, he's best known for writing the Green Hornet and *Terminator:Burning Earth*, with Alex Ross, for Now Comics back in the 80s. Today, he keeps busy writing and editing new pulp anthologies and novels via his Airship 27 Productions. (http://robmdavis.com/Airship27Hangar/airship27hangar.html).

He won the Pulp Factory Award for Best Pulp Short Story of 2011 for "Vengeance Is Mine" which appeared in *The Avenger – Justice Inc.* from Moonstone Books.

You can keep updated with his latest projects by visiting his personal website at –
(www.airship27.com)

TAKEDOWN

By Bobby Nash

Richard Ruby was having another one of *those* days.

He had put in several long nights at The Ambassador Palms Hotel, where he'd been hired by the manager; a fidgety little man named Eugene Roberts. To Rick, it appeared that he was one step away from hysterics. Rick had offered to buy the man a drink in the hopes that it might settle him down, but he'd promised Edie a few weeks earlier that he would try to keep his drinking under control, especially when he was working a case. She was a sweet kid and a whiz around the office, but this temperance kick she was on lately was becoming a pain in his backside, but he had trouble saying no to her so he promised to cut back on the booze while on the job. It was no easy task, but so far Rick had managed to keep his word, which wasn't easy sitting just a hop, skip, and a jump from the hotel bar for hours on end.

The Ambassador Palms Hotel was considered by many as one of the New York City's most exclusive four star places to spend the night. Rumor had it that the pillows in the suites were so soft it was like laying your head on a cloud. Rick was curious, but although the hotel was willing to pay his fee, he couldn't afford to spend an hour in one of their deluxe rooms, much less spend an entire night. "It's a shame I won't get to try one out firsthand," he'd remarked when he took the gig. The Palms was just the sort of up-scale place where Carla St. Clair would have enjoyed a rendezvous. Carla's daddy, the Virginia sugar tycoon, would have flipped his lid knowing that a lowly little private investigator like Rick Ruby had even been allowed to step across the threshold into the lobby. Of course, daddy's disapproval of Rick only made the P.I. more attractive to his daughter.

Rick's client had noticed a lot of new faces, most of them he described as women of questionable repute. Roberts had told him that "*those women*" had been spending a lot of time in his hotel, although none of them had actually rented a room. He wanted the P.I. to find out who the new players were and what they were doing in his hotel. He was certain that they were high-end prostitutes, but he couldn't act without proof.

That proof had been fairly easy to get as Rick had been able to corroborate the manager's assumptions fairly quickly. Stopping the girls wouldn't accomplish anything, Rick knew, and he'd told his client as much. Running off the girls wouldn't stop their boss. He'd simply have a new batch working the hotel the next night. He had to find the boss and convince him to back off and know that The Ambassador Palms was off limits.

Roberts was afraid that this unwanted element was going to hurt his business. The Ambassador Palms was a classy high-priced hotel, but they fostered a reputation for being a Christian run business. The manager didn't want details. He just wanted whatever tomfoolery was going on to stop. He had actually used the word "tomfoolery," which had made Rick laugh, although he quickly covered it when he realized that the man wasn't kidding.

He had instructed Rick to "*get the goods*" and "*shut them down*" by any means necessary without disrupting the hotel's clientele. Keeping things quiet was important. That was why he had come to The Ruby Agency instead of the police.

Rick took the case for several reasons.

First, it seemed like an easy gig on the face of it and he couldn't think of a single good reason to turn down easy money.

Second, he hadn't paid Edie Rose in weeks. She had only threatened to quit four times, but eventually he knew he was going to push his luck with her too far and she would walk. Rick wasn't sure he could function, let alone survive, without Edie Rose there to take care of him, even though she spent too much time on the all but pointless task of trying to save his soul.

Third, with all the downtime he had between cases of late, he'd alternated spending his time in the company of a couple of young ladies or drinking. After listening to his secretary complaining about his drinking all day, the last thing he needed to do was hear it at night, but Belle had been on his case about the size of his bar tab the past few nights. Even though he wouldn't have to pay the tab, thanks to his playing house dick and bouncer for Belle's bar, even he was starting to think he'd been hitting the bottle a little too much. Belle didn't like him spending quality time between the sheets with her girls either, but she let that go because it didn't cost her money.

Plus, she wasn't stupid. There was a slim hope that he might give up the booze, but there was no way that Rick Ruby would lay off the dames. He would rather cut off his own arm first.

Fourth, and maybe the most important, was the need for a new pair of shoes. He only owned one good pair and they were on the verge of falling completely apart. Who could trust a private dick that couldn't afford a new pair of shoes?

After five days with very little sleep, Rick was exhausted. It was his sixth night camped out in the lobby of the hotel. The first two nights were a bust with nothing out of the ordinary going down. He caught his first glimpse of the woman he began to think of as Raven because of her deep black hair on the third night. She was a stunner, no doubt about it. Rick didn't necessarily have a type, as evidenced by the vastly different women he orbited on a regular basis, but if there was one type that he always fell hard for, it was hers.

The manager's assumptions appeared to be right on the money as far as he was concerned. Rick had spotted Raven in the lobby every night for the past three nights and now he caught a glimpse of her stepping out of the elevator. Despite himself, he felt his breath catch at the sight of her. If not for being there on business, he would have sidled up next to her and asked for her name.

But he was there on business so he simply followed her instead.

He gave himself a four count before following through the lobby doors out onto the sidewalk. Rick slipped into the pay phone box and dropped a dime in the slot. While dialing the phone, he watched Raven and her friend, whom he assumed was in the same line of work, stand on the sidewalk and waited for their rides. They were the kind of women that was hard to miss.

There was no one on the other end of the line, which Rick knew when he dialed his office. It was generally empty after three a.m. unless he was sleeping one off there, as he did most nights. He spoke into the phone quietly, a pretend conversation with his empty office to provide cover as he kept Raven in his sights.

Rick reminded himself to add the dime to his expense report.

• • •

Lacy Blake was tired.

Stepping out of the elevator into the lobby of the Ambassador Palms Hotel she was not at all surprised to find a beehive of activity. The Palms was four stars all the way. The concierge took great care of their guests, whether it was their first visit to New York City or if they were frequent visitors. The hotel had a rich and storied history and frequently made the "best of" lists in various trendy magazines and was a preferred destination for movie stars, politicians, and businessmen from around the globe.

If she were not aware of the fact that it was just a bit north of three o'clock in the morning, the hustle and bustle of the lobby certainly wouldn't have given it away. It had been just as busy before sunset when she'd arrived. Small groups of men in business suits clustered together in conversation, some muted and considerate, some filled with boisterous laughter, and others downright intimate with a lady friend.

Lacy sighed and noticed more than a few of the men and women turn to look her way as the clacking of her three inch heels against the marble floor drew attention to her presence. She wore a long coat that fluttered around her ankles as she walked, exposing her long bare legs with each step while accentuating the painfully uncomfortable heels with straps that ran up her leg. The front of her coat was cinched tight, buttoned just high enough to expose ample cleavage. Her stark black hair bounced playfully around her shoulders in rhythm with her steps.

Although her look had been carefully designed for just such a response, mentally, she hoped that none of them would work up the nerve to approach her before she made it across the lobby to the front doors. The last thing she wanted to deal with at the moment was some drunk jerk trying to put the moves on her so she kept her pace brisk, but steady. Increasing her stride, while tempting, did more harm than good. She had an image to uphold, after all.

Lacy breathed a sigh of relief when she made it to the lobby exit without incident. A small playful smile tugged at her lips as she stepped out into the cold New York winter night. Standing in front of the hotel's valet stand was a woman she had gotten to know fairly well over the past few months.

"Hey there," Lacy said to Ariel Webb, who waited impatiently at the curb.

Ariel was a couple years younger, not to mention several inches shorter, than Lacy with a dancer's physique and a playful demeanor that made her seem even younger. She was a big hit with many of the agency's clients, especially when she put her hair up in pigtails as she had them tonight. Lacy suspected that she was also wearing the oft-requested plaid skirt and white blouse schoolgirl uniform under a long coat similar to her own. Her porcelain skin added to the sweet and innocent image that so many of the Johns preferred. Personally, Lacy didn't understand the appeal of the Catholic Schoolgirl look, but to each pervert his own, she decided.

"You have a good night?" Lacy asked.

Ariel gave her that tight, almost embarrassed smile that had fired many a man's libido as she opened her coat to reveal the naughty schoolgirl outfit she was wearing, much as Lacy had suspected. The red plaid skirt was so short that no modest person would be able to bend over in it. However, in their profession modesty was rarely a job requirement. In fact, it was rather frowned upon. Despite her youth, Ariel had been in the business a few years already, which was quite an accomplishment in an industry that tended to use up and spit out its employees rather quickly.

"Nice outfit," Lacy teased.

"Damn conferences," Ariel laughed.

"Tell me about it. What is it about these things that brings out the freak in these guys?"

"Who knows, but it's good for business. And they usually tip well."

"Not the guy I had tonight," Lacy groused. "Bastard was so tight I'm surprised he didn't squeak when he walked."

Ariel laughed at the joke and wagged a finger toward Lacy. It was her turn for show-n-tell. "Okay, let's see it," she said. "I showed you mine..."

Lacy sighed, but unbuttoned her coat and held it open to show off the tiny French maid's outfit she wore underneath.

"Happy?"

"Very much so," Ariel said playfully as a limousine pulled to the curb and stopped. The valet moved quickly to open the door. "I believe this is your ride, Lace."

"Good," Lacy said as she stepped closer. "I'm ready to go home and get out of this outfit... again," she said with a wink.

"Lucky for us the classics never go out of style, huh?" Ariel asked.

"Right. Lucky," Lacy said as she stepped into the warm limo. "I'll talk to you tomorrow, kiddo. Get a good night's sleep."

"Good night, mademoiselle."

She smiled at her young friend through the glass before the valet closed the door.

"Where to, Miss Blake?" the driver asked.

"Home," she said as she laid her head against the seat and closed her eyes in an effort to ward off the headache that was starting to build in her temples. "I'm exhausted. Calling it a night. There's a long hot bath calling my name."

"Yes, ma'am," the driver said before pulling away from the curb.

As soon as the first limo pulled away a second one slid in to take its place. The valet moved to the door and repeated the same process for Ariel Webb. "Ma'am," he said as he held the door for her.

As Ariel stepped into the limo she ran a slender finger along the valet's jaw line. Despite his macho exterior, he blushed as she called him, "Cheri." Once inside the car and the door closed, she blew the valet a kiss. It was the closest thing to a tip he would get from her tonight. Her employer kept the valets and concierge at New York's finer hotels paid so the girls didn't have to. It would only draw unneeded attention from law enforcement.

"Home, Miss Webb?" the driver asked without turning to look at his passenger.

"Are you kidding?" Arial asked as she stretched playfully, offering the driver a little show in his rearview mirror. "The night's still young."

"Yes, ma'am."

"And I really need to get laid."

• • •

 Rick Ruby hailed a cab.

"Where to, Mac?"

"Follow that car," Rick said, pointing at the limousine that pulled away from the lobby entrance.

"Are you for real?" the cabbie asked.

"Yes," Rick said.

"I've always wanted someone to hop in my hack and say that."

"There's an extra ten spot in it for you if you don't lose them," Rick said.

"You got it, boss." The cab pulled away from the curb and fell in behind the limo, keeping a few cars between them.

"Not too close," Rick warned.

"Relax, Mac," the cabbie said boisterously. "That ten spot is already as good as in my pocket."

Rick knew he wouldn't be relaxed until he had this case sewn up and collected his fee. His efforts to follow one of the ladies back to their boss had so far met with limited success. Rumor had it the ladies of the evening were handled by Claudio Tommasso, a big time gangster with the Tommasso crime family, second only to his brother, Bennicio. So far he had found no proof to back up those claims, but it was a safe bet. This was the first opportunity he'd had to follow the one he had started to think of as Raven and he couldn't afford to lose her trail.

Twenty minutes later, the cabbie pulled to the curb beneath a broken street lamp and set the brake on his old jalopy "Looks like this is your stop, Mac," he said.

Rick watched as the chauffeur opened the door for his passenger. Shapely legs slipped out into the night, followed by one of the most beautiful women Rick had ever seen. Considering he spent most of his nights surrounded by the ravishing beauties in Belle's Bar that was saying a lot.

Raven walked up a short flight of stairs, unlocked the front door to a townhouse the likes of which Rick could only dream of ever affording, and slipped inside. As soon as the door closed behind her, the driver climbed back behind the wheel and left.

Rick scratched his chin with a knuckle, felt the two days worth of growth there and reminded himself he needed not only a shave, but a shower as well. A hot meal and a nap wouldn't hurt either. He'd been on the job for a few days and had slept little during that time, but much like Rick's favorite poet, Robert Frost, there were still miles to go before he slept. That one line had stuck with him after he read it out of one of the books Donna Dixon kept in her dressing room at the Boom Boom Club. He'd run across it one night while waiting for her after one of her sets.

The poem had really stuck with him.

Now he used it like a mantra.

Rick opened the door and stepped out into the night, thankful for the cover provided by the broken light. He peeled of a couple bills, including the bonus he'd promised, and handed them to the cabbie. "Here you go," he said. "You did good work. Try not to spend that bonus all in one place, all right?"

"No promises," the cabbie said with a hearty laugh. "You sure you don't want me to wait on you?"

Rick would have liked nothing better, but after peeling off the fare and bonus, he only had a couple of George Washingtons left. He wouldn't be able to afford keeping the meter running, much less get back home. "I appreciate it, but I'll be okay," he said instead. "I'll probably stake the place out until morning."

"Suit yourself," the cabbie said. He put the car in gear, but turned back to Ruby before pulling off. "Look, there's an all night diner about a block south of here. I'm heading over for a bite to eat. On my way back out I'll swing back by just in case you need a ride."

"Thanks," Rick said. "I appreciate that."

"Catch ya later, Mac," the cabbie said and pulled off into the night.

Rick Ruby watched him go, smiling. "Enjoy your breakfast, Mac," he said. The area where he'd been dropped off was what he liked to call upscale middle class, which basically meant this is where folks with good jobs ended up as they worked their way up the ladder of whatever business they worked. Before the Stock Market crash back in '29, homes in this neighborhood were twice as much as they were now, but still more than a lowly P.I. like Rick Ruby could afford.

If the woman he came to know as Raven lived here then she was doing mighty fine for herself or she worked for someone who was, not that Rick was judgmental. He knew full well that if not for the generosity of Belle he would have probably been out on his can a long time ago. Perhaps Raven had her own version of Belle to keep a roof over her head. Either way, after spending many a night sleeping on the small lumpy mattress in his apartment or the ratty old sofa in his office, Rick envied anyone who could lay down to sleep in such comfortable digs.

Rick's usual method of detecting was to take the direct approach, which usually ended with either fists or bullet flying. This time, he decided to try a different tack. He found a bus stop bench nearby. Pulling a newspaper out of the overflowing trash bin next to the bus stop sign, Rick settled in on the bench so he had a good view of his quarry's townhouse and pretended to read.

He yawned. It was going to be a long night. Suddenly, Rick wished he'd asked the cabbie to bring him back a cup of piping hot coffee.

• • •

Lacy Blake had never been so happy to be home.

Pushing open the front door to the townhouse she made her way through without turning on the lights. Peeking around the curtains, she watched the limo pull away and disappear. Except for a taxi letting out a guy across the street, the street was empty.

She let out a breath and felt the tension of the day start to fall away. Unbuttoning the coat, she let it fall open as she reached for an inside pocket with her right hand while she tossed her keys into a small decorative glass bowl on the table next to the door where they landed with a small clink.

In the dark, she didn't see the man reach out and pull the small chain on the side lamp until the bulb's brightness burnt away the shadows.

That didn't mean she didn't know he was there.

The intruder sat comfortably in the end chair, one leg crossed over the other, as if he didn't have a care in the world. He didn't even flinch at the sight of her pointing a handgun directly at his head. Instead, he smiled.

"Don't even think about…" she began, her voice trailed off when she saw who was waiting for her in the dark.

"Busy night?" the man asked, his eyes falling on the skimpy outfit visible beneath her open coat.

Clearly irritated, Lacy blew out a breath even as she let the gun fall to her side. "Dammit, Reardon!" she shouted. "What the hell is the matter with you? You're lucky I didn't shoot your sorry ass."

"Now, now, Agent Blake, is that any way for a lady to talk?" Reardon said as he stood up from the chair where he had been sitting. "Especially

"You're lucky I didn't shoot your sorry ass."

to her boss." As he had every other time they had spoken over the past few weeks, Agent Tanner Reardon wore a crisply pressed suit and tie, neither one overly expensive, but also not cheap ones either. Working for the Bureau of Investigation paid better than most jobs, but not enough for expensive suits. The only thing he spent big bucks on was the lengthy trench coat that so many agents like him seemed to enjoy wearing, which was at that moment draped carefully over the back of the chair.

Like Reardon, Lacy Blake was an agent for the Bureau of Investigation, reporting to the Department of Justice. As one of only a handful of women to break through to the rank of agent, Lacy Blake was constantly pushing to prove to her colleagues that she could handle the job. Those she had worked with the past year knew what she was capable of, but she had only been assigned to Reardon's investigation less than a month earlier and he treated her like a rank amateur at best, a buffoon at worst.

In his late thirties, Reaerdon looked like the stereotypical G-man with his pomade slicked back hair dyed black to cover the gray hairs that had started to pop up around his temples. Reardon had made his career working for the Bureau and un-apologetically saw it as a boy's only club. If not for the fact that his undercover investigation had crossed into the field of prostitution, he would have undoubtedly prevented her transfer to his division. Instead, Lacy went undercover as a high-class prostitute working at the Palms, where she had gathered intelligence on not only her potential customers, but also on the other working girls and those who pulled their strings.

Agent Blake kept the gun in her hand, but no longer pointed it in her handler's direction. Weapon at her side, she walked to the bar that separated the kitchen from the dining room. "What are you doing in my apartment?" she asked as she dropped ice into a glass with her free hand.

"What do you think?" he asked, following her across the room. He leaned on the edge of the bar. "Has there been any further development in the case?"

Lacy laid her gun on the counter then poured herself a drink. She did not offer one to Reardon. She took a steep drink, held it a moment, then swallowed. The burn felt good after the long night she'd put in working at the hotel.

"Well?"

She sighed and put the glass back down on the counter hard enough to rattle the ice cubes that remained. "Not since I gave my report to Donovan an hour ago at the hotel," she said. "The meet is still on for tomorrow night.

If everything goes as planned then it's a good bet the big man will be there and we can collar him."

Lacy walked past him, pacing the room as she continued. "Speaking of Agent Donovan," she started then blew out a tired breath. "Look, I've been undercover for almost a month and you always set up these dates for me with the service so I don't have to... you know."

He smiled at her discomfort.

"I appreciate you helping with my cover, but..."

"Yes?"

Lacy whirled around to face Reardon, who was still watching from the bar where she had left him. She wondered if he could tell just how tired she was as it was almost 4 a.m. Then she wondered if he would care if he could tell.

"Donovan is old enough to be my father," she added. "And he has two left feet! Couldn't you just once send one of those single young agents you've got in the office down to pretend to be my date for dinner and dancing? Maybe that one that always stares at me when I come into the office could do the next one. Him, I think I might enjoy debriefing."

Arms crossed like a stern college professor; Reardon leaned against the counter, amused by her complaint. Lacy stopped pacing and put her hands on her hips. She still had on her coat because the last thing she wanted to do was give Reardon the satisfaction of seeing her in the French Maid's uniform.

"I see," he said. "In other words, you're looking for a real date?"

"Exactly!" she agreed, hoping to surprise him with her candor. It had been tough playing the roll of sexy mistress of the night without finding the attention arousing. "I must be the busiest prostitute in the city who's not having sex," she added.

"Well, if that's all you need," Reardon added with a smirk.

"Don't even think about it."

"You don't know what you're missing, Blake."

Agent Blake leaned against the bar next to him. "I can imagine," she said.

"Your loss."

She yawned. "I hate to be rude, but I have a meeting with these guys in..." she looked at the clock on the wall. "In a few hours and I really need some sleep. Unless you've got something worth telling, get out of here so I can go to bed."

"Do you know where the meeting is taking place?" Reardon asked, all business now.

"No. Just when."

"A car is coming by to pick me up at ten. After that, contact will happen at the hotel. The big man's got a reservation under an alias. I wasn't able to find out which one. Maybe one of the boys could go in as a bellhop or something."

Reardon picked up his coat from the back of the chair he had been sitting in earlier and headed for the front door. "Then I'll let you get your beauty rest," he said. "I'll have spotters on you before the meeting. Hopefully, we'll be able to keep a tail on you. Unless you think you could hide a transmitter somewhere on you."

"Not with these guys," she admitted. "They give paranoid a whole new meaning. Then again, the government is after them so..."

Reardon stopped at the front door, a hand resting on the knob. He turned back to face her. "Look, all joking aside, you be careful tomorrow." He stepped out the open door and into the night.

"I will, mom," she said before closing the door. "Scout's honor."

Once he was gone, Lacy let her forehead rest against the locked door. He was good at his job, but Agent Reardon had a habit of annoying her. She blew out a breath, but felt anything but relaxed. She was too exhausted to feel much of anything. She turned off the lights and made her way to her comfortable bed where she collapsed into it without even bothering to take off the degrading costume her cover required her to wear.

She was asleep as soon as her head hit the pillow.

• • •

Rick Ruby watched the man leave Raven's apartment and couldn't help but wonder if this was the lady of the night's mysterious boss. The plan had been to stake out her place and hopefully tail her to the boss. He hadn't expected the boss to have been inside waiting for her.

If he had a car nearby, there was little chance of the P.I. being able to tail him back to wherever it was he came from. He was beginning to regret having sent the cabbie away, but the ol' Rick Ruby luck held. The guy hitched up his collar against the early morning chill and started down the sidewalk.

Rick waited until the man got a good lead on him then fell into step far enough behind him to follow, but not look like he was actually following him. He wanted a cigarette so bad, but refrained. Lighting up would draw attention to himself and the smell of the cigarette's smoke might also give him away, neither of which would help him stay on his quarry's trail.

After walking a couple of blocks before the man popped into a small store that was open all night and Rick took advantage of that to light up a smoke. He was almost finished by the time the man came out a short time later carrying a brown paper bag held in one arm and a steaming hot cup of what he assumed was coffee in a disposable cup in his other hand. Although he wasn't much for walking, or getting much exercise at all, Rick was glad that the man hadn't hailed a cab. In the wee early hours of the morning like this, getting a cab was difficult at best. Finding two on the same street one right after the other was all but impossible.

Once the mark was half a block away from the store, the P.I. stubbed out the cigarette on the sidewalk with his shoe and followed.

After another three blocks, the man turned into an office building. It was the last place Rick would have expected. Running prostitutes was the kind of business that one expected to take place in back alleys and darkened street corners, not in a high rise office building for all to see. He was beginning to think there might be more going on than a simple prostitution ring.

After a few minutes to make sure the man wasn't coming back out, Rick moved in for a closer look. The building was much like any other office building in the city. It was made of concrete, brick, steel, and glass. He made a note of the address on the door in his notepad once he was safely out of sight of the door. There was no doorman on duty that he could see, but Rick had been a private detective long enough to know better than push his luck. He walked to the corner and ducked down a side street before leaning against a wall to make a notation in the small notebook he carried with him everywhere.

Come morning, he would run a check on the address and hopefully get some answers for his client. He yawned. He pushed off from the cold brick and headed back to the street. He barely had the cash to cover it, but he'd try his luck with a cab. As exhausted as he was, Rick wasn't so sure he was up to walk all the way back to his apartment.

He walked back onto the sidewalk and was startled when he saw the man he had been following standing there as if he'd been waiting for him. That's when Rick sensed the presence of two more men behind him.

"Hi there," the man he had been following said around a smile as the two behind him grabbed him and pinned his arms tightly behind his back. There was a pinch against his neck and the world began to spin around him like a blender.

Rick tried to lurch forward, but the bruisers held him tight. All he could do was double over as a wave of nausea gripped him. He vomited right there on the sidewalk, thankful he had passed on the cabbie's offer of breakfast. Rick hated to waste good money on food only to throw it up. His head heavy, Rick somehow found the strength to lift his chin in defiance. He refused to pass out in front of these bastards.

The Cheshire-like grin of the man he'd been tailing smiling at him was the last thing Rick Ruby saw before the lights went out.

• • •

"Who are you?"

At least that's the question Rick Ruby thought had been asked. He sat slumped forward in what he assumed was a chair, but something held him tight across the stomach otherwise he was sure he would've hit the floor by now. The room was made of concrete blocks with the most drab paint job he had ever seen and made only worse by the stark bright light from bare bulbs. The brightness of the room made his eyes hurt, which was something since he hurt all over. Whatever they'd hit him with had really put the whammy on him. All he wanted to do was sleep, but he had a feeling his captors were not going to let that happen.

He was right.

A backhanded smack across his cheek set off a series of bombs bursting in air behind his eyes that put the annual Forth of July fireworks celebrations to shame. The metallic tang in his mouth told him he was bleeding, but he was too groggy to spit. Instead, the P.I. slumped forward and let the spit and blood dribble to the floor. He hoped that feigning unconsciousness would buy him some time to come up with an escape plane.

Unfortunately, they weren't buying it.

"Up an' at 'em, pally" one of the bruisers said as he forcibly jerked Rick back into the upright position. Despite his efforts to the contrary, the battered P.I. couldn't stifle the pained grunt from being manhandled in such a fashion.

"Things will go a lot easier for you if you'd just answer the question," Raven's mysterious boss said, stepping in Rick's field of vision. He was blurry around the edges, but that Cheshire Cat grin was still firmly in place. Rick found it unnerving.

"I forget, what was the question again?" Rick mumbled, trying to sound cocky, but failing miserably.

A gut punch was his only answer.

He would have fallen out of the chair again if the bruisers standing behind him hadn't clamped their beefy paws on his shoulders to hold him in place.

Cheshire knelt in front of Rick so they could look one another in the eye. "We really don't want to hurt you," he said. "Believe it or not, we're the good guys. I'm Agent Reardon. I work for the United States government."

"You're a... G-man?" Rick asked, trying not to laugh at the absurdity of his situation. In the back of his mind he heard one of his favorite film star's voice telling him, "*Well, here's another nice mess you've gotten yourself into, Ruby.*"

"That's right," Reardon said, once again pacing back and forth in and out of Rick's line of sight. His head hurt far too much to follow the man's incessant back and forth. "That means I've got the power to toss you into the deepest, darkest hole I can find and leave you there to rot until The Rapture if you don't start cooperating and answer my damned questions."

Risking another bout of nausea, Rick lifted his eyes to look directly at his captor. "What was the question again?" he asked with a pained smirk.

Reardon chose not to rise to the bait and hit him again. "You don't work for Tommasso, that much is a given," he said instead. "Hey! Pay attention." The agent slapped Rick across the face, not hard, but enough to refocus the P.I.'s attention back on him. "So who are you? And don't test me. My patience has reached its limit."

"Ruby," he muttered.

"What was that?"

"My name's Ruby," he said. "Richard Ruby."

"Now that wasn't so hard, was it, Richard?"

"You'd be surprised."

"Why were you outside Lacy Blake's home?"

"Who?"

"Don't play dumb, Mr. Ruby," Agent Reardon said.

"I'm not playing, G-Man."

"I don't believe you."

"How's that my problem?"

"You do not want to trifle with the United States Government, Mr. Ruby."

"No I don't," Rick said. "You, on the other hand..." He smiled.

"Why were you following Agent Blake?"

"I'm telling you, I don't know who that is."

"You're going to have to do better than that, Mr. Ruby. I saw you outside her house. You followed me from there."

Rick's eyes widened. "That dame's a G-man?" he said.

"Why were you following her?"

Rick's brain whirled with new information. He switched tactics. "You've got eyes, don't you?" he said. "That broad's a stunner. I thought maybe she and me could paint the town some night, but I couldn't get up the nerve to ask her out. I mean, look at me. What chance do I have with a woman like that?" he said, playing the role of infatuated loser to the hilt.

"Absolutely no chance," Reardon said.

"That's what I figured," Rick said. He breathed a sigh of relief as if getting out of this predicament with all of his teeth still intact was all but assured.

He was wrong.

"Recognize this?" Agent Reardon held up a wallet in front of Rick. It took him a second to realize that it was his. That meant that the G-Man knew all along. He knew Rick's name, his address, and his profession.

"It does look familiar," Rick said playfully. "I was wondering where I left that?"

"What's a two-bit private dick like you doing looking into one of my agents?" Reardon asked.

"Two-bit?"

"Who hired you? Was it Claudio Tommasso?"

"That's a bit harsh, don't you think? I know I'm not the top of the heap, but two-bit? Man, that's mean?"

The Cheshire grin returned. "Oh, you've not seen mean yet, Mr. Ruby."

"Neither have you."

"Who. Hired. You?"

"Roberts. Hotel manager."

"Why?"

Rick snorted a laugh. "He thinks he's got a hooker problem."

"Why's that funny?"

"Because what he's actually got is a G-man problem. He'd probably be better off with the hookers. At least they can be reasoned with."

"I've had enough of this clown," Reardon said, cocking his head to the side, a signal to one of the goons standing outside of Rick's line of sight. "This guy don't know squat. Get him out of here."

Rick tensed against either a gunshot to the back of the head or another blow to his kidneys, but was surprised when neither came. Instead, there was a sharp prick against his neck, followed by a familiar sensation as a thick solution was pumped into his veins where it burned like molten lava. The P.I. strained against his captors, but thick hands held him firmly in the chair.

Rick's vision blurred at the edges until all he could see once again was his interrogator's pearly whites glowing sinister against the gloom of his dungeon. He couldn't help but wonder if this was it, if this was his last night among the living. If it was, he was very disappointed. Rick always thought he would go out surrounded by beautiful women, not surrounded by oily government agents in need of a shower and a breath mint.

Rick laughed at that. Or at least he thought he did. He couldn't guarantee that any part of him was moving. His arms felt like lead weights pulling him down. *If I'm going to die, then at least I'll go laughing*, he thought as everything around him went dark. Then, he felt the hard hands that had been holding him let go and Rick Ruby fell into a deep dark hole into nothingness.

• • •

By the time Rick Ruby opened his eyes it was late afternoon.

"Rick?"

He could have sworn he heard an angel calling his name, the soft lilt of her voice beckoning him toward a blinding light. He squinted against the glare, his eyes barely open more than slits against the brilliant illumination. For a moment he wondered if the pounding in his head meant that he was dead, but he just as quickly dismissed the notion. *There's no way that being dead hurts this bad*, he decided. As for the angel calling him forward, he realized that it didn't belong to one of the Heavenly Host, but to a more Earthbound angel, Edie Rose Adams.

And she was angry.

"Rick."

Edie Rose was his secretary, his research assistant, and his conscience. Although the latter was not in her job description, Mrs. Adams' baby girl had made it her mission in life to save Rick Ruby's soul. Out of all the people in his life, himself included, young Edie Rose seemed to be the only one who believed that Rick Ruby had a soul worth saving. He loved her for it, but did very little to make it easy on her. If she was going to save him she would have to do it in spite of himself.

He closed his eyes against the glare of afternoon sunlight streaming through the office window that was in dire need of a good cleaning. He couldn't believe he was alive, much less back in familiar surroundings. He had no memory of how he got back to the office, much less inside.

"Rick!"

Edie Rose slapped him once, twice across the cheek and was about to go for a third swing when he reached up a hand to stop her.

"What?" he mumbled, his mouth so dry it felt like he had been chewing on cotton all night. "I'm up. I'm up."

"You look terrible," she said matter-of-fact.

"That's good, because I feel terrible," he slurred.

"Were you drinking again?" she asked, not quietly. Disappointment dripped off every word.

""No," was all he could manage.

"I don't believe you."

"Honey, I've not touched a drop. I swear." He held up a hand hoping she would take the hint and lower her tone to something less akin to fingernails on a chalkboard.

"Look at you, Rick," she shouted, which he wished she would never do again because the words reverberated like a jackhammer inside his already buzzing brain. "What was it this time, huh? Some floozy you met in the hotel bar? You were supposed to be working, Rick, not out drinking yourself into a stupor!"

It had been a long time since he had seen her this angry.

"Miss Williams doesn't charge us much for the office or your apartment, but she still wants what's due, Rick," Edie Rose continued. "Or should I say, what's past due. She came by here this morning looking for you."

"And?"

"And I lied to her and said you were out working on a case."

"I was."

"A case of scotch doesn't count," she retorted.

Rick blew out a breath. There was no way he would win this argument. "I'll talk to Belle," he said. "Don't worry."

"One of us has to," she shot back.

"What's that supposed to mean?" Rick asked. He pulled himself into a seated position, a move he instantly regretted as the room began to move beneath his feet like an ocean wave. It was all he could do to keep from retching. Thankfully, it had been many hours since he last ate, else he might have made a mess. And something told him that his secretary was not in the mood to clean it up even if he had.

"It means one of us around here needs to be an adult and make sure our bills get paid. In most businesses that would be your job as the owner," she said. "Instead, you're out drinking when you should be working. We haven't had a paying client in weeks, Rick. We can't afford to lose this one."

"I swear, Edie Rose, I wasn't drinking," Rick said, even though he knew it was hopeless. It was clear from her demeanor that she was in no mood to listen, much less give him the benefit of the doubt. "And I'll take care of the rent too. Belle will understand."

With a snort of derision, Edie Rose turned on her heel and stormed out of his office, clearly finished with the conversation.

"Oh, baby, don't be that way. I'm sorry."

"Baby?" she countered angrily, turning back to face him. "I'm not one of your floozies, Rick. Please don't treat me like one," she said, lowering her trembling voice, tears threatening to well up in her eyes. Aside from worrying about his drinking, Edie Rose objected to the number of women that paraded through Rick's life like a revolving door. He assumed it was a byproduct of her Christian upbringing. He had no desire to stop spending time with the fairer sex, but he had made an effort to keep his personal life out of the office.

It wasn't easy.

Especially considering the office sat above a jazz bar filled with beautiful, willing women. There was a reason Rick spent his off duty hours hanging out at Belle's, and it was not the scintillating conversation skills of Broom Stick.

Despite the four-alarmer going off in his brain, Rick got to his feet and padded across the cold floor toward his assistant. That was the first time he'd noticed he was barefoot and wondered if he'd taken them off or if someone else had. "I'm sorry, Edie Rose," he said honestly. "You know I don't think of you that way. It's just a habit. Whenever a woman is mad at me I try to sweet talk her. The way my head's pounding right now, and I swear to you that I was not drinking last night, it was just instinct. I'm sorry. Truly. Forgive me?"

"It's okay. I … wait a minute," she said as a thought hit her. "Women are always mad at you. There's not a week goes by there's not some irate woman comes through that door wanting a piece of your hide."

"And now you know why I'm always such a sweet talker," he said with a playful smile.

"Practice?"

"Exactly."

Despite herself, Edie Rose cracked a smile, though she quickly tried to cover it. "You're a rat, is what you are," she said, but without any trace of anger left in her voice.

"Also true," he said.

"Speaking of angry women," Edie said, changing the subject.

"Oh?"

"Miss Johnson stopped by to see you."

"What did she want?"

"I'm not one of your floozies, Rick."

"Don't know. She wouldn't tell me, but she acted like it was important," Edie said. "Said she had some information for you and you only."

"I had her ask around to some of her contacts about this mess over at The Palms," he explained as he headed back into his office and plopped down on the couch. "Lounge singers and ladies of the evening often share the same customer base. I figured she might know something that could help me."

"I'm sure she hears all kinds of gossip," Edie said just loud enough for him to hear it. He knew she was just being catty. Edie liked Evelyn Johnson well enough and often stopped in at Belle's after work on the nights she performed to listen to her sing. It was Rick's relationship with her of which she disapproved. He wondered if it was Evelyn's job or the color of her silky smooth skin that Edie objected to, but he was too smart to ever broach the question. She would put up with a lot, but not that. And he couldn't afford to lose Edie Rose. His business would fall apart without her and that was a fact. She was the glue that held the office together.

"I'll head down and ask her," Rick said from his office as he pulled back on his shoes. Sleeping off the headache would have to wait. Besides, he knew that if he played his cards right, Evelyn Johnson might just kiss it where it hurt, and to Rick there was no better cure for what ails you than that. That woman's lips could start a forest fire.

Rick made his way down to Belle's, the jazz club and bar below his office. A shrewd businesswoman, May Belle Williams owned and operated the club where Rick served as the house detective, provided protection for Belle's girls when they needed it, and put the kibosh on trouble when necessary. Although the business was still listed in her late husband Parker's name, Belle actually owned the entire building, which made her not only Rick's boss, but also his landlord.

Thankfully, she liked him.

And he her.

Theirs was a partnership made in Heaven. In exchange for cheap office space and free food and booze at the bar, Rick was there whenever Belle needed him. He was the house detective, protection for Belle's girls, and bouncer whenever the need arose. The rest of the time he was a professional barfly, a job description that fit him to a T. Rick loved a good drink and he often thought he got the better end of the deal.

Especially after he met Evelyn Johnson.

Evelyn was the star attraction at Belle's. Whenever the sultry singer was on the bill, the place was packed to the rafters, standing room only. Evelyn's voice was silky smooth, just like the rest of her. Rick had seen many a man entranced by her beauty and voice as they worked in concert. Evelyn didn't simply play to the audience, no sir. Her music made love to them.

Luckily, Rick wasn't the jealous type.

He counted himself lucky that an angel like Evelyn Johnson would even spare a second glance his way, much less talk to him. The fact that she so heartily welcomed her into her life and her bed was still a mystery to Rick. Whatever the attraction, he knew he would be the envy of every man in the room if they knew in whose company he spent many of his nights. Of course, they could never know. Despite that fact that they were both single, consenting adults there were still some out there who would not understand their relationship.

Although, Rick had to wonder about those people. How could anyone look at a gorgeous dish like Evelyn Johnson and not want her simply because her skin was darker than their own. Trying to understand that point of view made Rick's head hurt so he no longer even tried. Sometimes he even welcomed the prejudice because it meant fewer suitors vying for attention from the lovely Miss Johnson and less competition was always a good thing as far as Rick Ruby was concerned. He was happy to keep her all to himself.

It was still early enough in the day that when he walked into the bar so it was quiet. The ever-present Bruce "Broom Stick" Strickland was at his usual spot behind the bar, taking advantage of the lull to catch up on the morning newspaper. When he saw Rick enter from the side door stairwell, he reached for a glass, but the P.I. waved his friend off even though he was dying for a beer. He could also go for a shot of the hard stuff, but Edie Rose was already mad at him. The last thing he wanted to do was make her even madder by reeking of alcohol when he returned to the office. The last thing he was in the mood for was another one of her angry temperance lectures.

"Evelyn?" Rick asked Broom Stick.

"In the back," the barkeep answered.

"Thanks."

"Watch your back. She's in a mood," Broom Stick added as Rick passed the bar.

"Thanks for the tip," Rick said before ducking behind the curtain that disguised the side-stage entrance.

The side stage entrance led into a hallway that ran the length of the room from the front where Broom Stick stood at the bar all the way to the stage at the back. On one side was the auditorium wall. On the other were dressing rooms for the performers. Belle made sure her talent had a place to prepare or to hide out between sets if they needed to get away from it all. As one of Belle's brightest shining stars, Evelyn Johnson rated her own private dressing room.

Rick knocked twice.

"What?" came an angry voice from the other side of the freshly painted door. Aside from pouring a mean beer, Broom Stick was a skilled handyman. He had spent the past few mornings adding a new coat to the dressing room doors. Belle liked to keep her place looking fresh and clean.

"Evelyn," he said softly. "It's me, honey."

The door yanked inward and Rick felt his breathe catch at the sight of her. As always, she was a vision of loveliness, but instead of the slinky gown she performed in nightly, she was wearing a sheer robe with fur around the cuffs and collar.

"You look like something the cat dragged in," she said as soon as she saw him.

"So I've been told," he said. "You, on the other hand, look like an angel."

"Flatterer."

"I only speak the truth."

"Get that silver tongue of yours in here," she said, grabbing him by the collar and pulling him into a lip lock so intense it could have melted wax.

• • •

An hour and a half later, Rick left Evelyn Johnson's dressing room.

He had a smile on his face and a spring in his step as he headed back to his office, a complete turnaround from the exhausted mush who had come down the stairs less than two hours earlier. Rick was even more tired than before, but he didn't care. Thanks to Evelyn's magic fingers, his muscles no longer ached as much as they had when he first awoke. Not only had she made him feel so much better, but her contacts had come through for him as well.

There was much work to be done and very little time to do it.

The rest of the afternoon was a blur. Later, he would vaguely recall talking with Edie Rose about something, but she was still mad at him so it was a brief conversation followed by her going out to an early dinner. He'd contemplated offering to take her out to eat, his treat, but decided that would only make him look guilty, which he wasn't. At least not this time. He hoped she would forgive him in time.

His head pounding from the lack of alcohol and the beating he'd taken the night before, Rick barely made it to his apartment before passing out.

He collapsed onto his bed fully dressed. He was out like a light before his head hit the mattress.

Edie Rose was gone by the time he woke and returned to the office. Rick had hoped to see her, but was also thankful not to have to dive back into an argument with her. She had left his messages on the desk in his office. He sorted through them, but nothing stood out as overly important so he decided to return any calls he needed to the next day. It was a short walk back to his apartment to bathe, shave, and put on a fresh set of clothes that didn't look like they had been slept in later and he was once again heading across town to The Ambassador Palms Hotel.

He arrived before the sun dipped completely behind New York's sky-scraper canyons. Then, Rick spent the better part of an hour trying to re-lieve his client's fears with promises that the case was proceeding apace and that he had learned a good deal the night before and that he hoped to have things wrapped up soon. The bruise beginning to purple on his chin made it harder to convince Mr. Eugene Roberts that he was on top of things, but as he so often did, Rick simply kept on swinging and wore the man down until he changed the subject.

"I assure you, Mr. Roberts, I'm real close to wrapping this thing up for you," Rick said as he glanced at his inexpensive watch for the third time. "In fact, I should probably get into position. It wouldn't do for you-know-who to see us together."

"You're right, of course," Roberts said hurriedly as he straightened his neck tie, a nervous habit Rick had noted a few days before. "Please, don't let me impede your progress, Mr. Ruby."

"I appreciate that," Rick offered, turning to leave.

"My pleasure, sir," the manager said.

Rick turned back to face his tightly wound client. "We'll talk later," he said reassuringly. "I'll have this buttoned up soon. I promise."

With a nod, Roberts moved off to attend to his duties. As Rick watched him leave, he hoped that he'd just made a promise he could keep.

• • •

Even though he had promised Edie Rose that he wouldn't, Rick popped into the hotel bar and ordered a scotch, hold the rocks. He hoped the sting of alcohol would help remove the fog from his brain from whatever his attackers had injected into him earlier that morning. Whatever it was, the effects felt like a hangover, only without the fun that went along with earn-ing it.

Edie Rose was already pretty hot under the collar and that little voice in his head whispered, *how much madder could she really get*? Even though that little voice had gotten him into more hot water over the years than he'd care to admit, Rick saw wisdom in the words and tossed back the drink then ordered himself a second. He fought the urge to complain about the cost, having been spoiled by far too many free drinks at Belle's. Of course, since this was a work expense, he would make sure the cost of his drink was added to Mr. Robert's bill.

A newspaper tucked under his arm, Rick took a seat in one of the lobby's extremely comfortable chairs and nursed his drink while perusing the sports section. If all went as planned, he hoped he wouldn't have to wait long.

As usual, things did not go as planned.

A couple of hours passed and evening turned to night. Rick resisted the urge for another drink as he read the newspaper a third time. Repeated readings had not improved the news that stared back at him in black and white. Even the crossword puzzle hadn't offered him much distraction and had not killed near as much time as it should have. He was bored. Never a good thing when on a stakeout.

Not for the first time, he wished he had picked up one of the pulp paperbacks Broom Stick kept beneath the bar. Rick wasn't much of reader, but he did occasionally enjoy stories about Earthmen traveling to distant planets to rescue gorgeous scantily clad alien princesses from green bug-eyed alien monsters.

He was about to start on his fourth trip through the news of the day when he caught sight of his quarry.

She was hard to miss.

The woman he'd come to think of as "Raven" didn't walk through the lobby so much as she glided through it. If not for the clacking of her heels against the polished marble floor, he might have thought she walked on air. She moved with purpose. If she noticed the stares from both men and women as she passed, she gave no sign. Or she simply didn't care. Yesterday, Rick thought she had an air of mystery that made her so appealing.

Now he knew it was all an act.

Rick waited until she passed before he pushed himself free of the confines of the comfortable chair where he had been camped out for the past few hours. He winced as his back reminded him that he wasn't as young as he used to be when it spasmed from sitting idle too many hours without getting up to move around. He should have known better. In spite of the pain in his back, Rick weaved through the obstacle course of chairs, plants, people, and small tables scattered about the open lobby until he fell into step behind the woman.

He stepped up next to "Raven" as she pressed the elevator call button.

"Hi there," Rick said, a playful smile on his face.

"Not interested," she replied without turning to look his way.

"How can you say that? You don't even know what it is I've got to offer."

This time she turned to regard him. Her lip curled up in contempt as she saw the detective's wrinkled clothes and coat that was frayed around the edges. No way were they in the same ballpark, much less the same league. "Oh, I think I know what's on your mind, buddy," she said. "And trust me, it's not going to happen so you can just tell your story walking, all right?"

The elevator arrived with a ping and the doors parted. She stepped inside without a second glance in Rick's direction.

He followed her inside and stood beside her, both of them facing the lobby through the open door.

She sighed loudly. "You really are pushing your luck, aren't you?"

Rick smiled at her discomfort, but kept on the charm. "Oh, you have no idea," he told her. "I do some of my best work after my luck runs out."

She snorted in derision.

"Besides, I have two words guaranteed to make you talk to me."

"And they would be?"

"Agent Blake."

The elevator doors closed before anyone in the lobby could see her shocked expression.

• • •

From across the lobby, Ariel Webb watched.

Like everyone else, she couldn't help but notice when her friend, Lacy, walked into the room. It wasn't jealousy, okay, maybe it was a little bit jealousy, but there was something about Lacy that seemed out of place. Oh, she liked the new girl well enough, but sometimes her leggy friend seemed to have an air of being better than this life.

That was something Ariel couldn't understand. She loved her life. Having grown up with nothing, she had clutched onto this new life that working for Claudio Tommasso had afforded her. Normally not the type of man she would go for, Ariel found herself more attracted to the big man's power than his looks. With his ample girth and balding pate, she was surprised how often he had a gorgeous woman on his arm.

Apparently she wasn't the only one attracted to power.

And Lacy had power of her own.

She envied her friend her looks, and her height, if not her drive for power. Diminutive by comparison, Ariel Webb was petite and, as one of her regulars liked to call her, plucky. But Ariel was an up and comer in the business. Her aspiration in life wasn't as lofty as saving the world or anything like that. She wanted to be a kept woman. Having grown up with nothing, she had come to enjoy the life that being in bed, so to speak, with the mob had provided her. She wouldn't give it up without a fight.

Ariel was one of Mr. Tommasso's favorites, a position she worked hard to maintain despite all of the newcomers to the business. Whenever Claudio was in town he made it a point to stop by and see her. A surprise phone call to her apartment the night before had alerted her that the big man was in town and heading to the Ambassador Palms Hotel that night to personally check on the operation.

Of course, his assistant had told her that her presence was requested and that she should bring a friend.

Ariel thought tonight would be a great night for Lacy to meet the boss.

She was about to head over to catch Lacy before she got in the elevator, but stopped short when she saw the man in the rumpled jacket sidle in beside her. No way was he one of her regulars, Ariel knew. Like her, Lacy only dealt with high end clients, not the rabble that normally cruised by the street corners looking for a good time.

Whatever else this guy was, he was trouble.

Once they walked inside the elevator, Ariel made a break for the stairwell door. With any luck, she would beat them to the floor.

• • •

As soon as the elevator doors closed, Lacy Blake made her move.

Planting her right arm against the annoying man's chest, she pushed his back against the wall and catching him completely off guard as the elevator lurched into motion on its upward climb. With her free hand she pulled a gun from a holster strapped to her inner thigh and brought it up for him to see.

Instead of pleading, as she had expected him to do, the man chuckled. "That was pretty impressive," he said. "They teach you that in junior miss g-man class?"

"Who the hell are you?" Blake asked, leaning in close and keeping her voice low.

"Name's Ruby," he croaked in spite of the pressure on his chest. "Richard Ruby."

"Who do you work for?"

"Not who you think?" he said. His eyes fell on the bare arm pressed against his chest. "Do you mind?"

Agent Blake holstered her weapon then reached into his jacket and removed the P.I.'s weapon from his shoulder holster. Once he was disarmed, she eased off the pressure and took a step back in case he made a play to retrieve the gun.

He didn't.

"That's better," he said moving his shoulders to work out a pain in his back. "I think that little move of yours might have saved me a trip to the back cracker."

She didn't smile. "You were going to tell me who you work for," she prodded.

"Oh. That." He slowly pulled a business card from his shirt pocket, careful not to spook her since she still had his gun pointed at him. "I'm a private detective. The hotel manager hired me to find out of there was a prostitution ring operating out of his hotel." He looked her over, starting at her shiny high heels, stocking-covered legs, short black dress that hugged all the right curves in all the right places. "So… have you seen any prostitution going on around here?" Rick asked. He did not even attempting to hide the sarcasm.

"You're in way over your head, Mr. Ruby," she said.

"That's what your goon, Reardon said too," the P.I. said. "And from the look on your face, I'm guessing he didn't tell you about me, huh?"

"No," she admitted, lowering the gun to her side. "He did not."

"Not surprised. He didn't strike me as the sharing kind."

"And you are?"

"Sometimes." The P.I. smiled. "Look, I have a client that needs to hear something from me before he calls in the cops. Whatever operation you're running here, I'm sure a squad of New York's Finest swarming over this place like a herd of bulls in a China Shop will throw a wrench in your scam, whatever it is."

"But you'll make sure that doesn't happen if I tell you what's going on, right?" Blake offered.

"Something like that," Ruby said as the elevator stopped at their destination.

Agent Blake motioned toward the opening doors with the gun. "You win. We'll talk."

"That's all I ask."

"After you," she said and followed Rick Ruby into the hallway. Once on the move, she stayed one step behind him as she told him the room number that was their destination. "It's up there on the left," she said once they were closer. "Here's the key," she said, handing it forward to rest on his shoulder.

The P.I. took the key, unlocked the door, and stepped inside.

Despite the darkness of the room, he immediately noticed that the room was not unoccupied. The man came out of nowhere, slamming the Ruby into the wall, stunning him. Then, the intruder lifted the battered P.I. and tossed him onto the bed where he bounced twice before falling to the floor on the opposite side.

A flip of the light switch and the room was awash with a soft yellow glow.

"We meet again, Mr. Ruby," a familiar voice said as Rick pulled himself up off the floor, holding onto the bed for support.

"I wish I could say it's a pleasure, Reardon," Ruby said.

• • •

Ariel Webb watched from the stairwell.

Her fear that Lacy had gotten into trouble had quickly been replaced by suspicion when she saw her friend walk the man from the elevator to a room that was not one of the ones in use by herself or any of the other girls. The fact that she held a gun on the man she had seen her with in the lobby was also odd. There were precautions in place to keep them safe. Mr. Tommasso saw to that. Any man who got rough with one of his girls answered to one of his men.

The smart thing to do would be to head back down to the lobby and have Tommy, one of Tommasso's guys, come up and check it out, but Ariel didn't want to sound an alarm unless she was sure exactly what was going on. Making Claudio or the organization look bad was a sure fire way to find herself out on the street and there was no way she was going to risk that without being one hundred percent positive that there was trouble brewing.

Once the coast was clear, she pulled off her high heels, stepped into the hallway, and padded across the carpeted space until she stood just outside the door she'd watched Lacy and the stranger go into.

She paused at the door and listened.

What she heard shocked her.

• • •

"I warned you to stay away from this," Agent Tanner Reardon shouted.

Before Rick could say anything, Agent Blake stepped between him and her boss. "Would one of you care to explain to me what is going on here?"

she snapped. "In case you haven't noticed, we're in the middle of an operation," she said pointedly at Reardon.

"I am painfully aware of that, Agent Blake," Reardon said, lowering his
voice to just above a snarl. "It's my operation after all. Now why don't you
get in position? Your next appointment will be here soon and we don't
want to miss it," he added.

She chucked a thumb over her shoulder at the P.I. "What about him?"

"I'll deal with Mr. Ruby," Reardon said.

"I wouldn't be so sure," Rick said, feigning a cocky attitude. "The odds
are a little closer to normal this time. You won't sucker punch me this time."

"Shut up!" Agent Blake told him.

"But I…" Rick started, but a stern look from the woman he had come to
think of as "Raven" stopped him short. "Sit," she said, and with a pained
smile, he did as he was told.

"What are you planning to do with him?" Blake asked Reardon.

"That's not really your concern now is it, Agent Blake?"

"It is now," she said, refusing to back down. "You're not going to hurt
this guy."

"Again," Rick added, ignoring the dirty look Reardon shot his direction.

"Again," Agent Blake parroted.

"Fine," Reardon said, backing down. "You want him, he's your problem."

"He's not our only one," she said.

"Why? What happened?"

"This guy claims the hotel manager hired him to find out what we're up
to here," Blake said. "I thought the hotel management had been read in on
this?"

Reardon shuffled his feet.

"Oh, what did you do?" Blake asked.

"It's nothing," Reardon said. "The Tommasso and Manelli families have
eyes and ears all over this city, Blake. We couldn't take the chance that
someone on staff here wasn't also on their payroll," he argued. "What we're
doing here is too big to leave to chance. The fewer people who know what
we're doing, the better."

Agent Blake blew out an angry breath. "Well, we've got a problem then,"
she said. "I mean, if this guy," and she once again regarded Rick, who had
taken a seat on the edge of the room's lone bed. "If a two-bit private dick
like this guy, no offense."

"None taken," Rick said in a manner that told her that the opposite was
true.

"You're not going to hurt this guy."

"If he got onto us, then it's a good bet someone else will too," Blake finished.

"I've got it under control," Reardon said.

"No you don't," Rick said. "Look, I've been watching you guys the last few days. You've got the whole room watching when you walk through those doors, doll, and trust me, I'm not the only one who has been out there more than once."

"If we… if I've been compromised," Blake started.

"You haven't," Reardon said matter of fact. He turned to the beefy goon who had tossed Rick around like a kid's toy earlier. "Get down to the lobby and check out his story. Let's get some more men down there." He cast an angry glance at the P.I. before adding, "just in case he's right."

"Yes, sir."

As soon as he was gone, Reardon slammed a hand against the wall. "If you've screwed up this operation, Mr. Ruby, so help me I'll bury you," he said.

"Look, pally, I'm not the one who screwed the pooch here," Rick said, getting to his feet. He was tired of being pushed around by the government man. "But I can help you out."

Before Reardon could fire off another less than helpful retort, Agent Blake interjected. "How?" she asked.

Rick pointed to the phone on the bedside table. "Let me call the hotel's manager, Mr. Roberts."

"What good will that do?" Reardon asked.

"Will you shut up?" Blake said. "Please continue, Mr. Ruby."

"I can inform Mr. Roberts that everything is under control and that after tonight his prostitution problem will be a thing of the past." Rick cast a smug look at Reardon. "As soon as you finish your business, you clear out the girls that aren't on your payroll. And this stays quiet."

Reardon started to answer, but once again Agent Blake beat him to the punch. "Deal," she said and pointed toward the phone.

Rick dialed the operator and waited. "This is Richard Ruby. I need to speak with Mr. Roberts, please. Trust me, doll, he'll want to speak with me. Just tell him."

While the P.I. explained the situation to his client, Agents Blake and Reardon conferred in hushed and quiet tones. "Do you trust him?" Reardon asked.

"Do we have a choice?"

"If he steps so much as a hair out of line," Reardon warned. There was no need to verbalize the rest of the threat.

"I know."

"Roberts is on board," Ruby said, hanging up the phone. "He's none too happy about it, but he's given me another twenty-four hours to wrap this thing up. You've got that long before he calls the cops. Something tells me that a couple dozen uniformed cops swarming over this place would screw with your operation."

"Point made," Agent Blake said. "Thank you."

"Any time, doll."

"Who are you after?"

No one answered.

"Come on," Rick said. "Before I became a '*two-bit* private detective' I was a cop. I might not be front and center on the game board, but I know this city and the players. I can help you."

"I don't think so," Reardon groused.

"It's clear you're either after the Tommasso or Manelli family since they are the chief suppliers of girls in this town. I've certainly had my run ins with both," Rick said. "Remember Derrick Shaunessey?"

"The name rings a bell. Mid-level thug for the Manelli's until he left town in a hurry last year. What about him?"

"I helped him pack," Ruby offered.

"Are you trying to tell me that you're the one who took down Shaunessey's New York operation?" Reardon asked. He was skeptical.

"That was me. Check with Jack McGinnis over at Metro Homicide. He'll back me up," Rick said. "Come on. Let me help you. Who's the target?"

"Tommasso," Blake said plainly.

"It won't be easy, but I know a few low-level guys who might be willing to flip on the next rung in the ladder for a few sawbucks."

"I don't think you understand," Blake said.

"Apparently not," Ruby said. "How about you enlighten me?"

"We're not after just any ol' someone in the Tommasso organization," Blake said.

"Then who?"

"Claudio Tommasso."

"Are you insane?" Rick asked. "You want to take down the number two man on the totem pole? Even if you manage to put the snatch on him," he looked at Agent Blake's outfit, "his brother will rain down hell on your team trying to get him back."

"You let us worry about that, Mr. Ruby," Reardon warned. "And I wouldn't get too comfortable if I were you. Just because you aren't handcuffed to a radiator somewhere doesn't mean you're a part of this team. We do not require, nor do we want, your help. You are here as a courtesy only. Try to remember that. One word from me and my men will bury you in the deepest, darkest hole we can find."

Rick looked at Agent Lacy. "He really loves the sound of his own voice, doesn't he?"

"You have no idea," she said and rolled her eyes.

"If you two are finished with your Laurel and Hardy routine, what say we get this show on the road?"

"Of course," Blake said. "I had better get into position. Everything ready?"

Reardon nodded and pointed toward the ceiling where a series of wires dropped to the floor. One of his men had a receiver on the hotel's round table and the wires plugged into it. Rick guessed that they were exactly beneath the room where Agent Blake was planning to meet whoever they were after. The wires were obviously attached to microphones hidden in the room above.

"I don't think my client is going to appreciate you drilling holes in his hotel," Rick said.

"Do I look like a give a good hot damn what the hotel manager appreciates?" Reardon snapped.

"I guess not," Rick said, holding his hands up in surrender as he sat back down. The P.I. could be brash, and quite often pushed his luck, but he wasn't stupid. Angering Agent Reardon was not the best plan for long term health. Rick had heard enough stories about G-Men like Reardon disappearing people. Although he had no proof, when you hear a story enough times it begins to have an air of truth to it.

The P.I. decided it was better to play it safe than sorry.

The phone rang and the agent with the microphones answered it. After a curt exchange, he said. "Target has arrived. He's on his way to the elevator."

"Get up there," Reardon told Blake.

"Right." She was already heading out the door.

Reardon pointed to the technician monitoring the microphone feeds. "You tell me the minute this goes sideways."

"Yes, sir."

"Are you expecting trouble?" Rick asked.

"Mr. Ruby, I always expect trouble."

• • •

Lacy Blake took the stairs at a run.

It was only one floor, but she was out of breath by the time she hit the landing. Not for the first time she silently swore to lay off the cigarettes, even though she knew it was a promise she would never keep. Taking a second to slow her labored breathing, she pulled open the door and stepped into the hallways.

"Lacy?"

She started, but quickly composed herself. Ariel Webb was leaning against an end table that sat against the outer wall near the stairs. Like Agent Blake, Ariel was dressed to the nines, from her newly coifed hair to the freshly shined high heels. As always, she looked stunning.

"Where have you been?" Ariel asked.

Blake barked a laugh, a trick she used to buy herself an extra few seconds to formulate an answer. "Oh, you know," she started, chucking a thumb back toward the stairwell door.

"Quickie in the stairwell, huh?"

She smiled, thankful for the readymade excuse. "It's a living, kiddo."

"Just don't let the boss catch you," Ariel warned. "You might be one of Claudio's top girls, but he'll have one of his boys slice you to ribbons if they find out you've been skimming off the top."

"Nothing like that, I assure you," Lacy said. "Cute bellhop. My last appointment left me..." she rolled her eyes toward the ceiling as if searching for the right word. "Unfulfilled," she finally said.

"Just watch yourself, Lace. I'd hate to see anything happen to that pretty face of yours."

"You aren't the only one."

"Has Mr. Tommasso gotten here yet?" Lacy asked.

"Claudio?" Ariel said. Blake noticed that she referred to him by his first name. "Not yet. I heard he was in the building though. Probably checking in with the guys. You know, business before pleasure. Have you met him yet?"

"I haven't had the pleasure," Blake said.

"Tonight's your lucky night then," Ariel said. "Claudio likes to sample his wares. He gets around to each of us eventually. Some more than others."

"Sounds like you speak from experience."

"What can I say?" Ariel gloated. "I'm that good."

"I've no doubt."

Ariel giggled. "Come on. I'll introduce you."

Lacy followed Ariel to the suite at the end of the hall, directly above the room where Reardon was set up with his listening devices. "So, what's he like?"

"Claudio is great," Ariel said, beaming.

"You like him." It wasn't a question.

"Yeah." She blushed. "I guess I sort of do."

Ariel unlocked the door and pushed it open. "After you," she said.

Agent Blake stepped into the room and immediately knew that something was wrong. A light snapped on in the corner and there stood Claudio Tommasso and two of his hired thugs.

Lacy spun back toward Ariel. "What's going on?" she started, but caught a fist to the face before she could get it all out. Ariel's punch packed more power than she would have expected from someone of her stature. It wasn't enough to knock her to the floor, but she would definitely feel it in the morning.

It was the second hit that knocked her off balance.

She dropped to the floor, the room spinning around her.

Before Agent Blake could catch her breath, Ariel planted a foot to her middle, causing her to curl up into a ball.

She was about to deliver another shot when a word from Claudio Tommasso stopped Ariel in her tracks. "Enough," he said and stepped closer.

Lacy looked up at the man she'd been sent to apprehend and wondered how it had all gone wrong. What had given her away? "How?" she managed through pained gasps for air.

"That's not the question you should be asking," he told her.

"No?"

"No. What you should really be asking, Agent Blake, is what happens next?"

• • •

"This is taking too long."

"Calm yourself, Mr. Ruby," Reardon said. The G-Man had reached his limit with the interloping private detective. If not for the time sensitive nature of the operation, he would have personal drug Rick Ruby out of the building in chains and dropped him in a deep, dark cell somewhere in the middle of nowhere, but at the moment there were more pressing matters.

"Are you getting anything?" he asked the technician working the recording equipment.

A shake of the head was his only answer.

Rick started to pace back and forth in front of the balcony door. The twinkling lights of the city that he usually found soothing were not having their desired effect. He felt pent up, restless. "I'm telling you, this doesn't smell right."

"The only thing that smells wrong here is you," Reardon said. "Now sit down and shut up."

Ruby fumed. "I'm starting to get sick and damned tired of you, G-Man!"

"The feeling's mutual."

"Shouldn't we hear her up there by now?" Rick asked.

Reardon's scowl deepened. "He's right," the agent said to the technician. "We should be picking up something other than static. I can hear footsteps up there."

"Maybe they aren't talking," the technician said, offering a shrug.

"Something's not right," Rick said. He was already heading toward the door before Reardon even noticed he was moving.

"Where do you think you're going?"

"To get your agent back," Rick said as he pushed aside the agent who had grabbed him earlier.

The agent moved to stop him, but a tiny shake of Reardon's head told him to let the man go. Ruby was out the door in a shot. Once in the corridor, he ran past the elevator and made a beeline for the stairwell.

He took the stairs two at a time, breathing heavily with each footfall. *Too many cigarettes and too much booze*, he heard Edie Rose's voice echo in his brain. He hated to admit it, but she might be onto something. The smokes he could probably do without, but he could picture no scenario that would make him stop drinking.

He stopped at the landing and peered through a tiny crack between the door and frame to make sure the coast was clear. It was, so he stepped out and counted off the number of rooms to find the one that sat directly above the room where Reardon was listening.

Rick put an ear against the wood and listened. He could hear muffled sounds from inside. It sounded like a fight. He reached into his holster for his sidearm and remembered that Agent Blake had taken it from him. It was now sitting downstairs on the dresser. He bit back a curse, but there was nothing he could do about it. There was no time to run back downstairs and retrieve his gun. Whether Reardon's boys could hear it or not, his agent was in trouble on the other side of that door.

Putting his shoulder into it, Rick slammed into the door once, then twice, before the tell-tale sound of splintering wood tore the door's lock out of the doorframe.

Rick found himself in the middle of a room almost identical to the one below. Claudio Tommasso stood there wearing a suit that cost more than Rick had earned the previous year. He puffed on a thick foreign stogie as he and his two bodyguards watched a woman kick Agent Blake. He recognized the girl from the other night when he had trailed "Raven" to her apartment. It was funny. It had only been last night, but it felt like it had been days since that happened.

His abrupt entrance had captured everyone's attention and all eyes were on him.

"Hold it!" Rick shouted. It was an empty threat, of course, as he had no weapon on him. He was certain that Tommasso's men were armed, however. That meant he had to move fast.

The P.I. launched himself across the bed at Tommasso's goons, angling his body so that he hit them both in the same attack, knocking them to the floor with him falling atop them. Before either could react, he delivered three heavy punches to the face of one until he felt the man's nose break and blood splattered across the wall and the sheets. The man sagged to the carpet, out of the fight.

Rick lashed out with his foot and caught the other on the chin before he could get back to his feet. The man groaned and dropped back to the floor.

Rick grabbed the gun from the holster of the man with the freshly broken nose and pointed it at his partner. "Just stay down," he said as he got to his feet.

The distraction was all that Agent Blake needed. She grabbed Ariel by the ankle and yanked, driving the youth bodily to the floor. It only took two punches to knock the fight right out of her.

Through all of this, Claudio Tommasso had watched. He made no move to run or to throw a punch. From all Rick had heard about the man, Claudio was a bureaucrat, not a fighter. He left that sort of thing to his brother, who ran the organization. Even though he was the number two man in the family, Claudio was little more than middle management. That was part of what made him the perfect target for Reardon's sting. The man's ambition to be top dog was greater than his ability to do the job.

Rick tossed the pistol to Agent Blake, who trained it on her target while he retrieved the second goon's gun. "You okay?" he asked her.

"Fine," she said though grit teeth. "Where's Reardon?"

As if on cue, Agent Reardon and his back up arrived at the door, weapons drawn and at the ready.

"So glad you could join us," Rick said, letting out a deep breath.

Reardon ignored the jab. "Well, well, well," he said as he stepped up to the prisoner. "Mr. Tommasso. I think it's past time the two of us had a little talk."

"I've got nothing to say," Tommasso said softly.

"Yeah. Well, we'll see about that," Reardon said. He pointed toward his men. "Get him out of here. And do it quietly."

"Yes, sir."

After the prisoner was escorted out, Reardon turned to Lacy. "Good job," he told her before following his agents out and closing the door behind him. He did not share the sentiment with Rick Ruby, however.

"Glad to be of service," Rick said to the closed door. "Schmuck."

Agent Blake stifled a laugh. "He might not say it, but I will. Thank you."

Rick blanched, his cheeks actually starting to redden like his hair. "Aw, shucks, ma'am," he said. "It weren't nothing."

"I'm just glad it's over," Rick continued. "Now I can collect my fee from Mr. Roberts and pay my secretary before she leaves me."

"I understand," Lacy said. "Before you go, there is still one more thing we need to do."

"Oh?"

"I need to debrief you." She smiled. It was the first time she'd smiled at him. He liked it.

Rick raised an eyebrow. "Debrief me?"

"Oh, yes," she said as she put her arms around him and pulled the P.I. close.

"Well, she's waited this long to get paid," Rick said as he reached over and turned off the lights. "What's one more day?"

• • •

In a modest office in Washington DC, a phone rang.

"Speak," the man who answered it said.

"This is Tanner Reardon," the voice on the other end of the line said. "We're on target. The suspect has been apprehended."

"Excellent work. I trust there were no problems."

"Nothing I couldn't handle."

"Very well. My agent will meet you in one hour at the safe house," the man in Washington said. "Once he's in position, we'll move forward as planned."

"Are you sure this will work?" Reardon asked. "I mean, impersonating Claudio Tommasso is risky. Are you sure your man can do it?"

"Trust me," the G-Man known only as K-9 replied. "My man knows what he's doing."

"What's his name, your operative?"

"You can call him X."

THE END

Opening the Tommasso Files

Rick Ruby has arrived.

It had been a good year for The Ruby Files, the book's title character, and the creative talent that worked on building this pulpy noir world Rick inhabits. As I type these words, it has only been a week since we learned that Rick Ruby won the 2013 Pulp Ark Award for Best New Pulp Character and that the book was nominated in several categories for the Pulp Ark and Pulp Factory Awards. To say that we're all excited about the nominations and the win would be an understatement.

With this story, Rick Ruby joins the larger pulp community. By that, I mean the ending ties in with another pulp hero published by Airship 27: Secret Agent X. This story is actually a prequel, of sorts, to the Secret Agent X story I wrote for the *Airship 27 Presents: All-Star Pulp Comics* book. It should still be available as you read this.

The story didn't start out with the intention of tying into the X story, which features X impersonating a mobster named Claudio Tommasso, who was turning state's evidence on the mob. In The Ruby Files story, Agents Blake and Reardon were after a mobster. Instead of creating a new character, I decided to use a character I was already familiar with. This is not the first time it has happened. The Tommasso and Manelli familes mentioned in the story have cropped up in several of my pulp tales across several publishers.

Once I decided to make the mobster in The Ruby Files story Claudio Tommasso, suddenly it all fit, as if that had been the plan from the beginning. I love it when the story flows together like that. It doesn't always happen like that—sometimes you have to make it go together kicking and screaming—but when it all falls into place like it did with this one, it's magic.

One of these days I may have to compile a timeline that follows these villain's stories as they run afoul of several pulp heroes. It's hard to keep a good mobster down.

Keep an eye out. I'm sure we'll be seeing these guys again.

Lacy Blake was also one I pulled from the files. Originally created to be a character in a modern day setting, her story had been shelved for awhile.

When the idea of a prostitution ring came up for this story, I knew she was the perfect choice. Good characters have a habit of not staying locked away in the idea file for long.

• • •

Bobby Nash's life is nothing at all like Rick Ruby's, but he does enjoy visiting it from time to time. Instead, Bobby spends his days as an award-winning author of novels, comic books, short stories, novellas, graphic novels, and the occasional screenplay for a variety of publishers and production companies. He is a member of the International Association of Media Tie-in Writers and International Thriller Writers. On occasion, Bobby appears in movies and TV shows.

Bobby was named Best Author in the 2013 Pulp Ark Awards. Rick Ruby, a character co-created by Bobby and author Sean Taylor also snagged a Pulp Ark Award for Best New Pulp Character of 2013. Bobby has also been nominated for the 2014 New Pulp Awards and Pulp Factory Awards for his work. Bobby's novel, Alexandra Holzer's Ghost Gal: The Wild Hunt won a Paranormal Literary Award in the 2015 Paranormal Awards. The Bobby Nash penned episode of Starship Farragut "Conspiracy of Innocence" won the Silver Award in the 2015 DC Film Festival.

For more information on Bobby Nash please visit him at: www.bobbynash.com

A Tree Falls In a Forest

by Sean Taylor

Rick Ruby screwed his eyes shut and let the colors swirl so tightly he couldn't distinguish one from another. "Ave Maria" skipped like a broken record in his head. His body lurched like a falling boxer. His legs gave out. Then the rest of him did the same.

"Heya, Donna," he said between heavy breaths.

Rick felt the blonde dancer's weight shift above him.

"Heya yourself, Rick." Then again, as usual, he had done most of the real work, not that he minded.

"That was nice."

"Always is, Rick."

"Think you can do it again, you know, that thing with the…"

She slapped his chest, then twirled the red hairs there between her fingers.

"No time. I've got to see Eddie in an hour." Her smile fell just a little in spite of the way she tried to hide it. "We've got an… appointment."

Rick propped up on his elbows, pushing them behind him so he could almost reach Donna Dixon's ruby pout. "You know I don't like you seeing Eddie. He's bad news."

Donna grinned. "And you know I don't like you seeing Evelyn." She traced her lips with her tongue. "Or Claire, little Miss Moneybags. But particularly Evelyn. I don't like the way she wants to own you."

"Yeah, but just knowing Eddie is gonna get you killed one day, most likely."

"Sure, but knowing Eddie gets you the kind of information you, ahem, pay me for."

"Touché."

"Rick?"

"Yeah, honey?"

"Pass me the sheet."

"I've seen you naked before."

"Sure, but a girl likes to maintain some sense of mystery after the stage is emptied."

135

"Yeah, sure. I guess. I'll trade you for the phone in that case."

"Deal."

Rick bunched the top-sheet in his meaty grip and jerked it free of its bonds at the bottom of the bed, then handed it to Donna. As he did, she returned the favor with the telephone. He reached for it, but only got hold of the handset, and the rest of the phone fell onto the bed, clanging like a bicycle bell as it hit the bare mattress.

"Oops," she said.

"Oops my eye. You did that on purpose."

"So says the big tough private dick."

"Yeah, yeah. Well, I'll be keeping my eye on you just the same, Donna."

"Just your eye, baby?" Donna asked with a giggle as she turned and sauntered toward the bathroom. As she walked away, she let enough of the sheet fall away behind her to expose her porcelain backside.

"You're a naughty one, you," Rick said. He dialed the number for the office. It rang three times, and then Edie, sweet Edie who knew him as well as anyone and still thought the world of him, answered with a strained sing-song.

"Rick Ruby, Private Eye."

"Edie?"

"Rick!" she shouted, her voice suddenly emptied of the songlike bounce and filled with anxiety in its place. "Where have you been? I've tried calling you everywhere."

"I've been with Donna," he said. No sense in lying after all. Not to Edie. Never to Edie. "Getting information." Okay, maybe a little bit of a lie. "Why? What's wrong, sweetie?"

There was a short pause, and it sounded to Rick as though Edie were crying and trying to get her composure. "It's Evelyn, Rick. She's at Belle's, and it's not good at all. It's her brother, Rick. He's dead."

"Morris?"

"Yeah, Morris."

"What happened?"

"They hung him, Rick. They hung him from the roof of the Grand downtown."

"Who hung him, Edie?"

"Nobody knows for sure, but Evelyn says it was the Klan."

"The Klan?"

"Yeah. The Klan. He was a jazz man, Rick. Just back from Paris. Things are different in Paris."

"Damn. He didn't…"

"He did. She's the one who reported the hanging."

"Meet me at Belle's. Close the office. Just get the hell down to the club. Now."

"I'll see you in thirty minutes, Rick." She sniffled loudly. "And Rick?"

"Yeah?"

"I'm sorry. I know how special Evelyn is to you, in spite of…"

"Thanks. Just meet me as soon as you can. We've got to keep Ev from doing something stupid and making this worse than it already is."

• • •

The air inside Belle's normally smelled of alcohol and pain and regret. But when Rick entered the double glass doors, he couldn't smell the alcohol at all, and he knew exactly why.

Evelyn sat crying over a table in the middle of what was typically the dance floor, and Edie sat beside her, an arm over the tall singer's mocha shoulders. She wore a long black dress that fit her like a curtain fit a theater window, nothing like the slinky outfits she usually wore when he caught her act, or the far less than even that she wore when they caught each other after her act.

Edie, on the other hand, wore a smart suit that still couldn't hide the fact that she was all woman. Rick wondered for a moment if he had ever even seen her in anything that wasn't smart. Someday, he thought, someday she's going to walk out in something different, and by God, he just knew he was going to have to shoot a man in cold blood just to keep the girl from being looked at wrong.

He tried to laugh at the thought, but the atmosphere of the club left the sound stillborn in his throat. He heard Evelyn's tears, even from as faraway as the doorway, and as much as he wanted to turn around and run, he knew that would be the wrong choice.

Perhaps that's why his first step toward the crying singer surprised him. Damned if he could explain the things he did when he was too sober to do otherwise.

"Evelyn?" he all but whispered when he reached the table where she and Edie sat.

"Rick!" she bawled as she jumped to her feet. "Thank God you're here."

"I was… busy," he stammered. "Sorry."

"I know just what you was, baby, but I'm glad you're here anyway. It's the Klan. The Klan strung up my brother."

Rick wanted to glance at Edie, wanted to know what she had told Evelyn, wanted to know if the singer had learned the truth that he had been wrapped in Donna's arms and sheets while her brother was being strung up for all the well-dressed white folks walking down Broad Avenue to see.

But he couldn't.

Evelyn looked him dead in the eye and locked him there. Her gaze held no passion but vengeance. It held no love save the lust to see the man who killed her brother get his and get his good. Rick held the stare and didn't smile. After a moment, she opened her grip and dropped three one-hundred dollar bills on the table in front of them both.

"What's...?" Rick started.

"We were going to take a trip, you and me, but you just didn't know it yet. Go off to some place where the color of a man's skin and the color of a woman's skin didn't matter so damn much."

"I mean..."

"No." She still refused to let his gaze unlock from her own somehow, and the contact made Rick fidget. "I was saving up, but now this money is to pay for your services. You're going to find the man who killed my brother. I want the one that tied the rope and the one that pushed him off the top, and every damn one of them that watched it happened."

"Evelyn, honey, I would do that for you anyway. You don't have to pay me. You never have to pay me, baby."

"I ain't paying you to *find* them, Rick," she said. "The trouble is, in spite of you not being able to settle down, your problem is that underneath all that trouble you are to me, underneath every bit of that, you're a good man. You're too good a man."

"I don't understand, Evelyn."

He looked away just long enough to get a peek at Edie. Her eyes went wide. Apparently she had figured out what he hadn't yet.

"Like I said, baby," Evelyn practically cooed at him. "I ain't paying you to find them. I'm paying you to kill them."

Rick sat down. As he did, he used the motion as an excuse to keep his mouth shut.

"Now do you understand, baby?"

Rick tightened the screws on his lips even more and looked at the ceiling. The tile he had promised Belle he would work on last weekend still needed touch-up paint, but Belle hadn't busted his chops about it yet. In the end, just like always, he was pretty sure that Broomstick would end up on the rickety ladder to make sure it got fixed. Some things just didn't change.

"Rick'll find 'em for you, for all of us, Evelyn," Edie said, the comfort of years of religion having trained every word as they dripped like the land of milk and honey from her sweet tongue. "But that doesn't mean we have to..."

"It's okay, Edie."

"Rick."

"It's okay."

"But the good book. Thou shalt not kill."

"I've killed before, and for lesser reasons than this."

"But that was self-defense, Rick, or even more, defending someone else."

"Doesn't matter."

"Evelyn, you can't ask him to do this."

"I didn't say I was doing the thing or not doing the thing, Edie. All I said was it was okay. Now stop. Please."

Rick felt a shadow behind him. The shadow reeked of lilacs and fresh-laundered cotton. His shoulder grew gooseflesh when the shadow gripped it tightly and squeezed. "Rick, I'm glad you're here."

"Of course I'm here," he said.

"Of course Rick's here, Belle," Evelyn said after her long silence. "I told you my Rick wouldn't let me down. Not if the whole world all around me did, Rick Ruby would never let me..."

"Now hush, girl. Mourn if you need be doing so, but that don't mean you need to carry on like some kinda natural born fool."

Good old Belle, Rick thought. She knows the truth. Rick Ruby lets everybody down...even when, hell, especially when he does the right thing... and only a fool would believe otherwise.

"Belle, she wants Rick to..." Edie said, but Belle shushed her.

"I know exactly what she wants. It's the same thing all of us want."

"Belle?" Edie asked.

"But wanting it and trying to make it right ain't the same thing, ain't never been the same thing, and some of us know better."

Rick knew without even taking his eyes of the ceiling that Belle was looking at Evelyn when she spoke.

"Sorry I wasn't here," he said to no one in particular.

No one responded.

He let his gaze drop back to the table and those around it.

Edie caught his eye, and he quickly looked to the floor. He wasn't sure what was stronger, the guilt that Evelyn's faith in him brought on or the pathetic smallness that Edie's disapproving expression gave him that made his heart wrinkle up like a raisin.

Not that it mattered.

Nothing mattered now but seeing that the jackass who killed Morris got what was coming to him. And even if that didn't assuage his regret, then it might at least take the sting out of it long enough to take Evelyn out to that paradise she had been saving up for.

"Well, I'm sorry just the same," Rick said to the no one who had demanded an apology. Maybe it was for him. Maybe no one cared. "When's the wake?"

"Wednesday," Belle said, letting go of his shoulder. "Here. We're gonna close the joint for the day in honor of Morris."

Evelyn shuddered beside him. He heard more tears whimper out onto her face. He reached across the table and took her hand.

"Who do we know at the Grand?" he asked Edie. "Who do we really know who could get me into the girl's room?"

"Carla's daddy has a permanent place there, Rick."

"Someone a little... closer to the ground, honey. Somebody willing to walk away for a few dollars."

"I'll see what I can drum up, boss," she said, placing her hands over his and Evelyn's. "Don't worry, Evelyn. Rick won't let you down."

"Rick lets us all down, honey," Evelyn whispered. "That's why we love him. We can't help it 'cause he only lets us down in the tomcat things that he don't know any better about."

Rick cleared his throat.

Edie forced a smile.

Evelyn pulled her hands from beneath them both. "I need a drink, Rick. Get me a drink, baby."

"I don't know if now is…"

"Get me a drink, baby." Evelyn grabbed his hand and pulled it toward her. "Please. I need a drink."

Broomstick spoke up from the bar. "I'll get you both one. Hell, I think maybe we could all use a shot of the good whiskey tonight. You in, Edie?"

Edie shook her prim and proper head. "No thanks."

"None for me, Bruce," Belle added. "I need a clear head tonight." She was looking at Evelyn again as she spoke.

"Got it, boss-lady," Broomstick said.

Rick watched as the lanky black man pulled glasses from the overhang to the bar top with the speed of a rodeo sharpshooter, then swung up a clear bottle made brown from the light flickering through the liquid inside and popped the cap and emptied the bottle into the glasses with the fluid curve of a master sculptor. Moments later, the glasses were full and the bottle had disappeared again beneath the bar.

"Come and get 'em," Broomstick said.

They did, Evelyn leading the way, dragging Rick by his captured hand. Edie sauntered behind, trying to keep up with Belle's wider step.

"I count five glasses," Belle said. "And only three mouths wanting this stuff."

"A toast," Broomstick said. "To Morris. Not even our little missionary could say no to that, could you, Edie?"

Edie flushed red, but shook her head and took hold of the smallest glass of whiskey.

"Well," Belle said, "can't argue with that."

"To Morris, the best damn jazz man in town," Broomstick said, raising his glass.

"To Morris, may God have mercy on his soul," said Edie, and lifted hers as well.

Rick waited for Belle, who nodded, then added, "To Morris, damn him, he could sure blow one hell of a horn."

Rick raised his glass. "To Morris. He was a good man in a stupid world."

All eyes were suddenly on Evelyn. She was crying again, her chest fluttering in the formless black dress. She wiped her tears away. "To Morris," she said, "who had the misfortune to be born a man so he couldn't get away with it."

She quickly poured the whiskey down her throat and wiped her mouth clean with her sleeve. The rest of the group looked around at each other, uncomfortably aware of the unspoken double standard that Evelyn had dared address out loud. And she was right. Had Morris been a woman and his white woman been a man, his "crime" against society would have gone more or less overlooked, another failure of the white man to control his rutting and not the taking of a woman's so-called virtue.

"The hell with it," Rick said. He downed the whiskey in a single gulp. "Here's to you, Morris. I promise I'll find the bastards who killed you."

As the liquid flowed smoothly into his belly, the rest of the glasses clinked and he heard Belle simply say, "To Morris."

"To Morris," Evelyn said again, then crashed to the floor in a heap of black cotton at Rick's feet.

• • •

"How's Evelyn?" Rick asked into the telephone of the lobby of the Grand Hotel.

"She's sleeping," Belle said, "and your Edie hasn't left her side."

Rick smiled. He was pretty damn sure Belle was doing the same. *His* Edie. Like hell.

"It was just a case of nerves, honey. Don't let it bother you. Hell, I'd been waiting all night for it to happen. I'm just glad you were there to carry the fool girl upstairs to her room."

"The woman's name again?"

"What?"

"Morris' woman."

"Oh, right. Gertrude Horscutt. But if she's smart, she's left town or been sent away by her people."

"People hire me for a reason, Belle. And if I've learned anything, it's that people are rarely smart about murder."

"People hire you because they listen to the radio shows and go to the movies too much."

Rick laughed. "You're probably right. Lucky for them, I didn't learn how to do my job from a radio writer."

"Lucky for me too, Rick. There's a lot better ways I could make good money on that room of yours upstairs."

"Office."

Rick surveyed the lobby, but it didn't do anything but sit there and let people walk all over it. Two gents in suits and top hats walked from the door to the desk, followed by three young bellhops, each loaded down with at least three pieces of luggage. At the desk, the staff stood and waited for them. An elevator dinged opposite the desk, and a pale man in a cheap suit exited it and walked toward the door.

"Office with a bed in it. Makes it a room to me, honeylamb."

"Suppose so."

Rick reached in his coat pocket for a pack of Camels. Fresh pack. He opened it and tapped out a single cigarette. "Well, I guess I need to get to work. Check in on Evelyn for me, okay."

"Don't you worry none, Rick. Just get this bastard that killed Morris. You hear me?"

"Loud and clear, Belle."

Rick started to remove the receiver from his ear, but Belle's voice stopped him. "And Rick?"

"I'm here, Belle."

"Listen."

"I'm listening."

The man in the cheap suit exited the Grand. Another man in a similar suit stood up by the door and followed.

"But hurry."

"About Evelyn..."

"Yeah."

"She's special, Rick. She loves you. But *you* don't have to watch her drink herself to sleep and cry all over my tables when she knows you're…"

"Sorry, Belle. My man's leaving."

"I get it, Rick."

"It's not that. It's just…"

"Just go, Rick."

He put the receiver back on the phone and clenched his fists. Damn it, he thought. Evelyn knew as well as he did how things went in the world. Hell, didn't Morris' death prove that? And Belle, damn it, Belle should know the way of things better than any of them.

Rick followed the second man outside. He stood just outside the door talking to the man in the cheap suit. The first was thanking the second and turning to walk away down the sidewalk. The second leaned against the first for support, then shook his head and muttered, "Sorry 'bout that. Stupid leg's acting up again."

The first walked away, and the second stepped toward the Grand Hotel door and right into Rick.

"Hello, Skipper," said Rick, taking him by the wrist. He reached inside the man's coat pocket and retrieved a gold pocket watch. "Still at it, I see."

"That was my dear old grandfather's, Ruby."

Rick flipped it over. "And just, pray tell, what was your dear old grandfather's name?"

"Hmmm... Well, grandma'am always called him... Hmmm..."

"Richard?"

"Right. Richard, same as yours, my friend."

"Then I'll return this one to Thomas."

"Fine. What do you want, Ruby?"

"Just want to see justice done, Skipper."

"What will it cost me this time?"

Rick handed the watch back to Skipper. The other man looked up, relaxed his expression and his dark mustache danced a bit on his upper lip. The wrinkled eyes softened and took on the closest thing to a smile they could manage.

"The murder suite. I want to take a look around."

"I'm sure I have no idea what you're talking about."

"Don't play coy with me, Skipper. It's not your color. Doesn't look good on you."

"Don't know nothing about any murder."

"Maybe Thomas would like his watch back after all. Besides, I know you're casing this place all the time. If something happened here, you already have the wallet of the guy involved."

"I told you, Ruby, I don't know..."

"The corpse is Evelyn's brother."

Skipper shut the hell up and his face looked wound as tight as the gears in his head.

"The singer?"

Rick nodded.

"All right, but I wouldn't do this for just anybody, Ruby. And you let her know it was me who helped you out." The lust in the small-timer's eyes as he spoke about Evelyn made Rick want to throttle him and follow it up with a punch to the kidneys.

He held his tongue. "What do you know, Skipper?"

"The police have cleaned it out already."

"Tell me something I don't already know. Something solid enough to hang a coat and a hat on."

Skipper motioned down the street. "How about a glass of something cold on the outside that gets warmer on the inside while we talk?"

Rick nodded again. His wallet wasn't fat, but this was personal. "Fine. But just one. Too early in the day for me to see the bottom of a bottle."

"Doesn't sound like the Rick Ruby they talk about on the streets."

"I don't like it any better than you, but a job's a job."

He followed Skipper's cheap suit two doors down and into a stairwell that led into a shadow about eight feet lower than street level. The shadow smelled like loneliness and lust and a woman's voice sang something about love lost and a two-timing dog of a man. Rick felt the place was as much like home as anything he could have imagined.

Skipper opened the door, and a little bell dinged. Rick grabbed the bell and held it against the door as he entered and closed it behind him quietly.

"Two brandies," he called to the bartender.

The old man at the bar smiled and wobbled his head in what could have been a nod or just a case of worn-out neck muscles.

"Make one a Scotch," Skipper whistled to the old guy.

"Make 'em both brandies," Rick corrected, and the bartender wobbled his weak neck at him again.

"Getting me mixed up with the Fords again, Skipper."

"Can't blame a guy for trying."

"Maybe you can't. I can."

"You hurt me, Ruby. I thought we were being friends here."

"My friends pay for their own liquor, or even better, mine."

Skipper raised an invisible glass between them. "To my favorite enemy then."

"So," Rick started, interrupting the thought with a cough, "what did you see last night?"

"Well, I'm no stool pigeon..."

The hell he wasn't.

"...but when I heard the stiff was a colored man, I figured the coppers would try to pin it on the Klan, but I didn't see the first piece of white cloth in the hotel last night."

"What if they were trying to keep it quiet?"

"Since when do they keep anything quiet, Ruby?"

"First time for everything, I hear."

"Whatever helps you sleep at night."

"What else?"

The old guy placed two glasses of brandy on the bar. Skipper looked at his like an old friend just met and picked it up and downed enough of it to give his throat a fit. When he finished coughing, he thumped his chest like a gorilla. "Good stuff."

Rick took a sip then put his glass back on the bar and let it crawl a step away on a circle of condensation. "What else?"

"Well, I don't know which colored man got killed, not that I can tell one from another unless it's a colored woman, but I did see one swanked up darkie getting in the elevator with Mr. Joseph Martin."

"The banker?"

"The only Mr. Joseph Martin I know who has a regular suite at the Grand."

"Point taken."

"Anyway, I ain't one to read things into things, but it sure looked to me like those two..."

Skipper cleared his throat and stifled a laugh.

"...gentlemen knew each other."

"How so?"

"Let me put it to you this way, Ruby. Ain't no rich white man so liberal or progressive he calls a black man by his last name and a mister in front, at least not living in the Grand, there ain't."

"Go on."

Rick waited for Skipper to take another long draught of brandy, followed by another deep cough.

"I could get used to this."

"Not out of my pocket, you couldn't. Go on."

"Well, I thought to myself that was pretty curious, so I climbed on the elevator with them, and when they noticed that, they clammed up damn fast, but not before I heard something about Paris, France, and about something they both owed somebody else."

Rick took another sip.

"It's good, right? Sure it ain't worth another of this fine brandies?"

Rick slid what was left of his over to Skipper. It made waves back and forth in the glass, but was smart enough not to jump ship. Skipper slapped Rick on the back.

"Did you hear who they owed?"

"Not a word of it. And they got off on separate floors, so I just guessed I was barking up the wrong tree and followed the colored man. Figured one of 'em in a fancy suit with his own room at the Grand would be easy pickings."

"And?"

"And I was right. He had a diamond watch and two hundred dollars in his coat pocket. But I feel bad about it now. I really do, since you know the guy."

"Never met him," Rick said. "Just said he was Evelyn's brother. Hell, you probably know more about him than I do." Rick let the thought linger for a moment to see how heavy it got. When it felt too light, he continued. "Where's the watch?"

"Fenced it. No telling where it is now."

"Fenced it to who?"

"Delmonte, down by the docks. Runs the..."

"Runs the shoe repair workshop. Delmonte and me, we've..." Rick thought better of revealing too much. "We've met."

"And that's all the story I've got, Ruby." Skipper took a long swig from Rick's glass. "Hope it helps."

And I hope you choke on that brandy, Rick thought. "Me too," he said instead.

He even let the bell ding at him on the way out.

• • •

Victor Delmonte was a tall man with a full head of black hair who should have been more handsome than fate had allowed him to be. From behind, people assumed he'd have a face like Clark Gable, but a fire when he was a kid had left him with a face scarred with hard lines and white blotches all over his skin. That's why folks who worked with him called him Victor "The Snow Leopard" Delmonte. Actually, folks who preferred not to work with him called him the same thing, only they usually did it from the wrong end of a .45.

Rick Ruby didn't, however, call Victor Delmonte by his whimsical nickname. Rick Ruby called him Vic. Because Rick Ruby knew how the Snow Leopard hated to be called Vic.

"Hiya, Vic," Rick said as he entered the workshop. "Been a while."

"Unless you want some shoes repaired, flatfoot, I'd advise you to turn around and show me an empty room again."

"You're behind the times, Vic. I haven't been a cop for a while now."

"Once a flatfoot, always a flatfoot."

Rick reached inside his coat and pulled out his license. "Strictly freelance now, Vic." He even stressed the shortened name and winked as he said it.

"I don't know nothing about nothing."

"Don't need to convince me. I just came here about a watch."

"I don't fix watches."

"This one doesn't need fixing."

"I don't sell watches."

"I didn't say I was looking to buy a watch."

"Look, flatfoot, I'm busy. Tell me what the hell you want or just beat it. I don't have time to read detective stories right now."

"I'm here about a watch. A diamond watch. And you're gonna give it to me so I can give it back to the woman it belongs to."

"I don't have any woman's watch. Try a boutique downtown."

"It isn't a woman's watch. It's a man's watch, and I'm not leaving without it."

"Damn it, Ruby. I gave you what you needed back then. You're not gonna start hassling me all the damn time again, are you?"

"Depends on a watch."

Victor Delmonte got silent for a few moments. Rick picked up one the pairs of shoes on the counter and put them back down. "Ironic line of work, Vic, particularly for a man with a broken soul."

"Yeah, yeah. You're still a comedian."

"Hiya, Vic. Been a while."

"So..."

"God damn it. But this is it. No more. After this, we're done. I don't ever want to see you again."

"No promises, but trust me. I'm not fond of seeing you either, Vic."

"And for the love of God, stop calling me Vic. If any of my people were to hear you..."

• • •

Evelyn met him at his office door in nothing more than a man's white dress shirt, unbuttoned, open down the middle, exposing the loveliest expanse of exotic landscape he could ever want to see.

"Hi," he said.

"Hi, Rick," she said.

"Looks good on you, but it's probably not appropriate for church."

"Who said I was going to church, Rick?"

Rick shook his head. It was a bad time to exercise the angel on his shoulder. "I've got something for you."

"I've got something for you too, baby."

"I..."

She smiled and leaned against his suit. The warmth of his own skin made him start to sweat. It had help, he realized, from the nakedness of her skin too. Damn that angel.

"Not now," he said, but she didn't move.

"Why not now?"

"I can't."

"I bet you can."

"You know that's not what I mean. I mean it's not right. I don't want to take advantage of you when you're like this, when you're grieving."

"Belle said we all grieve differently."

"Not like this."

"You're no fun, Rick."

"Tell me about it."

She kissed the nape of his neck.

"I found his watch."

She kissed him again. "Whose watch?"

"I found your brother's diamond watch."

"My brother never owned a diamond watch in his life."

"I've got a fence that says different."

"Then you've got a fence who's lying to you."

Her fingers fumbled at his tie. He gave the angel a glare. Moments later he watched his tie flutter to the floor.

"Wouldn't your room be better for this, Ev? This is my office. I have to work here, and the last thing I need…"

"This isn't about what *you* need, Rick."

She had his top two buttons open and her breath was already tickling the red curls there.

"Look, Ev, you know I …"

"I know you what, Rick. Want me? Think about me? Care about me? You can't even say it, Rick. But you can damn sure show me." Her voice had built to a timbre that almost sounded like a freight train bearing down on him, but she stopped and looked up from her work on his buttons. "Please," she said, and the freight train derailed right in front on him.

"I want to talk about your brother's watch."

"I told you, baby. My brother never owned a diamond watch, not a day in his life. He would've told me. He was vain about that kind of thing. Proud as a peacock."

Her hands were at another button, one not on his shirt.

"Ev…"

"Ssshh."

He glanced at the angel on his shoulder, and the little fellow winked at him and shrugged. Rick took a deep breath, and knew he was a bastard, but damn it, he was Evelyn's bastard for as long as she needed him to be.

Morning came early for both of them, and he woke up with Evelyn snoring softly on his chest. He squeezed her ebony body against his and kissed her forehead sweetly, silently. She stirred against him and said a word made up completely of the letter M.

"Mornin," he mumbled.

"You're a good man, Rick Ruby," she said.

"You're the only person who believes that, baby. I'm not a good man at all. I'm a selfish bastard, and I'll never be any better."

"You only tell yourself that to take away the guilt."

"I only tell myself that because I'm selfish bastard."

She kissed his chest. "That's just your shield, baby. Just like one of those Knights of the Round Table. You can fight any dragon this old city throws at you as long as you think the world would be better off without you." She propped up on her elbows, using his chest as a table. "The minute you start believing you're worth keeping around and actually matter to other people, that's the day you stop being any good at what you do. That's the day you stop doing whatever it takes to catch the bad guys."

"You listen to the radio too much. Hell, you should write for the radio, baby. That's good stuff there."

"Make fun if you want to, Rick Ruby, but the truth is that I know you. I may be the only person who does. I can't have you, not the have and hold, sickness and health kind of have, but even if all I can do is steal you from someone else's bed for the rest of your life, you and I both know I'm the only person who knows you. And that makes you mine, whether anyone else knows it or not."

"I'm yours, Ev. You've got me boxed and wrapped like a fur coat at Macy's during Christmas. Would you like a bow for that package, Madam?"

Evelyn laughed. "It's more fun to unwrap some presents, Rick."

"I'm going to hell. My poor Irish mother will never forgive me."

"At least you'll be there to keep me company."

She lay down again on his chest. He wanted to ask her about the watch, but her gentle breath through his forest of red curls convinced him now was not the time. Instead, he simply enjoyed Evelyn's warmth as her body seemed to do its best to melt into his and become one flesh.

"Baby?"

"Yeah, Ev?"

"Belle's having the wake tomorrow night. So get your good suit cleaned."

"I'll get Edie on that as soon as I check in with her."

He wrapped one hairy arm around her shoulders and stared at the ceiling with his eyes closed.

The city came to life outside, with its clatter of lost souls and modern chariots. All the while, Rick waited for the one sound he knew was coming sooner or later…the inevitable ring of the phone to tell him the city had found another dragon for him to slay.

• • •

Jack "Mac" McGinnis was at his desk, just as Rick hoped he would be, but his pet bulldog, Robert Perry, was on the leash again, growling at anyone who walked into the yard. The phone rang, and Mac picked it up, leaving Rick to entertain the younger cop.

"Hi, Bob," Rick said to Perry as he approached. "Do I need to throw you a raw steak, or can I talk to the boss?"

"Oh hell, not you again," Perry said. "I was hoping you were still busy helping Dick Tracy in the comics."

"He has my number when he needs me."

"What do you want this time, Ruby?"

"A minute with your boss, Bob."

"Damn it. I told you my name is Robert."

"Right."

"And Jack is my partner, not my boss."

"Does he really let you believe that?"

Mac shot them both a warning glance.

"He's on the phone."

Rick nodded.

Mac's second glance indicated a third would be shot with actual bullets.

"He's on the phone," Perry repeated.

"Sure. How are the wife and kids, Bob?" Rick asked, knowing full well that Perry's wife had left him two years ago and taken the kids with her to her mother's in Chicago.

Perry only glared and refused to play along.

Rick smiled.

"Jack will be done in a minute. Have a seat."

"Any coffee ready?" Rick asked.

"In the hallway."

"Good. I like mine black, thanks."

Perry looked like he wanted to say something that might cost him a job, but instead he sighed loudly. "Fine. Be right back."

Mac hung up the phone as Perry left the office. "You know, Rick, one day you're gonna meet Robert in a dark alley and he's gonna forget he's a policeman."

"He'll have to get in line, Mac."

"I'm sure he will." Mac grinned. "So, what can I do for you today, you old has been?"

Rick sat up straight in the chair in spite of its age and state of disrepair. "I'm working the murder at the Grand. The stiff is Evelyn's brother."

"It was Klan. We've got witnesses."

"So I hear. I want to speak to them."

"Sorry, buddy. Can't. We're keeping them hidden, somewhere the Klan can't get to them. That's bad business, ratting out the sheets."

"That's what I figured. But I think that may be the wrong angle."

"How do you figure?"

"That's just it. I don't figure it, not just yet. All I have is a hunch, and it could be nothing more than bad stew from yesterday."

"Coffee. Black." An arm like a boxer cut the air between Rick and Mac, and a dark mug of even darker liquid clanked on top of Mac's cheap desk. "What kind of stew?" Perry asked.

"Voodoo stew, complete with shrunken heads and live snakes. Who cares?" Mac said, wiping a drop of sloshed coffee off the desk with the underside of his tie. "Where's mine?"

"Only got two hands, Jack."

"Well, think you can take at least one of 'em out to the percolator and get me a cup?"

Perry nodded and Rick yawned.

"Am I boring you, Rick?"

"Didn't sleep much."

Mac laughed. "Be careful. I'd hate to see you end up like Evelyn's brother."

"I'm sure I don't know what you're talking about."

"I'm sure you don't either. But word gets around." Mac sniffed the fresh coffee stain on his tie and made a face like he'd been hit in the nose with a mallet. "As bad as always. Why is it you can only get a decent cup of coffee in New York at a diner?"

"You should try the coffee at Belle's."

"Not while I'm on duty."

They laughed, and Mac leaned forward and braced his elbows on the edge of the desk. "So, tell me about this hunch."

"Tell you what... I'll play ball if you will. Let me have a peek at the witness statements, and I'll give you everything I've got.

"You know I can't give…"

"It was worth a shot. What *can* you tell me?"

Mac took a deep breath. He looked at the ceiling and waited for it to give him advice, it seemed. While he waited and stared, Perry returned with the third coffee and put it down on the desk. Mac leaned forward again, took a sip, and made the brick-face again. "At least it's consistent."

"What's Ruby fishing for this time, partner?"

"Back on the leash, bulldog. Let the grown-ups talk."

"Cool it, both of you. I'm thinking."

Rick took a long, slow drain from the mug and set a half empty cup of coffee on the desk when he was done. Perry stared at his as if it was going to send him a gold-stamped invitation to drink it. Mac grabbed a pencil and tapped it on top of his desk.

"I can't say too much, but I can skim the newsreels for you. But that's all, okay."

Rick nodded. "Anything will help, Mac."

"And I expect the same from you, Rick."

"Fair enough."

Mac popped his knuckles. "Okay. I've got two witnesses that recognized two men going into the elevator just before the time of death. Both men were identified as low-ranking Klansmen, grunts. The only reason we know that is that both witnesses are former Klan."

"Former?"

"They found religion. Swapped one club for another, I guess."

"Okay. Got any proof of that, other than the witnesses' word for it?"

"They don't exactly keep public records, Rick. And if a man has the guts to come forward and go turncoat on the Klan, well, that's not something he's likely to do unless it's true. It's like trading a punch in the face for a slug in the gut."

"The Klan's an awfully big shortcut for real justice though, if someone was to try to frame it as a patsy."

"You're starting to sound like something out of the magazines. Have you forgotten how investigations work here in the real world, Rick?"

Rick shook his head. "Just enjoying the freedom to think around them. That's all." He grinned. "Names?"

"Can't give you that. Told you already."

"Not the witnesses. The suspects."

"I wish I knew. We're working that angle now."

"Do the papers know?"

"They suspect. And like you said, the Klan wears a pretty big target on its chest. But nothing official."

"Okay."

"What are you thinking, Rick?"

"Not sure yet. Just trying to fill in all the blanks on the application, Mac. You never know what could be important later. What about the woman?"

"The woman?"

"Horscutt. The white woman."

"Can't find her. And calling her family only got me the butler. They're touring Europe, and all the safe money is on her skipping the country and joining them right after this mess blew up."

"The rich go on holiday and the rest get dead. That's a story I've heard too often."

"I hear yah. Now, tell me about your hunch."

Rick dug through his pocket and pulled out the diamond watch. "Here's my hunch."

"A watch?" Perry asked.

"You get a gold star, Bob."

"Rick..."

"Sure, sure. Something about it just doesn't add up. It's supposed to belong to Evelyn's brother, but she insists he never owned one."

Mac scrunched his face to think, then opened a drawer and pulled out a file. He thumped it down on the desk and opened it, rummaging through it like a kid looking for buried treasure.

"Says here he had just come back from Paris. It's possible he got it there. I hear these jazz blowers can make a killing there."

"Could be. Like I said, just a hunch."

"It's never just a hunch with you, Rick."

"Like you said, I'm not a cop anymore. I've forgotten how real investigations work."

Mac laughed. Perry pulled up a chair.

Rick opened his mouth to speak, but the phone rang, cutting him off.

Perry grabbed it. "Jack McGinnis' desk," he said.

All the pink in the young cop's European face drained away. He handed the phone to Rick.

"Rick Ruby, what can I do f..."

"Rick!" Edie's normally calm voice was dressed up in the rags of madness and hysteria.

"Edie, what's wrong? Slow down and tell me what's..."

"It's Evelyn, Rick.

"What about Ev?"

"She's missing!"

Rick didn't respond. He just handed the phone to Mac and got the hell out of the police office.

• • •

Edie was pouring a Scotch when Rick burst through the door, her eyes red and tired and stained from crying. Even her smart, efficient dress looked exhausted. She called out to him and held the drink up for him to see it. He growled and told her to put it down, then beat a path to her table and ignored the rest of the folks around.

"Rick."

"What happened?"

"Rick."

"What happened to Evelyn?"

"Rick." Edie grabbed his jaw and jerked his head to the left. Two older guys in expensive suits sat at the corner table, smiling at him, *directly* at him. One had a thick head of silver above a face only a grandmother could kiss goodnight without closing her eyes. The other grew only a patch of gray above each ear and left the middle of the road as clean as the streets in the nice part of town. "These... gentlemen..." She swallowed the word like it was a rotten onion. "…would like to speak with you about the case."

"Edie," he said. "I don't have time for this."

One of the men lifted his coat open just enough to reveal the butt end of a .38.

"I think you have time to spare them a minute or two, Rick."

"Damn it," he muttered. Then he jerked the Scotch off the table and took a few seconds to drain it until the glass was lonely. He clanked it down loudly and stomped over to the table where the two were waiting. The younger of the ancients kept his hand inside his coat as a warning.

Rick dismissed the warning. He was a barely a breath away from feeding the old man the .38.

"Mr. Ruby," said the eldest. "It's a pleasure to meet you."

"What the hell is this about? Where's Evelyn? What did you do with her?"

"I'm afraid I don't know what you're talking about, sir. Mr. Wilcox and I," said Scattered Patches of Gray, "am merely interested in securing your services."

"Fine. I'll play along. Will you need photos or should I set you up to watch?"

"I afraid I don't follow, Mr. Ruby."

"When I find who Grandma is sleeping around with. You guys are here for the 'Catch Her in the Act' special, right? The one they advertise in the classifieds."

"Mr. Ruby, I was told you were a man who could be depended upon."

"Depends on what you need a man to be depended upon about."

Thick-Silver, Wilcox apparently, tapped noticeably inside his coat. Rick nodded and grinned.

"Don't mistake our civility for patience, young man," Thick-Silver said. "I've got a steady hand and a good eye for someone with life under his belt."

"And I've got a girl who isn't here with me. So do we have to do the song and dance again, or can we shoot straight to the point?"

"It's okay, Mr. Wilcox," said Scattered Patches. "Very well, Mr. Ruby. We are members of a proud and prestigious organization dedicated to the preservation of the American way of culture. As such, we are often misunderstood by those who consider themselves more progressive, even though it only reflects their own lack of practicality."

"Sounds to me like we're still dancing." Rick popped his neck with a rattle of loud cracks. "The turnip truck dropped me off earlier this week, so I've got a good idea who you two gentleman are."

"As such, a recent murder has cast some rather undue negative attention on our organization."

"Hanging a man from the Grand can do that."

"Do not tell me, Mr. Ruby, that you too believe this tommyrot."

"I told you this was a waste of time," Thick-Silver spat, nodding toward the door.

Scattered Patches shook his head.

"You've heard the rumors. You know as well as I do he keeps up with a nig…"

Rick didn't wait for the old man to finish the thought. Instead, he held down the man's arm that disappeared into his coat, then let him have it with the other hand. Thick-Silver's jaw complained with a sharp crack and led the old man away from the table and into the floor. He reached for the pistol, but Rick already had his coat halfway off and had his arms tangled up behind him in the sleeves.

Rick didn't have time to reach for his gun, but a nearby bottle of bourbon made the same point as the pistol, and even punctuated the statement when he broke it against the edge of the table and shoved the jagged glass teeth against the old man's neck.

Rick glanced toward Scattered Patches, expecting to see another pistol pointed at him, but the older man remained in his chair, quietly sipping on a clear drink. Either water or vodka, Rick figured.

Just beyond them, at the bar, Broomstick was already reaching for Sweet Angel, the double-barreled shotgun he kept there for emergencies. Rick shook his head no, then let the broken man go, and he fell into the floor, his face landing in the puddle made by the whiskey from the broken bottle.

"I don't mean to be uncivil, but my girl is missing, and I've got a good idea you two geezers have something to do with that."

Rick stuck out his hand to help Thick-Silver off the floor, but the old guy refused his hand and scrunched up his face with a scowl. "No thanks. Don't know who that hand might have touched…or where."

"Mr. Wilcox, we are here to ask for Mr. Ruby's assistance, not to insult him. A man need not always be judged completely by the company he keeps."

Rick took a seat and called out to Broomstick for another Scotch. Edie looked across the bar and nodded for the lanky bartender to go ahead. Another moment, and she walked it over to him without asking the others if they wanted anything.

"She's a pretty little thing," said Scattered Patches, "but I'm sure you could be equally happy with her in your bed…"

"My services." Rick stared at the glass without drinking. "You said you wanted my services."

"My people had nothing to do with this murder, Mr. Ruby. And I want you to prove that."

Rick stood up, taking his drink with him. "It's been a pleasure, gents, but I'm afraid there's nothing left for us to talk about."

Scattered Patches grabbed his wrist. "Our money is as good as anyone else's." He quickly moved his hand to the fabric of Rick's coat.

"I don't need your money to find out who killed Morris Johnson."

"Whether or not you need it, it's important to my organization that people know we are innocent in this incident." He cleared his throat, long and loud, almost making the pause a new member of the conversation. "And that we're willing to pay to prove it."

"Where's Evelyn?"

"I promise you. We had nothing to do with your singer's disappearance."

"You'll forgive me if I don't believe you."

"You have my word as a gentleman."

"Is that what they call a gentleman down south?"

"I will make a deal with you, Mr. Ruby."

"I don't make deals with killers."

"I assure you…"

"Keep you assurances."

"I know many people in many places in New York, of importance both politically and in regards to less savory indulgences."

"What a surprise."

"In addition to paying your regular rates, I will also ask around and see if I can help you find your singer, though I still say you'd better off with…"

Rick's glare cut the old man off.

"Do we have a deal, Mr. Ruby? Two heads are better than one, as they say."

"They say a lot of things, but that doesn't make it true."

Scattered Patches took an envelope from inside his coat and thumped it onto the table. Edie gasped. Broomstick stopped wiping the glasses for a second at the sound and glanced under the bar again. Rick shook his head, and the lanky bartender returned to his work, never letting his attention drift fully from the action at the table.

"That looks like a lot more than my daily rates," Rick said.

"Consider it a bonus."

"Consider it a bribe. Anybody can see it. And if you wanna play ball, then you're gonna have to play by the same rules as anybody else. All I'm gonna take from you is my regular retainer plus expenses."

The old man reached for the envelope, but Rick stopped him.

"I don't understand."

"All you're paying *me* is my regular wage, but I think the rest should cover your rental of the bar for our business and a few drinks."

The old man smiled, then let it creak into a grin. "You're a wise man, Mr. Ruby. I'm glad to have you on our side."

"Ain't on nobody's side, especially yours, and you're going to pay the gentleman at the bar personally after I take my cut."

"Of course."

"And you're going to call him sir when you do it."

Scattered Patches winced and squeezed his hands into fists.

"Your call."

"There are plenty of other investigators we could hire, Mr. Ruby."

"But none like Rick Ruby," Rick said. "Like your dance partner said. I've got something none of those others don't, and you need the good will and the publicity."

"And what's that?" asked Thick-Silver.

Scattered Patches glared at him. "Don't be stupid, Ernest."

"Oh." The other man's eyes lit up in recognition. "The singer."

"Said it yourself," said Rick. "Everyone who matters knows it, so I'm your only option."

"Very well, Mr. Ruby. It's all for the greater good."

"I've changed my mind," Rick said, shoving a few hundred dollars in his pocket and handing the rest back to Scattered Patches.

"I don't understand."

"Not completely changed my mind. Just decided I want the other fellow there to pay the gentleman at the bar instead."

Thick-Silver grunted but said nothing.

"Very well. But be warned, Mr. Ruby, you play a dangerous game."

"That's why it helps to have marked cards."

Scattered Patches handed the remaining money to Thick-Silver. "Ernest."

"You can't…"

"Now, Ernest."

"But…"

"Now. Ernest. Please pay the… gentleman at the bar."

"Yes, sir."

Rick stood up and walked back over to Edie. He was a heel. He knew it. He could have just taken the money. He should have just taken it. But sometimes the universe needed him to be a heel. So he did. The universe could thank him later. Not that he expected it to. The universe was a fickle bitch and she didn't give two dirty pennies what he did for her.

"Thank you for letting us borrow you establishment," Thick-Silver said as he handed Broomstick the money.

"You're very welcome," said Broomstick.

"Ernest?"

"Thank you... sir." The older man muttered.

Broomstick shoved the envelope of cash under the bar.

"You're still welcome, both you and your friend," he said.

Rick sat down next to Edie and poured himself a Scotch.

"Welcome to get the hell out of my bar," Broomstick said as politely as Rick imagined a rat might say to mongrel alley cat.

The two old men flashed Rick a loaded smile, then rose and exited the bar. The bell on the door jingled after them for a few seconds, and when it finished, Edie exhaled.

"We'll find her, Edie. We'll find her."

"Are you really taking their dirty money?"

"Why not? If you feel bad about it, ask Broomstick to let you borrow his rag and soap before we put it in the safe."

"Rick, don't kid me. I'm scared." She rested her head against his chest. His own chest started to shudder next to her. "I'm really scared this time."

"I'm scared too, baby."

She looked up through eyes that were already leaking onto her porcelain face. "Are you?"

He squeezed her to him and kissed her forehead like she was a kid sister. "Yeah, I think I really am this time."

• • •

Rick needed to clear his head and line all the facts up in a way that made some kind of sense. He fought the urge to just hang out at the bar and drink himself to sleep and wake up in a brand new world where Evelyn wasn't missing, Morris wasn't dead, and Edie wasn't growing up so damn put together.

He needed to think.

He needed to add everything up and figure out just what the hell was going on.

An arm slipped inside his and slowed down his steps along Waterford Ave. A voice like sugar cane and brandy cooed at him. "Fancy meeting you here, Rick."

"Welcome to get the hell out of my bar."

He didn't turn. He didn't need to.

"It's a public street, Donna. Good to see you too."

"Can we talk? I mean, somewhere less busy."

"I don't really have time for this."

The blond laughed. "Lighten up, Rick. I heard about Evelyn's brother. Just to show there are no hard feelings, I asked Eddie if he'd heard about the hanging after I finished rehearsing yesterday."

"And?"

"And we need to go someplace more private."

"Where?"

"Fairgrounds."

"Fairgrounds?"

"Ferris Wheel."

"Ferris Wheel?"

"Sure," Donna purred. "What's more private than a romantic view at the top of the world?"

Rick stopped, took a deep breath, and then wrinkled his nose. "I really don't have time for any games right now."

"Yeah, yeah, I know. Your precious Evelyn wants you to find her brother's killer. And I want to help. But I'm not putting myself at risk to do that."

"Eddie?"

"I wish it was just him." She glanced around before continuing. "But if what he told me is true, this is bigger than even Eddie. Bigger than his boss probably."

Rick grabbed her hand and all but dragged her across the street in the direction of the fairgrounds. She clicked on her high heels as fast as she could to keep up, the trim of her hat blowing behind her like a royal sash.

"You're in luck," Rick said.

"In luck, Rick?"

"I just got paid."

"Good. And one other thing. Another freebie for you, just because I feel like I owe Evelyn."

"She's missing."

Donna stopped, pulling against Rick's arm to stop him too. She looked at the ground as if she wanted it to look back. "I'm sorry. I didn't know."

"I'll find her."

"I know you will."

"I'd find you too," Rick added.

"I know." But something Donna didn't say made him feel like a bastard for even mentioning it.

"I want you to find her. Maybe this will help."

"Shoot."

"The woman Evelyn's brother was sleeping with."

"Yeah. Gertrude Horscutt."

"She's still in town."

• • •

Rick rang the doorbell and resisted the urge to straighten his loose tie. The door opened promptly, and a black gentleman in a shiny black suit asked if he could help him.

"Not unless you're Joseph Martin."

"He's in a meeting and can't be disturbed, I'm afraid."

"He's in something, but I'm sure it ain't a meeting."

"He left word that he's not to be disturbed."

Rick produced his license from his coat pocket and held it in front of the butler's eyes. "I'm here on business myself."

The butler studied the license. "I'm sorry, Mr. Ruby. Mr. Martin is not to be disturbed."

Rick pushed past him and stopped in the grandiose foyer. Marble figures lined the walls, one in each alcove, and between the alcoves hung romantic paintings from the masters, none of which appealed to Ruby.

"If you don't leave now, sir, I will have to call the police and have you arrested."

"Go ahead. While you're at it, ask for Jack McGinnis. Then he and I can talk with Mr. Martin together. We can even get his rookie in too and make an uncomfortable date of it."

The butler's shoulders dropped, and he suddenly looked a few inches shorter.

"Promise I won't get you in trouble. I just need a few minutes of Joe's time."

"Joseph, sir. No one calls Mr. Martin 'Joe.'"

"Got it. So, is Joe upstairs in a…" Rick cleared his throat loudly, "…meeting with Miss Horcutt?"

The butler's eyes sparked and widened, telling Rick he had just hit the center of the bull's-eye, but the man said nothing.

Suddenly a loud squeal erupted from upstairs. Both Rick and the butler looked up and traced the sound to an open door to the left of the stairwell.

"Stop that, Joe!" the female voice squealed again.

"No one, huh?" Rick asked with a grin. "Don't mind me. I'll see myself up."

Rick felt a meaty hand on his shoulder.

"I'm afraid I still must ask you to le…"

Rick whispered, "If you people care about Morris Johnson, you'll let me go."

Something sparked again in the butler's eyes, and in the second his hand loosened its grip, Rick pulled away and headed to the stairs. He glanced back to see if the other man followed him, but he remained as still as one of the marble figures.

Rick took the stairs without running, gripping the bannister just to enjoy the feel of the shiny, polished wood. No way he'd get splinters from this one, he thought, not like the railings at Belle's. When he reached the top, he let go and headed to the open door. He entered without knocking.

"Afternoon, Mr. Martin," he called out.

From behind, Gertrude Hoscutt was one of the most beautiful women he'd ever seen. And it was a good thing too, because with a name like Horscutt, she had a hell of a lot to overcome. Money or looks would have been enough, but lucky little Gertrude seemed to have been blessed with both.

She sat upright in the bed facing the headboard of what Rick assumed was Joe Martin's bed. Her alabaster back was covered down to the middle by a curly mass of black tangles. Her lower portion, Rick acknowledged tactfully, matched the creamy tone of her back and sat atop the lavender sheets, silk, he assumed, in a pleasant upside down heart shape. Morris had done very well for himself as a black man. Not only that, he'd done it before a man like Joe Martin.

Joe propped himself up on his elbows and looked around her knees with a glare that could melt stone.

"Who the hell are…"

Rick grinned.

"Oh hell. Not you. What do you want this time, Ruby?"

"Just have a few questions for you and the lady."

"How'd you get in here?"

"Don't blame your man downstairs. I can be awfully pushy."

"Don't have to convince me."

"I assume the lovely lady you're in a meeting with is Miss Gertrude Horscutt." He didn't let his tone make the statement into a question.

The woman turned her head and gave him a profile view. Unless she had some kind of disease on the other side, the face was that of the marble Venus in the foyer. The package was consistent. He'd have to admit that.

"Hello," she said without an ounce of shame. "It's a pleasure to meet you."

"The pleasure is all mine, Miss Horscutt."

Joe cut in. "Hey, this is all well and good, but do you mind if we do this in the sitting room instead?"

Rick nodded, and went downstairs. Within a few minutes, Gertrude joined him in the sitting room, covering herself in a luxurious white robe with a rose petal print that stopped at her knees and left her calves and tiny feet bare and exposed.

"I meant what I said upstairs, Mr. Ruby," she said, walking to the bar. "It is a pleasure to meet you."

"Likewise."

"Rumor has it you're a man who likes a good Scotch."

Rick laughed. "I probably wouldn't know a good Scotch if it introduced itself by name, but I'm more than a little fond of an average Scotch."

"So… I suppose you want to talk about my late lover, Morris Johnson?"

She poured two glasses and brought them over. After handing one to Rick she sat down across from him on the divan.

"Actually, yes."

"Does my candor surprise you, Mr. Ruby?"

"Please, call me Rick."

"Great. Does my candor surprise you, Rick?"

"You don't seem too bothered by the death of a man you call your lover."

"I don't suppose I am. I'm like a man that way, I suppose. A lover is just a lover, Rick. It sure is fun while it lasts, but you shouldn't try to get too attached."

"Sure hope Joe has the same idea." Rick swallowed something that tasted way too much like guilt. "Anyway, how did you two meet?"

"In Paris. He was playing with one of the bands, and I wanted to show my father I could make my own damn choices in life."

"The old walk on the wild side. Wouldn't have taken you for a stereotype."

"A stereotype would have found a pickpocket or a gambler."

"Point taken."

"We had a good time, lots of good times, and when I found out he was in New York with the band, I decided to look him up."

"Tell me about that night."

"Not a lot to tell. I met Morris in his room. We made love. Then I left. Next thing I know, I'm reading in the papers that he spent the rest of the night hanging out of his window."

"I see."

"What do you see?"

"I see a man I don't want in my house drinking my expensive liquor with my girl," said a voice from behind them.

Rick turned to see Joe Martin standing in the doorway. He had dressed in a pair of black pants and a white shirt and suspenders. Gotta look the part, Rick figured, assuming he hadn't felt like making time enough to put on a tie.

"If it's any consolation, I can't tell the difference between this one and the cheap stuff down at Belle's."

"Then I need to shoot my importer."

Rick grinned. "I'm going to assume that was a joke."

"Of course it was a joke. Don't be stupid."

"Too late. I've made a career out of being stupid. No reason to stop now."

"What do you want, Ruby?"

"Morris Johnson."

"What about him?"

"What do you know?"

"He was apparently one hell of a horn player."

"That it?"

"I keep my nose clean, Ruby."

"Not clean enough."

"I didn't know the man."

"Never met him?"

"Of course I met him. Rode the elevator with him at the Grand the night he died."

"Didn't think I might want to know that?"

"Don't rightly care what you want."

"Look, Joe, I just want to find the man..." Rick avoided glancing at Miss Horscutt. "...or woman who killed him."

"The police already know who killed him."

"The police don't know what I know."

"And what's that, Ruby?"

Rick drew a triangle in the air between them. "I've got three dots that make a pretty perfect triangle, only none of these dots seems to want to stay connected long enough to build a pyramid."

"Care to put that in English for the rest of us?" Joe spat.

"Sure. I've got Morris Johnson hanging from the Grand. I've got a rich white woman who wants to sow some wild oats at home and abroad. And I've got a powerful local businessman who calls a black man Mister."

"I never called that man..."

"Got a witness who says otherwise."

Joe bit his bottom lip. "Who cares? Probably a slip of the tongue. A man in my position gets used to speaking to people a certain way."

"A man in your position gets used to speaking to *certain* people a certain way."

"Regardless, Ruby, what's all this supposed to add up to?"

"Right now it adds up to a missing woman and a found watch."

Rick glanced to Joe and then to Miss Horscutt then back to his glass of Scotch. Neither flashed with any recognition.

Joe cracked his knuckles. "What watch?"

"Just a little something even a jazzman fresh from Paris couldn't afford."

"And your point?"

"No point. Just trying to build a pyramid to hang the killer from the top of."

"A pyramid has four sides, Ruby," Joe said, pouring himself a glass of something dark and bitter enough to foul up the air of the room.

"Geometry was never my strong suit. Was too busy taking sharpshooting."

"And the missing woman?" Miss Horscutt asked, tilting her head with a smile to show off the glimmer of diamond earrings and a slender jawline.

"A singer. Morris' sister."

"Evelyn?"

Rick nodded.

"Morris talked about her a lot. I hope you find her. I'll do everything I can to help."

"Appreciate that."

"Do you have the watch, Rick? Perhaps if it's that expensive, I might be able to tell you something about it."

"Thank you, Miss Horcutt." He dug into his pocket and pulled out the watch.

"Please, call me Gerty. All my friends do."

"I already have too many friends, Gerty." He handed her the watch, and she inspected the diamonds first, then the face, then the band.

"It's been specially fit for his wrist," she said. "You can tell by the number of links in the band. Several have been taken out to make it a perfect fit."

"Pardon me for asking, but did you give Morris the watch, Gerty?"

"It was a fling. If I gave away a watch for every fling I've flung, I'd have a watchmaker on account."

"Well, it was worth a shot."

"Is that all, Ruby?" Joe asked.

Rick gave the room a once-over. Nothing but books he'd never read for the most part, book cases he could never afford, leather chairs and a divan that looked like something out of a Carole Lombard film.

"Well?" Joe said, glaring and tapping his foot against the floor. He poured the bitter stuff into his mouth, coughed a bit, then resumed his glare.

"Tell you what. If anyone should contact you, or if you think of anything else, can you look me up?"

"Absolutely, Rick."

"Whatever you say."

"Say, Joe?"

"What, Ruby?"

"I changed my mind."

"Changed your mind?"

"About the Scotch. I can taste the difference."

"Good for you."

"I think I prefer the cheap stuff."

"Oh?"

"This one tastes too much like the ground in a stable."

"Yeah?"

"Or maybe it's just the company."

Miss Horscutt laughed. Joe called for the butler to please escort Rick Ruby the hell off his damn property.

At the door, the butler stopped Rick and asked him if he got what he needed.

"Maybe. We'll see."

"I met him once. Morris, I mean. Had to call him Mr. Johnson. I thought that was the damndest thing I've ever heard."

"Here?" Rick whispered.

"Here," the butler responded.

"But he came in through the back door, and he left the same way."

"That it?"

"That's it. I only took him to the sitting room and saw him out. He gave me two dollars and invited me to his show at The Marquis, told me I should find a way to Paris if I ever could."

"Probably not a bad idea. He didn't do too bad with that plan."

"Not until he came home again. I hope that helps, Mr. Ruby."

"I hope so too, pal." Rick stepped outside and let the door close behind him. Damn, he thought. He never once asked the man his name.

• • •

Good old Mac was waiting in the park just like he'd promised. And early too. A good ten minutes early according to the watch that was or wasn't the property of the late Morris God-Rest-His-Soul-and-Damn-He-Sure-Blew-a-Mean-Horn Johnson.

He walked the cobblestone path to the bench where Mac sat.

"Been waiting long, Mac?"

Rick took a seat beside him.

Mac made a noise that sounded more like a storming bull than a friendly hello, but Rick ignored it. "So, what's all this?"

"My hunch was right. It's not the Klan."

"I've got witnesses."

"Whatever you've got, it's all a frame job. And a beautiful one. The kind that's easy to walk around in and live inside and never know it isn't reality after all."

"What do you know, Rick?"

"The locals… they're keeping their noses clean for a few weeks."

"How clean?"

"Spotless, except for some gambling and some minor inconveniences to keep the cops busy."

"Why?"

"Because they don't want the extra attention. Something's up."

"You're telling me the hanging of a Negro jazz man for sleeping with a white woman isn't just another Klan murder?"

"I'm telling you that whatever Morris was involved in goes a lot deeper than either of us thinks, and that this whole Klan ruse is just that, a paint-up job to keep the police looking in the wrong places."

"Rick, you're sounding…"

"Yeah, I know. I'm sounding like a radio show. But you know as well as I do that I don't know what evil lurks within the hearts of men. I'm just a guy with a license and sense enough not to pin the tail on the first donkey that walks up to the station."

"Careful, buddy. Somebody might get the idea that you don't think I know how to do my job."

"It's not that. It's just that I get the feeling somebody gift-wrapped this one for you and there's pressure to accept the gift."

"Rick…"

"It's okay. Politics, I know. I used to have to play the same game. That's part of the reason I got out."

"So what's this really about?"

"Eddie MacDonald is running scared. And he's not the only one."

"And just why is that?"

"I don't know." Rick pulled out the watch again. "But I know it's got something to do with this. I can't shake it that this watch means a lot more to this case than just a way to keep time."

"I trust your hunches, Rick, but you know the way it is. I can't move on something until I have some kind of proof."

"Mac, Donna's scared too."

"Donna?"

Rick raised his eyebrows, then cut one toward his ally.

"The dancer?"

"She prefers the term 'entertainer,' but nomenclature aside, yeah, that Donna."

"How so?"

"For her life. And Eddie's."

"So, tell me about this watch again if it's so damn important."

"I found Horscutt. She was with Joe Martin."

"Yeah. We found out she was still in town yesterday. Her family wants her to stay out of it, and she wasn't there when the murder occurred. So she's clean."

"She's not clean, Mac. She's trying to sell me a story about a bad girl sleeping on the wrong side of the tracks. Only she can't keep the details straight."

"How so?"

"Well, she's painting herself as some kind of Sheba who keeps men like pets, only she told me that she and Morris 'made love.' Every other word made her out to be a female tomcat. But there was something that slipped through when she talked about sleeping with Morris."

"And that's important how?"

"I think she really loved him, Mac. And not only that, there's the watch."

"This damn magic watch again."

"She said it was adjusted to fit the guy who owned it. Specially fitted."

"And you want to see Morris?"

"I want to see Morris."

"Can't let you do that, but I'll tell you what. Let me take the watch and I'll try it on him and let you know."

"Thanks, Mac. You're the best."

"Tell the Mayor."

• • •

The back stairwell to the office was dark, but that was nothing new. Better to keep the lights off when he wasn't there. No sense in running up the electric bill when he already cut so deep into Belle's liquor costs.

Rick shoved his key in the door and turned the lock. It clicked and clinked and tumbled and the door swung slightly ajar. Rick pushed it open and reached for the light switch.

As he did, something dark and hard crashed into his skull.

That's when the lights truly went out.

He awoke in the rumble seat of a roadster with his head throbbing and his eyes trying to figure out the difference between the honest-to-God sky and the dancing stars that tried to block it out. He tried to wipe his eyes, but found his wrists bound behind him.

"I appreciate the cab ride, but I can't exactly reach my wallet right now," he said.

The driver didn't respond.

"Oh, this is going to be that kind of trip."

The driver glanced back and gave him a warning glare, then faced the road again.

"Guess I'll just have to talk to myself."

"It would be in your best interest to keep your big, fat mouth shut, Shamus."

"Oh, believe me, you've got the wrong man then."

Rick tested his legs and found them bound at the ankles and knees.

"A regular boy scout, aren't you?"

He tried to sit up but a sharp turn threw him back to the seat.

"So, where are we heading?"

No response.

"Over the river and through the woods. Won't Grandmother be surprised to see us show up?"

"Keep it up, wise guy. Just try me."

Rick thought of at least six smartass comebacks, but decided against them all. Maybe it was time to shut the hell up and just see where this trip might take him. With any luck, Evelyn would be at the end of the road.

After another fifteen or so minutes, the roadster pulled into an alley on the East side of town, and, from the smell of the air, just a mile or two shy of the docks. The driver opened the door and got out. He stood taller than Rick by at least a good foot, Rick guessed. He'd know soon enough. The man was bald with two long scars on his head and a clean face that held the kind of wrinkles that were created by time. This was a face carved by hard living and probably a little time in prison.

The man grabbed Rick by his shirt and lifted him from the rumble seat and stood him up beside the back of the car. Yep, a good foot taller. Without explaining anything, the man jerked a knife from inside his coat and revealed seven full inches of gleaming steel. Rick tried to back away, but his bound legs sent him falling against the roadster with a hard thud.

"Hold still, you fool," the man said, and the knife shot between Rick's legs and ankles, and suddenly he was free.

"That's one hell of a blade."

"Sure is, so don't try anything stupid."

"You're the boss."

"Not even close, but you'll meet him in a minute."

The boss, it turned out, wasn't half the man the driver was. He sat in an office chair in a small, dingy room off the alley, with a pair of glasses too big for his face resting on his nose, and a .45 sitting on the desk in front of him.

He nodded as Rick was pushed into the room. The driver led Rick to a single wooden seat in front of the boss, then placed Rick's .38 beside the .45. The two pistols framed a bottle of pricey Scotch in a familiar bottle.

Didn't matter how big the man was. With those two numbers at his beck and call, he could be the boss all he wanted.

Except for one important thing...

"Where's Evelyn?" Rick asked, shifting forward in the chair to take the pressure off his hands and wrists.

"We'll ask the questions," the boss responded.

Rick grinned. He was reading right off the script.

"Where is she? I ain't saying nothing until I know she's safe."

"Waldo." As the smaller man spoke, he motioned to the bigger one.

The bigger one slugged Rick across the jaw.

"Don't change a thing."

Another nod.

Another slug.

In his head, Rick's jaw cried out in pain, but Rick managed to keep own mouth shut. He spat blood onto the dirty floor. "Well?"

A third nod and another slug across the jaw. Rick felt a tooth jar loose and rattle around. "Should have listened to my dear old mother and gone into dentistry."

"I believe you have something I'm looking for, Mr. Ruby."

Rick smiled. "Why is it that all the guys who want to kill you or beat you up always call you Mister? You fellows are the most polite degenerates

...and revealed seven inches of gleaming steel.

a guy who have the displeasure of meeting. I really mean that."

"Would you prefer I have Waldo punch you again, or do you think a gunshot to your knee would be more effective to convince you of my sincerity in this matter?"

"Look, I don't even have to see her. I just need your word and a man of honor that she's okay."

"She is special to you?"

Rick nodded.

"But she…"

"She's black. Yeah. Lately people keep noticing that. Must be a lot of good opticians here in New York."

The little boss stood up. He was still a small man.

"I should have told Martin and the dame about the watch when I first got it. Could have saved me a day or two to meet you."

"If she's genuinely special to you, Mr. Ruby, I'd advise you to tell me where my property is. It wasn't in your office, nor was it on your person."

Rick laughed a hearty, loud kind of noise that in any other circumstance would have convinced the listener someone had told one hell of a joke. "You're going to love this, then. If you had roughed me up just twenty minutes sooner, it would have been yours."

"I'm not laughing."

"Then your funny bone is broken, because the watch…it's with the cops now."

Without any warning at all, another punch smashed into Ruby, but not his face. Instead he hunched over, grabbing the fist with his gut until it extricated itself from him and prepared for a second trip.

He spit more blood the second time.

"I'm still not laughing," boss man said.

"Hold on. It's hard to talk with my stomach in my throat."

The little man lifted his hand, and the driver stopped punching.

"Thanks."

"So talk."

"I can get it back. I'll have it brought to the wake tonight at Belle's. We can all switch dance partners there. You bring the girl, and I'll give you the watch as soon as I get it from my cop friend." No need to give Mac's name away if it wasn't necessary.

"Once I have it back, I'll make arrangements for you to get the girl."

"I'd rather ma…"

"Or I could just shoot her and make it a wake for two."

"Fine, fine. Just don't hurt her." Rick looked at the floor. "Please."

"You double cross me," boss man said, resting against the desk, "and the only way you'll see her again is dead."

"I hear you, boss."

"Good."

"So, who gave me away? Martin or the dame?"

The boss ignored the question and nodded toward the bigger man. "Take Mr. Ruby home. He needs to get ready for a wake tonight."

The little man at the desk jerked off the top of the bottle and took a long draw of Scotch. Rick's pyramid was suddenly a lot stronger with a fourth side after all, he thought.

• • •

The bar waited dressed in its Sunday best. Broomstick had mopped the floors and even painted the ceiling tiles Rick had never gotten around to. Belle had set out the good glasses and the best of the whiskey, and Edie had helped her all day to woman up the bar with flowers and cards. The place looked more like a florist's shop than a jazz joint.

All that remained was for the undertaker to bring the body from the coroner's office.

Two phone calls had set everything in motion; one to Mac and one to the other side of the law. Now he just needed to be on Lady Luck's good side for two hours. Just two hours. For Evelyn's sake.

Rick checked his watch. 6:35 P.M. Less than a half an hour before Morris made his arrival. Less than an hour before he hoped to see Evelyn again.

"You dress up nice, Rick," said Edie's soft, weak voice from the door behind him.

He turned and saw her standing like a silhouette in the doorway. A black dress reached the floor, exposing only her stockinged toes through the peekaboo cut in the front of her shoes.

"So do you," he said, and he walked over and hugged her.

She gripped him tightly and didn't let go. He could feel the warmth of her face where she had been crying. Hell, he could see the red puffy glow from the tears when she looked up at him.

"Everything's gonna be okay, kiddo."

She nodded against his chest. "I know."

"Honey, let go of the man before you break him," said Belle. She stood a few feet behind Edie and wore a dress that fit her like the Mississippi River fit a local map; winding and wide. Black, of course, but not the kind of black dress proper folk wore for mourning.

"Don't look at me like that, Rick. This wake ain't for crying. This one's for celebrating."

Edie eased up her grip around his waist but didn't let go completely.

"Afraid I'm not so good at celebrating a dead man," he said.

"Then you never learned how to have a wake New Orleans style. Morris lived, by damn, and that's what we're gonna celebrate tonight. Not that he got killed, but that he lived right up to the end."

"Belle?" Rick asked.

"What, baby?"

"What if I found out Morris was into something he shouldn't have been, something so dangerous and stupid it got him killed."

Belle laughed. "Then you're gonna keep your mouth shut until after tonight. You can ruin the man's reputation all you want after that."

"I don't want to ruin anybody's reputation, least of all Ev's brother."

"I know baby, but sometime there just ain't no way around a thing."

"I don't think I can do that to Evelyn."

"Listen, boy. You just make sure she gets home to us all safe and sound and stop worrying about whether or not she's gonna be mad at you about painting her brother a crook." Belle tapped Edie on the shoulder. "Now let him go, honey. You'll wrinkle his fine suit."

Edie let go and went to the bar and climbed onto a stool. Rick grinned as she crossed and re-crossed her legs to get comfortable and not expose too much leg.

"Don't worry, kiddo. Your virtue's completely intact in that dress."

"Rick…"

"Okay, okay. I'll stop kidding you."

The door clinked open, and all eyes turned to watch it. As they did, the second door opened along with it and the brown nose of a plain casket poked inside to get a sniff around the joint. When it edged in further, Rick counted the four men carrying it; three black men and one white, the boss he assumed.

"Where do ya want him?" asked the well-dressed white man.

"Right on the bar," Broomstick said, he voice leading the charge from outside.

"Looks like the guest of honor is here, Belle," Rick said.

"Looks like," she replied.

The mortician's crew gently placed Morris' box on the bar, and backed away. They nodded at Belle, and then the boss said they were sorry for her loss. Rick resisted the urge to tell him that she wasn't the dead man's sister.

"We'll be back in the morning to carry him to the graveyard," the man said. "Nine o'clock still fine?"

Belle shook her head. "Make it ten thirty, if you don't mind. When I send a man on his way to Beulah, I really try to give him a party to remember."

The man nodded. "That's fine," he added, motioning for his men to follow him to the door.

He and his workers had only been gone a few minutes when the doors opened again and seven dark-skinned men entered, laughing and singing and carrying musical instruments. The rest of Morris' band, he guessed.

"In the corner, Belle?" a tall, fat man with a guitar asked.

"Just like the old days, Talent." She turned to Rick. "Rick, I want you to meet Talent Jones."

"A pleasure," Rick said, walking over and reaching out his hand.

Talent took it, shook it vigorously, and let it go. "The cop?"

"Former," Rick said. "So, Talent huh? Interesting name."

"Interesting parents," the tall, fat man said with a grin. "I guess they had faith in me from birth. Just like Isaiah, plans from the womb, Mr. Ruby."

"Please, just Rick."

"You got it, Rick. Now if you'll pardon me, me and the boys will start getting set up so we can blow old Morris one hell of a path to Glory."

Rick walked back to Belle, Broomstick, and Edie at the bar, the end furthest from the casket he noticed. "I like him."

"Everybody likes Talent," Belle said.

"I just hope nobody gets hurt tonight, except maybe the bastards who caused it all."

Belle smiled and placed her hand on top of Rick's. "I trust you, son. I wouldn't let you do this if I didn't."

Rick placed his free hand on hers and squeezed, then let go.

They listened while the band rattled cases and tuned up.

Broomstick poured him a half a glass of bourbon. Rick lifted it, took a sip, and said, "No more for a while. I need a clear head tonight."

Broomstick laughed heartily. "That's why I gave you a drink. I want you to have the clearest head possible."

Rick shared the laugh and checked his watch again. 6:58 p.m. Time kept barreling on like a train. Clickety clack. Clickety clack. Whoo whoo. Too late to back out now.

A few minutes later, a beautiful woman in an elegant but tasteful black dress that revealed her silky, stocking-clad legs entered the room. She walked resolutely to Rick, nodded at Edie, said thanks for letting her know about the funeral, then promptly kissed Rick full on the mouth.

"Not the time, Claire," Rick said.

"It seems it's rarely the time lately," she said, "but let's not get into that tonight, sweetheart."

The kiss was still oozing guilt all over his lips when the door opened again and Donna entered the bar. She wore a blue dress that hugged her in all the places a dress was supposed to, and she glared at Claire, then waved with a smile at Belle and Broomstick.

"Thanks for coming, Donna," Edie said.

"Thanks for letting me know, kiddo. But if Eddie finds out, he's gonna have my hide." She walked over to Rick and hugged him then let go. "Still, I couldn't not come. It wouldn't be right."

"Well, that's one thing we can agree on," Claire said, returning the glare.

Donna cleared her throat and looked at Rick. "Well, more like two things, I'd think."

Thankfully, the tension between the two disappeared when the door clinked open again.

"You're taking a big risk if the Klan learns you're here," Rick said as Gertrude Horscutt entered the bar.

"I told her the same thing, Mr. Ruby, but she just wouldn't listen to reason," said Joseph Martin. His arm cinched her shoulders like a coat two sizes too small.

Gertrude glanced from Martin to Rick then back again, but said nothing.

"All the same, I'm glad you're here," Rick said. "I'm sure it means a lot to Morris."

"Means the world to him, I'm sure," Belle added.

"Who wants a drink?" Broomstick asked.

Martin and Gertrude joined the rest at the bar, and everyone other than Rick and Edie had a short glass of brandy.

"Best in the house," Broomstick said with a red hint of pride as he poured.

"I'd prefer you and Claire beat it after this drink," Rick said to Donna.

"Not on your life, Rick," the blonde said. "I owe this to Evelyn. And you."

"If she's not leaving, then I'm not leaving, sweetheart," Claire said.

"You're better than this, Claire. The last thing you need to do is lower yourself to my level."

"I guess you just have that effect on a woman." Her eyes flashed like daggers, then softened. "Rick..."

"Not now. But for God's sakes, at least you and Donna can…"

"Good evening, folks!" a voice yelled from the doorway.

Rick turned to see the skinny, short bespectacled man whose name he hadn't learned standing there with his arms spread wide.

The ape who had kidnapped him earlier stood beside him, holding a shotgun. He turned for just a moment to lock the doors.

"I hear there's going to be a lovely wake shortly, so I'll make this quick," the little boss man said. "All I want is the watch."

The boys in the band stood up and started toward the door, but the ape pointed the shotgun at Belle. "I wouldn't if I were you."

They stopped.

"Just have a seat, boys, and this will all be over in a minute." Boss man turned to Rick again. "The watch, Mr. Ruby."

"Let the girls go first. They don't have anything to do with this."

"Hell, Mr. Ruby, most of you here tonight don't have anything to do with this, but we can't let that stop us from sending a few of you to join dear old Morris in the afterlife, can we?"

"You bastard."

"That's what the nuns used to call me in the orphanage."

"Just as a favor for me. Let the girls go."

Boss man nodded at the ape, and the bigger man walked over to him.

"The watch?"

"The girls."

Big man buried the butt of the shotgun in Rick's belly, and he doubled over and hacked up a little bit of bourbon. It burned bad enough going down, but it felt like liquid lightning coming up.

"The watch, Mr. Ruby. I'd hate to turn this wake into another St. Valentine's Day."

Broomstick glanced at Rick, and Rick shook his head.

"Fine. Morris is wearing it. Just seemed right, you know."

"I should have guessed. Keep the gun on the woman. Ruby and I are going to see off an old friend."

Boss man motioned for Rick to lead the way, and he did as he was told.

"You know, they keep this casket closed for a reason. Hanging as long as he did can do a lot of wrong to a man's face."

"Kill the ghost stories, Ruby. I'm a big boy."

"Just warning you." Rick rested his hand on top of the casket. He drummed his fingers on the shiny wood. "Feel free to turn away."

"Stop stalling, Ruby."

"You're the boss."

"Don't forget that." Boss man motioned for him to open the case already.

Rick cracked open the top of the case a few inches and reached inside. "Damn thing's stuck a bit. Hang on."

"You're wasting time, Ruby."

"Or you could send the goon over to help me. They didn't plan for this thing to be opened, I guess, especially not after the autopsy."

"Nice try." He turned to his partner. "Keep the gun on the girl." Then back to Ruby. "Make room. I've got this."

"Suit yourself."

Boss Man joined him at the casket and pulled up. Rick did the same. The top of the box flung open and the tip of a police issue .38 poked out and rested a few scant inches from the small man's nose.

"Gideon Cleaver," said Mac from inside the coffin, "you're not nearly as tall as you look in your wanted poster."

"You forget..." the big ape with the shotgun started to say, then stopped when he heard the clicking of another gun.

"Rick didn't forget nothing," said Broomstick, holding both barrels of Sweet Angel, leveling them at the big man's chest.

"I'd put that down if I were you," Rick said to the ape. "Now this is the way I like it to happen, without all that bloodshed and double-crossing they always have to put in the magazines and on the radio."

"Put down the gun, Bert," the little man said. "Besides, we still have the girl."

"Not just one girl," Martin said, pulling a pistol on Gertrude and shoving it against her temple. "Keep these two idiots if you want, but I want that watch, fellows."

"Wondered when you'd show your true colors, Martin," Rick said. "But you can put that gun down. I know you and Miss Horscutt are in this mess together. You're not fooling anybody."

"I mean it. I will shoot her."

"I really, really doubt it."

"Okay, sure we were, but then she went and fell in love with that... man. I don't owe her anything anymore."

"Maybe. Maybe not."

"I mean it."

"Go ahead."

Someone knocked on the glass of the door.

Claire screamed.

Donna dove behind the bar.

The band scattered inside the bar.

Bert turned toward the door and accidently fired the shotgun through the wall near the piano.

Broomstick answered and clicked both of Sweet Angel's triggers.

Sweet Angel shouted her anger into Bert's chest.

Bert fell to the floor with a massive hole where there shouldn't be one.

Gideon Cleaver ran for the back door, but Mac fired the .38 and the little man hit the ground, screaming about his shot leg.

Rick checked to see that the girls and Broomstick were okay, then walked to the door.

"Stop, Ruby. I'll kill her," Martin said.

"Shut up, Joseph," Gertrude said and stepped away from Martin. He let the gun drop to his side.

Rick unlocked the doors and opened them.

"Right on time, fellas," he said.

Two old men in suits waited on either side of Evelyn Johnson. Behind them stood a group of four younger men in workman's attire.

Martin looked at Evelyn as if he had swallowed a puppy.

She fell forward into Rick's arms. He caught her and kissed her without a sound, feeling each fresh tear that rolled down to his lips.

Not one of the women at the bar said a damn thing.

"Right where you figured she'd be," said the eldest. "Thought we might have to rough up the butler to get him to believe we were on his side."

Rick looked up from Evelyn's shoulder to glare.

"Relax, gumshoe. It was a joke."

No one laughed.

"How'd you know?" Gertrude asked.

"Recognized a man's taste in Scotch, and took a long shot."

"Told him not to take the bottle," Martin muttered. "Stupid. Real stupid."

Rick took a good, long look around the bar, counted the bodies, both dead and living. So much for a bloodless wrap-up. Maybe the magazines and radio had it right after all. Still, it was a damn shame. Still, at least he hadn't had to pull the trigger this time. That was at least something. He took a deep breath.

"Thank you," he said to the two old Klansmen.

"Thank you for clearing our fine name," said the eldest.

"I didn't clear anything. You're still a bunch of murderous bastards in my book."

"Maybe. But we're not the bastards who murdered Morris Johnson."

"Doesn't change a damn thing," Broomstick muttered from the bar.

Belle sat down at the bar and took a drink from two of the glasses in front of her. "So tell me, Gertrude," she said. "Did you really love him?"

Gertrude looked ashamed. The look told Rick all he needed to know.

"At the end, yeah," Gertrude said. "But it was too late, and we both knew it. He wanted me to take the watch to the cops, for us to go straight and move back to Europe and get a place just the two of us, but Joseph was onto us."

Rick walked back to the casket to help Mac climb out. "What's the story about this damn watch anyway? I mean, sure it's diamonds, but not worth all this killing."

Gertrude dropped to her knees in the floor. Her eyes opened up like storm clouds. "Where's the watch?" she said weakly. "I'll show you."

Rick let go of Evelyn and reached into his front pocket and pulled out the watch from where he'd been hiding it since he'd gotten it back from Mac. He handed it to the woman on the floor.

She opened the back of the watch, then pried off a false back from inside the buckle and handed it to Rick.

Rick examined it and saw a sequence of numbers and symbols he didn't recognize.

"Looks like some kind of kid's scratching in the sand."

Evelyn walked to the bar to join Belle and Edie. Donna stood behind the casket with Claire.

"Thanks for coming," Evelyn said. "Hope you had one hell of a party without me."

Donna smiled. "Are you okay?"

"As okay as I can be."

Broomstick reloaded Sweet Angel and hung her behind the bar again.

Claire reached for Evelyn's hand. "I'm really sorry about your brother."

"Don't be, Evelyn said, straightening her shoulders with pride. "You heard his woman. He died a hero, or at least trying to be."

Gertrude sniffled.

"So what's with the symbols?" Rick asked.

Mac joined Rick and stared at the watch. "Code," he said.

"Right," said Gertrude. "It tells where to make a pick-up for jewels smuggled in from all over Europe. Martin was using the money he made from smuggling to keep the right politicians in office across the country."

"The right ones?"

"The ones who were open to bribes, the ones who could be trusted to look the other way when it counted."

"Let me see if I can guess the rest," Rick interrupted. "Morris and the band traveled around, and that left Morris free to share the location with each informant from city to city by changing out the back of the watch. Then he gets cold feet and falls in love, and when he comes clean with you about it, Joe here goes ballistic."

Gertrude sobbed openly, nodding.

"Keep your mouth shut, you bitch!" Martin yelled, and he raised his pistol at Gertrude.

Rick waited for the thunder to sound, but it never came. Instead, Joseph Martin slumped to the ground and dropped his gun.

Behind him Talent stood tall and taking up most of the light. In his hand was a long stiletto that dripped blood.

"It was me," he said. "I was the inside man. Morris stole the watch from me months ago and threatened to expose Martin. But then he met Miss Horscutt here and decided to play along for a while. I guess it's true what they say about the love of a woman."

Rick looked at Donna and grinned. Then to Claire, who tried to smile but was still too terrified. Then to Edie, who merely nodded at him.

Evelyn looked at the two dead men on the floor of the bar. She smiled and grabbed a half-drunk glass of brandy and lifted it.

"To Morris," she said.

"To Morris," Gerty coughed through her tears.

"What the hell," said Rick. "To Morris." He locked his eyes onto Evelyn's. There were no tears now.

"And to you too, Rick Ruby, the best damn dragon slayer in New York."

The door clinked again, and the mortician and his workers poked their heads in. "Are you ready yet for the real one?" the mortician asked.

"I need a doctor," said Gideon Cleaver.

"Damn you all, every last one of you," said Belle. "It's too damn bloody to have a wake in here now. Rick, get me a mop from the back, please."

"Whatever you say, Ma'am," Rick said. "Whatever you say." But before he did, he grabbed six hundred dollars from his coat pocket, three hundred of which he had taken from the two Klansmen.

"What's this?" Evelyn asked, as he offered her the wad of cash.

"A little something to boost your vacation fund."

She took the money and kissed him on the cheek. "I guess you do understand me after all, Rick Ruby."

"I never understood nothing, and I probably never will. But I guess it might be nice to visit Paris one day."

"A mop, please," Belle called out.

"Yes, ma'am," Rick said. "I didn't forget."

Belle was right again, as usual. There was an awful lot of blood to clean away.

THE END

Rick and Ray and Dash and Me
(Or Is It "I"?)

I'll admit it. Writing the story you've most likely just read—"A Tree Falls in a Forest"—was one of the most difficult things I've done in my writing career thus far. Let's start with the Klan. One does not simply write the Klan into a story without weighing his or her options and remembering the rules. They must be the bad guys. They must be bad people. But what if they're horrible, awful people, but not really the true bad guys? Well, that, as they say, can be a sticky wicket for a writer.

I also think that from the beginning I put far too much pressure on this story. It doesn't help that I was re-reading Chandler and Hammett at the time, and had this crazy notion that maybe one day good ol' Rick could sit among Phillip Marlowe and Sam Spade at the great dinner table of hard-boiled icons. (Even if he should. Just saying.)

In my mind, I wasn't just writing another story. I was trying to craft what I considered to be the penultimate Rick Ruby tale, the one story that if you wanted to understand who Rick is and what makes him tick—at least in my understanding of him as the co-creator of the character—then this is the story you'd need to read.

As such, it includes all the trademark traits and flaws that make Rick so real to me. His deep love for Evelyn. His inability to stop being a philandering louse. His battle with the bottle. His charm that somehow makes all this not really okay, but at least slightly tolerable. And of course, his ability to win the day by trusting his intuition and letting the bad guys think he's just a clueless oaf most of the time.

But not just Rick himself. I also wanted to make sure the totality of Rick's world was represented. A New York steeped in politics and violence. A culture of racism that prevents Rick from being truly happy. A family of his own creation that serves Rick as counselors and angels and devils as much as it serves him as friends.

In short, if this was the only Rick Ruby story you ever read, I wanted him to be as fully realized to you as if you'd read all of them.

Did I succeed? The hell if I know. But I will tell you this. The further I got into the story, the more I loosened up and let Rick and the crew just do their thing, the more the pressure seemed to finally fall away like broken chains. It was as if Rick himself told me to just relax and let him tell his own damn story. So I did. And that meant that when I finally re-read the piece from beginning to end after all the edits, I came to see it in a new light.

And that new light is this: I don't care anymore what you think of it after you read it. Really, I don't give one red-hot damn if you think it's the quintessential Rick Ruby tale or not. Because Rick told it to me. And I like it. No, I *love* it. And that has made all the difference, Chandler and Hammett the legacy of P.I. fiction be damned.

• • •

SEAN TAYLOR - is an award-winning writer of stories. He grew up telling lies, and he got pretty good at it, so now he writes them into full-blown adventures for comic books, graphic novels, magazines, book anthologies and novels. He makes stuff up for money, and he writes it down for fun. He's a lucky fellow that way.

He's best known for his work on the best-selling Gene Simmons Dominatrix comic book series from IDW Publishing and Simmons Comics Group. He has also written comics for TV properties such as the top-rated Oxygen Network series The Bad Girls Club. His other forays into fiction include such realms as steampunk, pulp, young adult, fantasy, super heroes, sci-fi, and even samurai frogs on horseback (seriously, don't laugh).

For more information (and mug shots) visit www.taylorverse.com and his writer's blog at seanhtaylor.blogspot.com.